Chapter 1

Julian and I had become the parents of twins, the boy we called Angelus Jax and the girl was Althea Argenti Alexandrov-Gustavo. They were born more human than anything from what we could tell.

We were sitting in the lounge one evening only 1 month after the birth with the babies doing the routine of feed change bed.

Ebony came racing up the stairs.

"There's a stranger walking up the driveway," he said, "I think it's that guy you didn't want here"

Talon went down to the security room to check it out and then came back up

There was a knock at the door.

Talon answered it.

"You shouldn't be here" I heard Talon say.

I finished what I was doing, I handed little Angelus to Mary-Anne and went to see who it was.

It was Sin in some poor business man's body

"What have you done?" Sin said looking at me as if he wished to tear me apart

"You will need to be more specific," I said looking at him like he was a mild inconvenience

"I could not pop in and check on you, I had to walk in here it has taken me days to find you" He tried to step in the door but couldn't as an invisible barrier prevented him.

"You cannot enter my home because you have not been given any kind of permission, and you have malicious intent," I said smiling at him

"I want my baby" he snarled

"And you can have them when you no longer pose a threat to

them," I said

"What do you mean by them?" Sin snarled

"I had twins," I said his face lit up

"Kids Daddy's home" he yelled as if they would come running to him.

"Sin do you know what a baby is?" I asked him

"Of course I do," he said looking more pissed off

"You do realize these babies are only 3 weeks old, they do not understand you, they cannot walk or even crawl," I said

"But they can talk for themselves right?" Sin said trying to look in and see them "after all they are born of a god"

As if right on cue Althea started her death scream of sleep, it was something she seemed to do some bedtimes.

I watched as Sin looked horrified and in pain

"What are they doing to it?" he screeched at me

"Darling let them cry it seems to hurt this cocksucker," I said to Julian in my head, I heard him laugh

"It's nothing," I said, "That is her way of saying, she thinks we're wrong and it's not bedtime"

"What?' Sin said looking confused

"It's how babies communicate...they scream and cry and whine," I said as Angelus started on his scream.

"Honey, can you come and do your thing?" I heard Julian yell from the lounge.

"I want to see my babies" Sin said trying again to get through the barrier

"No one can enter this house with malicious intent toward anyone else in this house," Talon said standing like a pissed off guard with his arms crossed

"You see Sin we are prepared this time, and they are not your babies, we had them tested for dna...it's all Julian and I" I said smiling "You could try through legal means to get them, but I think the council will heavily frown upon your claim, since it was rape by deception, and with malicious intent, and technically you made us have abominations, so they may throw on a charge of experimenting on and slavery of another being, and then kill the babies"

"You cannot keep me from them" He seethed "and there's nothing your council could do to me"

"I have every intention of making sure the kids know all about you," I said as both babies let off another ear piercing scream

"Who is making them do that?" Sin said his hands on his head as if it were causing him magnificent pain

"No one," I said, "it is what babies do, now if you will excuse me, I need to go and help settle them."

 I left Talon to deal with Sin and I went back to the babies.
Julian was holding Althea at arm's length admittedly so she would continue to cry, and Mary-Anne was doing the same with Angelus.
We calmed them down again and got them ready for bed.

After we had put them to bed we went back to the lounge.
Talon was sitting there watching tv

"So Sin has decided maybe it is better you raise them till they stop crying" He laughed "Apparently 5 minutes of them screaming was doing his head in, I told him that's nothing and he should hear when they really get pissy"

"I'm so glad they are really cruisey babies most of the time," I said cuddling up to Julian on the couch "cause their crying does my head in"

'I'm glad he left" Julian said "*and yes I am me," he said in my head*
I smiled and snuggled into him more

"So now we know for sure what Alipa was saying was true, what are we going to do with them?" Mary-Anne asked

"Well, we could move back to the castle, plenty of babysitters, and a good school." Silver said, not looking over enthusiastic about it.

"Or we could raise them to be normal," Julian said

"But they aren't hun," I said

"Well actually they kind of are," Talon said "I mean right now they haven't shown any special abilities or anything, and they don't even drink blood"

"Do you think if we find another place somewhere that maybe

Mat or Alipa could hide us from the likes of Sin?" I asked
"Well Alipa was able to ward this place pretty tight so I think so, we can but ask," Talon said looking a bit sad
"You miss her?" I asked Talon
"Yeah," he said knowing I meant Mat "I mean it's cool she has come out here a couple of times and you let me go there, but it's just not the same"
"Maybe you need to go home" I suggested
"Maybe, or maybe I could steal her and keep her with me" he grinned
"If only your sister hadn't made it a law punishable by death" Julian laughed
I smacked him.
"I think both of you should take a break and go see your loved ones," Silver said
"And who would help you with the babies?" Mary-Anne asked
"I'm sure we could find someone to help us," Silver said, "and you guys deserve happiness too."
"Well Brutus is being an ass at the moment so I have no interest in seeing him till he apologizes," Mary-Anne said
"Maybe you could go talk to him about what an ass he is being?" Julian said "you know being a male, he may not realize he is being an ass"
"He wanted me to go raise his babies," she said "We have only really not long started dating, I'm not having babies"
"Well it has been about a year," Talon said
"So you Mat are having babies now too, after all, you've been dating for 5 years," Mary-Anne said
"You know we can't" Talon said looking at her as if he would like to have babies
"Would you expect her to give up her job and raise them if you could?" she asked him
"Well yes and no" Talon admitted "she would have to stop working for some of the time after they are born obviously, but if she wanted to work after we could work something out I'm sure"

"According to Brutus and our last conversation, babies are womans work, like cleaning a house" she said

"Oh Brutus" I said trying not to laugh "he is silly boy"

"Even I know you do not tell a woman that if you want to keep her" Julian said "and I have made some pretty big cock ups in my time"

"He said he was going to call me again tomorrow, I told him not to bother" Mary-Anne said "I don't want someone who thinks I belong in the kitchen, hell I can't even cook"

Ivory wandered in the lounge.

"There's an SUV coming up the drive" he said "It looks like Brutus driving"

"Well there you go Mare" I said "now you can talk to him about it and tell him how you feel"

"I don't want to talk to him now, I need sleep. I have to get up to the babies in the morning," she said getting up she seemed very annoyed as she stalked out and up the stairs.

"Ok" Ivory said looking confused at Mary-anne's exit "also that Sin guy has been hovering near the edge of our perimeter since he left"

"Brutus nearly ran him over" Ivory said "Oh here is the big boy now"

Ivory was not wrong about big, Brutus was near 7 foot tall and built solid. I hadn't seen him in tiger form but I am positive he makes a great tiger too.

He knocked on the door and Ebony answered it letting him in. He came into the lounge.

"I am sorry to disturb you all, is Mary-Anne around, I need to talk to her" He said very politely

"She has gone to her room sorry Brutus, you are welcome to stay, all I ask is that you do not fight around the babies" I said

"She is really mad at me ah?" he said sitting down, he knew he fucked up.

"Yup" Julian said "word of advice, never tell a woman she is meant to stay home have babies and do housework, let that be her choice"

"Yet she is looking after your babies" Brutus said sulking
"It was her choice to help us, it is not really part of her job which is why we pay her extra for doing so, and she does not do house-work" I said defending us
"There's a big difference between raising kids and helping some-one raise their kids, beside she is still young, and if you really wanted to you could look at this as some hands on experience" Julian said nearly laughing I whacked him again (not abusively, just a slap on the arm)
"Really the women around me are equal opportunity woman, it's how I have trained the ones who were not and how I treat all my family, and how I expect my family to treat each other" I said
"Right so you'd support it, if the men all went home to play daddy and left the woman guarding shit?" he looked at me as if my head was going to start spinning
"Yes" I said "If the women were trained for it"
"So where are all your female guards? He asked
"We do have a couple, but we can only hire those who want the work, I don't care if they are male or female" I said "Hex,and Kerry are great at their job guarding, and hunting criminals"
"Talon trained them, and Savannah" Julian said smiling
"Oh yeah and there's Savannah" I said "so yes I can honestly say I don't care what sex they are I will hire them if they are good at the job"
"So I will work on not being sexist" Brutus said "but I really want to see her"
"Then go knock on her door" Julian said "And grovel a lot"
Brutus smiled at him and got up.
He didn't come back so I guessed they were making up, nights like this I am so glad we have sound proofing so good you can only hear what's happening if the door is open. Theirs stayed closed.
"Maybe we should get the kids into a more night time routine?" I said to Julian as we were headed to bed
"But they are like humans" Julian said

"Yeah and" I said "You know we are going to miss out on all the good bits, and we only get to spend a few hours with them each night, because they are weird babies who sleep"

"Maybe they sleep so well because they know how much they are loved, not just by us" Julian said snuggling up to me.

"If only they had been born more vampy" I said

"Don't worry hon we will work it out, we have time" He said smiling at me "I still think we could possibly get away with being normalish, move to the suburbs, plenty of vampires do that now"

The babies only woke up once that night, Julian and I played with them a bit, I was hoping they would sleep in for Mary-Anne.

Alipa was still here which was great, she spent a lot of time out in the woods collecting bits and pieces, she had decided to stay with us till our next family holiday in a couple of months.

Her self appointed task this evening was trying to work out how Sin had found us.

"It doesn't make any sense," she muttered "this place is warded and hidden up the wazoo, from all magical peering eyes, it should have just been a void to him"

"Maybe that's the problem" Brutus said carefully not wanting to piss her off

"What do you mean?" Alipa asked

"Maybe he couldn't find Silver so he looked for spots he found nothing?" Brutus suggested

"How could I have missed it?" Alipa said giving him a hug "your right, he probably looked at all the voids around the world and went looking into each, that explains why it took him weeks to find her"

"So how do we make sure that doesn't happen again?" Silver asked coming in the door to the security room holding Angelus, Mary-Anne was right behind her with Althea.

"We would need help" Alipa said "or Maybe start putting a void on objects, and leave them all over the place, I can make it so the object emits an area of void, but I will need Matiana's help"

The mention of her Talon perked up.

"So we need some objects to randomly leave all over the place, and Mat?" Talon asked, trying not to sound too eager "Any particular objects that would be better for it?"

"Yes you can ring your sweetheart and tell her we need her again" Alipa said smiling "And natural objects would be the best but anything is fine, I could enchant a plastic cup if I so desired"

"We don't use plastic anymore, but I get it" Talon said rushing back upstairs

"Silly boy could have used the phone down here" Alipa laughed looking at 6 cellphones and the landline right next to her.

The cellphones were all burn phones, just in case, we had a few boxes of them but only ever kept a few charged and ready to go.

"He's probably going to have phone sex as well" Mary-Anne laughed

"Ok well I shall go shopping online see if I can't buy up some crap to enchant" I said jumping on the pc "but we also need some kind of alarm that will go off when he comes near us"

"I can enchant something to do that, but it would be specific to a person" Alipa said

"What do you mean?" I asked

"I make a ring to be the alarm so you know when you are near him, but only you would know" she said

"Right so we would have to have a few so in case I can't warn others, someone else might be able to" I asked

"Yes" she replied

"Cool, I think I may send Talon elsewhere" I said "He can do his job anywhere and he wants to be with Mat so maybe I should send him back to the castle"

"That would be a good idea, but who will guard you?" Mary-Anne said

"There's plenty of capable people, maybe Brutus" I suggested Mary-Anne blushed

"I could do that if it's ok with Mary-Anne of course" Brutus said looking at her

"It has to be your choice Brutus, and please don't use me as a reason" Mary-Anne said

"To be honest it is getting a bit boring at Irena's, she really doesn't need me" he said

"Can you two work together and be a couple though?" I asked

"I guess so" Mary-Anne said "But you have to understand Brutus I need my space too"

"Of course darling" Brutus said "we should have separate rooms, after all we are not married"

Everyone looked at him in shock.

"Thank you" Mary-Anne said questionly

"Well there will be no doubt times I will be getting up or going to bed in the middle of the night when your sleeping and I would not want to disturb you since your looking after the bosses kids" he said

"Ok" Mary-Anne said taking a deep breath

"Do you guys think we can live a normal kind of life?" I said

"What do you mean?" Alipa said

"In the suburbs, letting the kids have human friends" I said "playing at the park"

"But you wouldn't be able to do that with them" Brutus said

"I just think it would be good for them to have some kind of normal, get them to know what it is like to live as a human" I said "Make sure they understand why they have to have humanity"

"Sleep overs would be serious fun" Mary-Anne laughed

"Hay mum I'm going to the vampires house for a sleepover" Brutus said mocking the idea

"Here's hoping they bring garlic" Ebony said walking in "So what is this about wanting normal?"

"For the kids" I said looking at my baby boys eyes he was watching me so intently.

Julian came in with bottles and took Althea from Mary-Anne and handed me a bottle.

"I just want them to be good people when they grow up" I said

"So you want us to work out how to live in the burbs and keep you guys safe" Ebony said

"I guess so, but you might be better off working with Talon" I said "I mean we won't need people with your guys skill set in the burbs"

"And you're sending Talon where?" Talon said coming back in the room

"Anywhere you want to go really" I said "But I think you are needed more dealing with the outside world than you are here, your skills are too good for this gig"

"Oh so I am a downgrade" Brutus said raising two eyebrows at me

"No offence Brutus but Talon is the very best at what he does, you are really good at what you do and would be more useful to us in the burbs" I explained

"Makes sense" he said smiling

"I can't agree to this," Talon said "The burbs, vampires?"

"There's a few decent communities now that have average joe vampires living in them, they are really treated as equals, but I also know they are pretty hard to get in to" Ebony said

"Yeah they are gated communities run by vampires" Talon said "And I don't think the twin antichrists will be safe"

"What?" I said thinking I must have misheard

"I am sorry sis but fact is they have a prophecy and a destiny of their own, and it's not great" Talon said

"What the fuck are you talking about?" Julian said

"Ivanovich told me there is an old prophecy that said something about twins born of the dead, he is trying to find it" Talon explained

"And if they were going to become evil, what did Ivanovich say you were to do?" I asked

"Nothing he said nothing, he just told me about it and that he would find it and get back to me" Talon said

"Is this when we first found out there would be 2 or was it when they were born?" I asked

"He told me about 3 months ago" Talon said "I didn't want to worry you about it, we are in a safe place here, but going to the burbs..."

"We would need complete new identities" I said "We have done well to keep out of the public eye so no one should recognise us anyway"

"Why are you so desperate to do this?" Julian said looking at me funny

"We have to get out of here and go somewhere no one would expect, so it will be harder for certain people to find us" I smiled

"You better keep your wings in and your back covered" Ebony said

"Anyone outside of family who knows us, know I am always by your side" Talon said

"I know" I said "Which is another reason you have to go, be with Mat, run the enforcers"

"And you will use these ...voids?" Talon said

"Yes we will drop them everywhere, we will get others to drop them too, so they are everywhere" I said

"I don't think it's a good idea" Talon said

"I am in two minds myself" Julian said "on one hand I see what Silver is saying, but on the hand I also see what Talon is saying"

"If we take the kids back to the castle, they will live an over privileged life and that leads to snotty entitled brats" I said "I do not want snotty entitled brats, because then when he comes back they will go with him, and they will create some kind of havoc the likes we have never seen"

Talons phone started ringing.

"Yeah" Talon said answering it "Oh hay Savannah"

"Hold on I will put you on speaker, Silver is here"

He pushed a button

"Ok Savannah go"

"Hay guys I hope you are doing alright with the babies" I heard her say

"Yeah so far so good" I smiled down at the now sleeping little boy in my arms "What's up hun?"

"Jay and I went to a thing at his dads pack and when we came home one of Jays exiled pack members had shown up, with a humanish girl, He found her half frozen on the mountain and brought her here because it was the closest safe place to take her, but she seems to have a connection to Declan, they both feel it, but now it is starting some distention in the pack, and we are not sure what to do" She said all in a rush

"Ok first hun take a deep breath" I said to her "What do you mean humanish?"

"Well to all of us she smells mostly human, but it's like there's something else, none of us can work it out." She explained

"Hay Savannah what's her name?" Talon asked

"We don't know, someone seems to have block her memory's and when she tries to remember it hurts her so much, when she does remember something she passes out from the pain" Savannah said "When she saw Declan for the first time she was so happy for a second and then she was screaming in pain and boom she passed out, but now she seems to feel safest with him, and he says she feels like home."

"I think we need to see her" Julian said "If someone blocked her mind and made it cause pain to remember then a very powerful vampire has been interfering with her.

"Ethan said when he found her she was still trying to crawl somewhere, muttering I have to find them" Savannah said "Declan thinks she was meaning our pack, Ethan thinks he is deluded and horny"

"Do you think it's Rain?" Talon said looking at me

"It could be, we didn't get to find out much about her in the other...thing" I said "Hey Savannah can you try and see if she answers to the name Rain"

"Hold on" she said we heard her say to Jay to go see if she knew the name Rain

"If she is we should let her and Declan come with us to the burbs" I suggested

"We still haven't made that decision darling" Julian said "It could be she might be to fragile for a normal life"

"Are you guys moving again?" Savannah asked

"Maybe" Julian said

"No we are moving, we just haven't figured out where yet" I said "Sin found us, so we are going to make it harder for him if he returns"

"That makes sense then I am surprised you haven't moved already" She said as my best friend and a big part of my family she knew all about what happened.

"He only found us last night give me a chance" I laughed

"Oh Jay is back" Savannah said

"Hay Silver" I heard Jay take the phone "I think she is this the Rain you mentioned, she just collapsed again soon as I said her name, she nearly hit her head on a table, if it hadn't been for my son catching her she would have been badly hurt"

"We need to get her to a powerful vampire, one who can undo whatever was done to her" Julian said looking at me with a kind gentle look. "How about we make the trip to see you guys?"

"Not a good idea at the moment, it would be better if we could get her to you, things here are a bit tense" Jay said

"Ok how about we meet halfway" I suggested "I mean we are traveling with newborn babies so it will take time to get shit sorted for them before we can even leave"

"Ok how about we meet somewhere in Nebraska" Jay suggested

"How about Omaha?" Talon said tapping on the computer

"Ok where when?" Jay said

"The Magnolia hotel, say 5 days?" Talon suggested

"Sure" Jay said "we can do that"

"Ok well we shall go and sort shit here and see you in 5 days" I said he hung up at his end

"We are going to need a winnebago thing" I said screwing up my nose "That would be the easiest with the babies"

"Yeah" Julian said "Eb's can you get on to that, we also need to pack everything"

"Well I booked a whole floor" Talon said "so glad they are happy to accommodate vampires"

"Ok well Talon you and the twins need to go back to the castle" I said smiling nodding at Ebony and Ivory

"Nope we stay till Mat goes home, she is coming over, damn it I will have to change her plans too" Talon said jumping back on the computer

"Well I shall go and start packing" Alipa said

"I'll find us a motorhome or two" Ebony said

We went about our evening, playing with the babies when they woke. Packing when they slept, we had accumulated so much stuff in the last 7 months being out here.

"We need to work out the kids stuff, what we need to take and what can wait till we find somewhere to live" I said going into their room when they woke up.

"Clothes, nappy's ...lotions potions and wipes?" Julian said laughing

"Yeah but they have so much" I said

"Ok" Julian said thinking about it "How about 1 month supply of everything?"

"Good start" I said

"But I don't think we should be driving round with the kids in the rv for to long" He said

"I think of it as a house bus, and this hippie chick loves the idea of going around the country in a house bus" I said

"Oh you're a hippie now?" Julian laughed

"Maybe more a gothic hippie" Mary-Anne said coming in the room Brutus was behind her "I'll take care of the kids stuff, I know what they use, what they don't"

"Thank you Mary-Anne" I said "How long do you think you will be helping us?"

"I have no idea" she said looking worried "Have I done something wrong?"

"Oh hell no" I said reassuring her "I was just thinking how impossible you would be to replace" I hugged her

"Oh" she blushed hugging me back "Thank you"

"Well I guess we have to go to bed" I said looking at Althea as I picked her up out of the bassinette "I love you my little princess" I said giving her a kiss on the forehead and handing her to Mary-Anne

I went over to Julian who had picked up Angelus and was saying good night.

We said our good nights and went to bed.

The next evening when we got up there was a huge Luxury RV outside, It was perfect.
A couple of our wolf guards had worked out how to fix the bassinets into the bed space that had its own little room, granted it was small when closed up, but we wouldn't have to move anything when we opened it up. I wasn't sure when that would be as we would be driving day and night to get it over with.
"So it's an 18 hour trip, we got vamps for night driving and wolves for day" Talon said "You guys can just sit back and do whatever, we do not have to sleep this trip as this vehicle has extra protections from the sun, but also we have bunk beds that close off" He showed me the fancy bunks where the vamps could sleep during the day
"We need to decide how many of us are really needed, and who is coming with us" Julian said "A group of vamps this big will draw suspicion"
"Goodpoint we are trying to go low key ish" I said
"Ok well I am going with you" Talon said "Mat is meeting us at the hotel, she's already left"
"Mary-Anne and Brutus" I said "Eb's and Ives, we need more wolf"
"Well I am driving" Colin said having come in behind us "I can let Hex drive some"
"Alipa, should come with us too" I said "and Jackson can fit too, but maybe we should take an SUV as well, so if we need to go somewhere we don't need to take the rv"
"Good idea darling" Julian said "So what do the rest get to do?"
"Holiday then back to work where Talon needs them" I said smiling
"We will need two houses side by side when we settle you know that ah?" Talon said laughing
"Yeah" I laughed " and we need to make fakes ids that pass while in transit"
"Don't be stupid" Talon said "Ebony and Ivory are working on them now"

"Oh yeah they asked me to ask you guys to go chose a name" Colin said

"Thanks Colin" I laughed heading back out the front door , this thing was so big inside

We went downstairs to the security room

"Good you guys came" Ivory said jumping out of his seat at his computer "I need names"

"Ok" Talon said "I will be Anton James St Clare"

"Suits you" Ebony said

"Thanks" Talon almost giggled

"Wait is that your..real name?" Ivory asked

"Yes it is" He said "No one will remember him, I was a nobody when Gustavo found me and I have been Talon ever since"

"That is a really nice name" I said "and yeah it does suit you"

"I will be Lucius Augustus Giovanni" Julian said smiling

"I will be Abigail Althea Giovanni" I said "This way kids keep their names, which reminds me we will need birth certs for them and stuff"

"I have already done that" Ivory said handing me over a pile of papers, there was birth cert, passports, social security numbers

"Wow thanks Ivory" Julian said

"Yeah I did them just after they were born, but I think the passport may have been a step too far, no one with a baby is going overseas a week after they born" Ivory said

"So where are we heading after Omaha?' Ebony said

"We will need two side by side" Talon said "So maybe find some new subdivisions?"

"But where?" Ebony said

"I have no idea" I said

"Not chicago, or alaska, or LA" Julian said

"How aboot Canada?" Colin suggested "I've heard it like New Zealand but bigger"

"And their equal rights record is pretty good ah?" Ebony said faking a bad canadian accent

"I found a place in new york that would fit us, seems canada are not into big houses, unless you want to run a hotel?" Ivory said

seeming excited "and there's a second place next door for sale"
"How many bedrooms and space around the house?" I asked
"10, and plenty , but we may need to fence it" Ivory showed me
the house it would have been perfect, in the bronx, new york
"And the second one is pretty much the same"
"Ok buy them, but we will need to make these enchanted things
to disperse everywhere, which means we need to find lots of big
houses where we can leave something" I said
"Hopefully Alipa can do that while we travel"Julian said
"Well this house will stay a void." Talon said
"Hopefully we can pull this off" Ivory said going over to printer
"Mrs Abigail Giovanni" he handed me the birth certificate
"Mr Lucius Giovanni" he said handing Julian his I.D
"And of course Mr. Anton st Clare" Ivory handed him his I.D "the
others have theirs I should have the passports by tomorrow"
"Ok well I guess we leave round midnight tomorrow" I said
"Do you really think it's a good idea to do this?" Julian asked
"Oh the place we found is a vampire friendly neighbourhood
too" Ebony said "hell the council there are asking for vampire
families to move in"
"They do know vampires don't have children ah?" Talon said
"Maybe they think all vamps are rich and that they will spend
big in that area" I suggested
"Yeah well our house cost 5 mil so yeah they like our money"
Ebony said
"Are there good child friendly services there?" I asked
"I have no idea" Ebony said " I didn't even look" he went back to
tapping away on the computer.
"Looks like the area has good schools" he said shrugging
"Ok well first thing I need you to do after the property is ours, is
make sure a builder goes in and fences the hell out of it, I want to
make sure we have our privacy and americans seem to not like
fences for some stupid reason" I said looking at Julian
"I totally agree, but what if there's some law against fencing?
Julian said
"I just double checked we can go up to 6 foot without a permit"

Ebony said smiling

"Great make sure the builder you get knows not to disturb any-thing on the neighbours properties but I want no gaps for neigh-bours pets to come over and I want chicken wire all over both sides of it," I said "when we get there we can electrify it if need be"

"What do you have against pets?" Talon asked

"Pets come over and so do their humans, when they look for them, some will use their pets as an excuse to be nosey I want that discouraged" I said

"And if the neighbours are vampires?" Talon asked

"Then the fence will be on at all times" I said smiling

The boys all laughed

"When did you get so cynical?" Julian asked

"When I lived twice in an unforgiving nasty world" I said

"Ok well let's get ready for the first part of this trip, if we are leaving at midnight we will be on the road for 18 hours straight, we will get there in the daytime, so Mary-Anne and Brutus will have to check us in. I will go ask Alipa if she can enchant some rocks for us to leave lying around on the way" Julian said

"Once we have Rain we will be going for a long 20 hour drive to our new home, the wolves or Mary-Anne will have to get the keys to the new house, maybe we could time it so we get there before the close of business or something" I said

"It's going to be a long week" Talon said as he started packing some of the things he wanted from down here "And I am not leaving you until I am satisfied with security at your new place" I smiled at Talon

"Thank you Anton" I said

We spent the rest of that night packing what we could and sort-ing out where to put stuff in the RV, Ebony arranged with the wolves we were leaving behind to have everything sent to the new place in a container once it was all packed up. Some of the wolves we were leaving behind wanted to stay on there, which was good because it gave us an extra layer of protection if Sin came back early.

Alipa did her thing on some stones and rocks and when Colin

had gone to town that day, he hid some of them on trucks and buses that were going any direction. He had even managed to get a rock into the car of some Canadians who were headed back home after visiting family.

The next evening we headed out, we were very fortunate as the babies seemed to like traveling.

When we arrived at the hotel, Mary-Anne went and checked us in and our wolves got everything sorted, the other wolves were not here yet and once it got dark us vampires went inside to wait.

The next evening Declan, Jay, Savannah and Rain arrived.

"SIL" Savannah yelled as she rushed to me to give me a hug

"Hay Sav" I said accepting her hug

Rain was mostly hiding behind Declan.

"Good to see you again Jay how have things been with the pack?" I asked Jay

"Not too bad, except some tools being overly paranoid" he laughed giving me a hug too

"You must be Declan," I said stepping around Jay.

Declan was very handsome, he was built like a wrestler but had long dreads this time around. He shook my hand

"It is a pleasure to finally meet the woman my father speaks so highly of" he smiled "This is Rain, we think" he said stepping aside so I could see the fragile little girl behind him, in the time before I thought her paleness was due to how she had lived, now I could see she was an Albino. I put my hand out to shake hers

"It is nice to meet you Rain" I said calmly

She cautiously took my hand and shook it, her touch was very gentle and at first she kept looking to Declan for approval. Then something happened.

She grabbed my hand tight as hell and looked at me confused.

"You are being hunted?" she said quietly

"It's ok Rain" I said trying to reassure her "I am aware and we have taken many precautions to make sure they do not find us" I patted her shoulder

"Can you help me remember?" She asked

"I don't know, but if we can't help you, I might know someone who can" I smiled at her "One thing I can assure you of none of

my people will harm you at all"
She did not look assured.
"Well shall we go to our rooms and catch up?' Savannah said "I for one am so excited to see you again Silver, so much has happened"
We headed up to our rooms.
"So what has happened?" Julian asked when we were in the elevator
"Well Jay and I went to all 4 of the big fashion weeks this year," she said, "and I finally got to debut at them all" her eyes went wide as saucers
We saw Jay roll his eyes and Julian laughed
"Why is that funny?" Rain asked confused
"I am sure Jay did not enjoy the fashion week shows as much as Savannah" Julian winked at Rain
"You can say that again brother" Jay said "She spent 4 weeks having a blast though so it was worth it"
"Aren't you glad I didn't make you go to every event I went to?" Savannah said smiling at Jay
"Very much so" he said
"So how did it go?" I asked
"Well I got orders from all of them, and some exclusive deals on fabrics, and lets just say my workers are going to be very busy for the next six months" she said
"That's wonderful news Savannah" I said
"And I am already working on next season" she said very excited
"I am so glad things are going so well" I said excitedly for her
"how's things with the pack?" I asked Jay
"I wish that was going as well as my wife's career " he said "things were chugging along nicely, which is why I went with my wife to Europe but my dad has been having problems with Trance again. When I go back I'm going to suggest to dad that we divide the pack let whoever wants to go with Trance go and they can find their own way"
"I can't believe that Lucian let that asshole stay alive after what he did" Julian said

"Well Trance kicked up all kinds of hell when Ethan found this one. "he said smiling at Rain "We were lucky Declan stepped in, Trance had it in his head she had to be turned or cast back out into the snow"

"Trance never was a bright spark" I said "so Rain, what are your plans now?"

"I don't know, get my memories back and decide from there" she said quietly

"Well I would very much like you to come with us," I said "we are in the process of moving and we have plenty of room. I don't want to try and help you till we are in a safe place. It can be a very hard painful process"

I saw her looking frantically Declan as if she was about to have a panic attack

"It's ok Rain. Silver and her people are good people." he said trying to reassure her. I sensed the bond they had...just like the other timeline

"If you can Declan, you are more than welcome to join us too" Julian said smiling

He looked at his dad. Who just nodded.

"Ok I will go with you Rain" he said taking hold of her hand.

"Your people won't start arguing because I am there?"she asked

"No in fact we were hoping you would agree we have fake I.d.s half made for you we just need a photo" I smiled

"Why fake I.Ds?" she asked so innocently

"Well we have a complicated family and there are some people like Trance who have trouble accepting complications. So we decided to go undercover and it will help keep you safe from whoever blocked your memory" I said

"Who's causing you guys problems?" Jay and Declan said together

"Just Sin" I said waving it off as if it were no big deal

"Oh," Jay said.

Jay and Savannah knew some of how I ended up pregnant, they just didn't know about us being thrown back in time by vampire lords who traded it for me.

"I thought you had managed to hide from him?" Savannah said

"Yup we did" Julian said "But I guess as he could not find her presence, he went looking for voids where he sensed nothing and there was only a couple then, now we have spread voids all over the place, so he will have to go visit each one by one."

"It is really just to protect the babies, even though he decided he no longer wants them till they come into their powers, which could be when they are 18" I said

"Only very few trusted people will know who we are and where we are" Julian said "Of course you two will know"

"So you're moving to the burbs to hide from Sin?" Savannah asked

"Yup" I said

"Even though some of us think it is a bad idea" Julian said

"And to be honest I didn't really give anyone a choice" I said feeling guilty at the rushed move, because I am now a paranoid person who gets very narrow minded and ignores others.

We all heard the cry of one baby followed by the other, Savannah and I went to get them.

"So what's it like being a mum?" she asked cooing over Althea

"I really haven't done much, they are more active during the day when I am not, and I could stay up with them but I have to drink so much blood and I end up exhausted" I said changing Angelus nappy. "Mary-Anne is doing a great job with them though"

"My god they are so cute" she said pulling faces at Althea. Althea just lay in her arms looking at her. Then Althea smiled.

"I honestly hate that I have to rely on others to look after them" I said swapping babies with Savannah so I could change Althea

"You could always raise them at night" Savannah suggested

"Yeah I could but that's not really fair on them, once they go to school and stuff" I said

"Home school could be an option, or moving back home" Savannah suggested

"I didn't even think about home school, but I want them to be socialized as well" I said "and I don't really want them to be raised like they are entitled and if I go home that is how they will be treated"

"Yeah I suppose, but they would be safe and around people who understand your situation" she said

"Except some won't" I said "I mean I am the first vampire ever to have had actual babies, they will become a target before they can even defend themselves"

"Are you planning on teaching them how to defend themselves?" she asked

"Well yes when they are old enough," I said, "and we have to see if they do develop any interesting powers"

"Oh my that will be fun" Savannah laughed "what if they can teleport and they start doing it when they are like 2?"

"Then we are fucked" I laughed

We walked out into the lounge area and Julian handed me and Savannah a bottle each

"I know this may be a weird thing to ask you" Rain said, "but you are not breastfeeding?"

"No I can't" I said "I guess being a vampire my milk never happened and boobs did not even grow"

"Oh I am sorry if I offended you" Rain quickly said

"You did not offend me dear" I said sitting down feeding Althea, Savannah copied me and fed Angelus "I understand that it is not a normal thing that has happened and people will have questions"

"We may have to tell people we adopted for a while" Julian said sitting next to me

"If only we lived in a better world where people could be more accepting" Savannah said

"Oh believe me this world is not so bad" I laughed

"Why on earth would a god do such a thing?" Jay said shaking his head "And then to turn around and try and take them away, babies need their parents"

"Everyone needs their parents" Savannah said "Oh that reminds me, my parents are coming to visit me next month, I am so nervous about it"

"You will be fine my love" Jay said smiling at her admiring they way she was with Angelus

"I know I will be fine but will they" she said "I mean they still don't know your a wolf, and they are coming to stay with your pack"

"How did they react to you being a vampire?" I asked

"They took it pretty well, turned out mum knew Damian from before dad" she said "and they have met Jay, once, but I just don't know if they can handle the wolf thing"

"I think they will be fine, they will see how well Jay treats you and love him for it" Julian said

"My father thinks its a bad idea having them over, but at the same time he wants to meet them" Jay said "he also doesn't like that Savannah happens to be a vampire but he loves her"

"I never picked your dad to be like that" I said

"Oh, he's not a vampist or anything, just not keen on not having more grandkids" Jay said, "and he is happy for us. He said love is too important to let the vamp wolf thing get in the way and it helps show others that it can be a positive thing"

"Sometimes I feel like an advertisement for vampire were beast relations" Savannah laughed "But that gets me more customers than most designers"

"It's good you guys have found a way to make it work" I said smiling at them Julian got up and took Angelus to burp him and have a cuddle. "I am so lucky, I had no idea how much of an effect having kids has had on me, in some ways I think I have softened but others I think...well if anyone tries to hurt those two they will die slowly and painfully"

"To be fair anyone who hurts a person in your very large extended family tends to pay with hellfire and brimstone" Julian laughed

I just looked at him

I noticed Rain and Declan were becoming more relaxed

The phone in the room rang and Talon answered it

"What?" he said not being very polite

"Who wants to see her?"

"Hold on I will check" he looked very dubious

"A guy is downstairs claiming to be Lucifer and demanding to see you" He said to me

"Oh and how the fuck did he find us?" I said

"We may have to ask him" Julian said getting up the babies had fallen asleep in our arms again

"Ok lets put these two to bed and I think Declan and Rain should probably go to their room" I said concerned "Only for your own protection, if it is Luci or someone else"

"Good idea" Declan said

"I will go with them" Savannah said getting up

"Would it be ok if I stayed?" Jay asked

"Yes Jay that would be fine," Julian said coming back in the room after putting Angelus to bed he took Althea from me and went back to the bedroom

"Ok send him up please" Talon said politely into the phone before hanging up

"Who is Lucifer?" Rain asked Declan on the way out the door

"Well you know the lord of hell?" I heard Declan say before the door closed

10 minutes later there was a knock on my door.

Talon went to answer it.

There was a man in a suit standing there.

"Ah, good you are here" he said making a beeline for me

Talon stopped him

"Get your hands off me" Lucifer said "Look I know this body is not ideal but I am Lucifer and I wish to speak with Silver"

"How is it you keep popping up and the angels have not attacked?" Julian asked

"Because I am not here, well I am but my body isn't" he said waving his hand as if it were insignificant "As long as the body stays in hell the angels won't come get me"

"So what can I do for you?" I asked him nodding at Talon to let him continue

"Oh, this is not about what you can do for me but what I can do for you" he said sitting on my couch

"I am not keen on making a deal with you" I said

"Oh no deal to be made" he smiled

"Then what do you think you can do for me?" I asked

"Hide you better" he said smiling

"Explain why I need to hide?" I asked

"Look we all know what happened to you, how you ended up with babies, how you sent me the hearts of the vampires who changed everything and used you, and how much you want to hide from Sin" he grinned "I too have some unresolved issues with Sin, he meddles with my business all the time and he has become more problematic in recent times"

"How is he messing with your business?" I asked

"He's taking people from hell and giving them a new life" Lucifer said looking agitated

"He's taking people out of hell?" Julian asked "Surely he can't do that without your help"

"Yes well he has been without my permission and well my father is absent forever so he's getting away with it" He said

"And why does this mean you want to help me hide?" I asked

"Well I can't stop him doing what it is he is doing but I can screw up his future" Luci smiled

"Ok Luci, what is he planning on doing?" Julian asked

"Please do not call me that" he said with a sneer "Anyway he is stealing my people and giving them life, but they are stuck in his realm, once he gets his hands on the babies he will turn those people into an army and take over your world"

"How can the babies help him with that?" I asked

"When they come into their power it will boost him a bit, like a battery, and if he has them he will drain one completely and boom armageddon not just for humans but for everyone" he explained

"Is that what you know for a fact or are you just going off some old prophecy no one knows about?" Talon asked

"It is what I know" he said confidently "I am not without my own sources you know"

"That's why he was so keen to get us back in time, so he could do what the vamps had done" I said

"Oh and there is a prophecy about your kid, however it only mentions one child, and I know he wrote it, then took it back in time when he knew you were pregnant" Lucifer said

Jay was looking confused

"What do you mean that's why he wanted you to go back in time?" Jay asked me

"Ok well I may as well tell you" I said "we lived through a timeline that was completely different to this one, some vampire lords got scared of the chaos they created and made a deal with Sin for a time travel spell to send the whole world back in time" I explained

"To be fair the idea of all the angels coming down to wipe everyone out may have been somewhat of an incentive" Lucifer added

"Part of the payment of that spell or whatever was me" I said remembering how angry it made me that someone could use me like that

"You see Sin knows things, like how his demonic creation abilities work well with vamps who are fae, and he knows even using Julian's sperm he could make some mega powerful child for him to drain" Lucifer said

"So what happened in this other timeline?" Jay asked

"It was awful, Silver was frozen for 30 years and defrosted into a world that had turned to shit, vampires controlled everything, your pack was run by Trance who often stole and tortured women and children from your pack, raised you as his own, and was just plain evil, Humans were either in the slums starving and dying or slaves to vampires, hospitals were used by vampires to source feeding stock, and the worst of the vampires enjoyed tormenting everyone with no restrictions" Lucifer said

"But doesn't coming back and changing things create issues?" Jay asked

"Well yes one issue being a vampire had twins" I said

"Silver and I worked very hard behind the scenes to make sure that some things happened, like meeting your father, helping him get back his pack and you and your mother from Trance, we took out a few vampires who would have caused a lot of problems for humans and us, some vampires who rose to power when we came out, were kept in check" Julian said

"And the council?" Jay asked

"Instead of controlling humans that were on the council we made sure the humans could not be controlled by any vampire, as we did the wolves" I said quietly

"They have done a very good job of keeping this world off the dystopian path of death that the world was on" Lucifer said

"So you knew Savannah would be abused by her sire?" Jay asked

"Yes" I said very quietly

"They had to" Lucifer said "Some bad things had to happen so things could be set right"

"In the other timeline Savannah was abused and used by many more than just her sire" I said

"How do you know things would not have worked out ok if you had stopped her sire?" Jay said seeming really angry

"It is my fault, I wanted all my family from that timeline to be my family in this one" I said feeling really guilty "Looking back it was rather selfish"

"No" Lucifer said "If you had interfered with Savannah she would not be the amazing woman she is today"

"How do you know?" Jay said

"Because much like Sin, I know things" Lucifer said

"Look really unless you can kill Sin or give us something so we know when he is near then I am not interested" I said

"You cannot kill a god" Lucifer said with disdain

"How did you find us exactly?" I asked

"Because I have my own skills" Lucifer said smiling

"Skills that Sin could make you use later to find us?" I pointed out

"No he couldn't do that" Lucifer said not looking so confident

"If he knows you can find us so easily then yes he will force you to do it" Julian said

"Don't worry Lucifer by the time the kids come into their

power we will make sure they are well trained enough not to let anyone take advantage of them" I said "But I think you should go, we have much to do"

"Like what?" he asked

"Like moving my entire family to some place in butfuck no where Europe and making sure you cannot find us again" I snapped at him

"Oh you seem a little touchy" Lucifer said snidely

"Yeah well I am overly sick of immortels trying to run my life" I said

"Well then I will go but if you decide you need my help feel free to call me, I believe you know how now" He said getting up and seeming very indignant "I shall see myself out"

He left and closed the door

"I am surprised he did not notice me at all, since he seems to know how to see through my voids" Alipa said from a seat in the corner

"I am shocked he did not notice you as well" I said "Now I need to know how he actually found us"

"Maybe we were seen here at the hotel by someone?" Talon said "I mean we haven't exactly been low key so far"

"How do we be more low key?" I asked

"We need smaller groups" Talon said "family in the Rv, the rest can split between cars and stuff, I suggest at some point in the middle of nowhere we split the rv's and have the one you start in go the opposite way, maybe to canada"

"Savannah and I could take it to Alaska" Jay said

"That's a good idea, if you don't mind" I said

"I don't mind but I want to know more about this other time" Jay said

"There's really not much to tell" Julian said

"It was a horrible world for all of us, much more brutal than this one and vampires helped fuck over the planet and we were attempting to fix it" I said

"How did you know we would be together here?" Jay asked me directly

"Honestly I didn't, but I did not have any choice in this. We had decided we would stay put, someone else did the ritual, I just paid the price" I said not looking at him.

"And the price was Sin getting you pregnant?" He asked

"That was part of it" Julian said "but we did not even know that till it was to late"

"We honestly thought we were clear" I said "But Sin used Julian and raped me"

"You mean like Lucifer was using that businessman?" Jay asked

"Yes" Julian said slightly angry

"I am so sorry Silver" Jay said "What happened to the people who did the ritual?"

"We hunted them down took their hearts and gave them to Lucifer" Talon said

"Why?" Jay asked

"Because he wanted them and he halted his plans to invade our world at my request" Silver said

"What?" Jay said confused

"I came across something meant for a demon, and the lords of hell thought god had done it, they were going to break through the doors to hell and rampage on the earth which would have brought the angels down to wipe the world clean" I said "It was my way of saying thank you and keeping the lords of hell happy and where they belong"

"So even when no one knows it, you were saving the world" Jay asked

"Please don't tell anyone" Julian said "Things are different now and we don't have to deal with that other time"

"But how did my father get back the pack in that timeline? And how did you meet me and Savannah?" Jay asked

"Does it really matter?" I asked "That timeline no longer exists"

"So you just wiped everyone you know?" He asked seeming shitty

"NO" I said getting angry "it was none of our choice, we just dealt with what we had the best we could, and if you must know Trance had the pack and he made damn sure you and your pack suffered a lot"

"How did you know you would make things better?" Jay asked calming a little

"We didn't, but we had hope" Julian said "and things turned out much better"

"I don't understand how you could have been payment for something you had nothing to do with" Jay said looking at me

"Because the vampire lords felt they owned everyone and everything, that I was a commodity to trade, after all Ivanovich had spent years trading in my blood, I think they really wanted to get rid of me for messing up their plans, but we stopped all the shit they created from happening" I explained

"But he still took his payment?" Jay asked

"Yes he raped me repeatedly over the course of 2 fucking months and I had no fucking idea because he used Julian's body to do it" I said I could feel the tears starting in my throat any more of this and I would be crying

"I am sorry Silver," Jay said, sitting back down "Why did you not tell us this when we met you?"

"Because that timeline does not matter, it no longer happened" Talon said "and honestly I think we all wanted to forget the horrors from back them"

"Look Jay I lost most of my family in that timeline because of one of those vampire lords, we all lost so many loved ones, when we woke up back here I just wanted to make sure none of it happened" I said "In this timeline, the one that matters, I have them all and more, I even tried to get to Savannah before her sire did, but I was too late, and it has been explained to me some things had to happen, we were going to stop vampires coming out but that would have messed shit up worse"

"How do you know?" Jay asked

"Because the powers that be would have taken control by force" Talon said "I know I was in the loop on both timelines, trust me this is better"

"In the other time Savannah was frozen for attempting to kill her sire, and her lover was killed by another, then she lived as a prisoner of yours before you two got together, in this line her lover was killed by her sire and when she took retribution she was not punished for it, and you found each other naturally" I explained

"You should be grateful that none of us had to live through the tortures and pain from that line, even Savannah did not get the same level of abuse from her sire here as she did there, and you have both flourished because of it" Talon said

"I am sorry I just …" Jay started

"Look Jay as far as Silver is concerned you guys are family from the time she met you in the other line and she has gone above and beyond to make sure you are as safe as you can be, because she protects her family no matter what" Julian said

"We would most likely be dead now if that line had continued" Talon said "I had to wait 30 years to meet Mat, and I do not regret a single moment of this timeline"

"Did you say Ivanovich was trading your blood?" Jay asked me

"Yes he was, he was forced to make more positive changes this time and his accomplices didn't have the chance to get to me, this time" I said

"So he doesn't know about what happened?" Jay asked

"Yes he does which is why he agreed to do things differently, his neck was on the line too" Julian said

There was a knock on the door.

We all froze, except Alipa who went to get the door.

Talon and Julian get ready to fight whoever has found us now.

It was Mat.

"Wow I did not expect this kind of welcome" She said putting her bag down, Talon ran to her and hugged her tightly.

"I missed you Mat" he said looking down into her eyes

"I missed you to darling, but what's going on?" she asked

"They are being foolish and arguing over things that no longer matter dear " Alipa said shuffling back into the room and to her seat

"I am going to go see Savannah and Rain" Jay said getting up "I hope you were right Silver and things don't go south"

"Tell Savannah I said hi and I will catch up with her soon" Mat smiled as he walked past her

"Yeah I will" He said walking out the door.

"What is his problem?" Mat asked after he closed the door

"He is caught up in what could have been instead of what is, he will be ok though" Alipa said

"So you guys needed me to help with something?" Mat asked shrugging off Jay's behaviour

"Yeah we need better protection from gods and lords of hell" I said

"I have the spells it is just the quantity of things I need to do the spells on is a bit much for one old hag like me dear" Alipa laughed

"Ok" Mat said "When can we get started, I have to get back as soon as I can the students go a little silly when I am not around"

"OH?" Silver asked

"Yeah last time I left when I got back some of the students had started an uprising, even though they had no idea what they were wanting or fighting for, it took me days to get it all sorted" Mat said "Lily and Luca are holding the fort this time so hopefully we don't have the same issue"

"Why didn't you tell me?" Talon and I said at the same time

"Because I dealt with it and didn't want to make a big fuss" Mat said shyly

"You are amazing Mat" I said

"You look very tired Silver" Mat said "Maybe you should go rest while your babies are"

"Yeah its not them who made me tired but thank you Mat for your concern"

"You lot piss off, Mat and I will get started on this" Alipa said "We have more than enough things to enchant so we don't need you lot around annoying us"

"Yes mam" Julian said jokingly "Come on wife to bed with you" he gave me a sly smile

"Ok we are going, we will leave tomorrow night all going to plan" I said "Thank you Mat for coming all this way to help us

out"
"Really I just wanted to see Talon" Mat blushed
"Oh yeah that reminds me, he will be going back with you too" I
said smiling
She looked delighted and looked at Talon who nodded
"After I make sure the new place is secure" he added

Chapter 2

The next evening we were all ready to go, Brutus had made sure we had a couple of extra cars and had worked out routes they could take to get to Brooklyn, he and Mary-Anne would be in the SUV going with us as they would be collecting the keys.

Jay and Savannah took the second RV and planned a route that was with us for part way and then they would go off to their home.

Everyone had been given random rocks and sticks to throw out the vehicle on their way, and small enchanted trinkets that they could give any kids they saw or slip into others cars. We were making sure the voids would appear everywhere.

Alipa was making packages to send overseas to people we knew with explanations on what to do with the things she was sending. All heavily enchanted.

Julian and myself had enchanted rings that could warn us if any godly beings (or demonic angels) were nearby.

It was a relatively boring drive with the most excitement being when the twins woke up.

We arrived at the real estate office that sold us the houses around 4pm Mary-Anne and Brutus signed the paperwork and got the keys. The estate agent insisted on taking them to the properties that were side by side, and then waiting for the vampires to wake up.

I woke up before any of the other vampires, Julian woke as I was getting dressed. We came out of our room and Mary-Anne and Brutus were sitting in the lounge area of the RV with the estate agent.

"Oh, I didn't realize we had visitors already" I said seeing the stranger sitting there

"Oh Abi" Mary-Anne said jumping up "Lucius" she nodded at Julian "This is Steve he is the one who sold us the houses, he

really wanted to meet you and make sure we were above board
and you really are vampires"
I hated people like this, nosey asshats who have to know everything.
"Hello Steve" Julian said "We are indeed vampires, and thank
you for letting our friends get the keys for us"
"You are aware they also signed all the paperwork?" Steve said
getting up and shaking Julians hand
"Well yes that is one reason we have them with us to make our
lives easier so we do not have to deal with humans who really
want to meet vampires" I said looking at him like he was an
intruder
"Well I see everything seems to be in order here I shall just show
you all around and then go" He said looking put out
"There's no need really we are capable of looking around our
new houses without a guide" Julian said "We are very private
people and would be grateful if you could just leave us to it" I
noticed a bit of a push in his voice
"Of course that is perfectly acceptable too, other vampires in
the area have a coffee group the first evening of every month so
if you want to meet more like you I would suggest going along"
he said leaving our RV.
Then the babies woke up crying.
"You have babies in there?" he said turning quickly back to face
us.
I had gone to get one of the babies and Mary-Anne had come
with me to get the other.
"Yes my wife and I adopted a couple of children to give them a
better life" Julian said carefully guiding the agent back to his car
"Vampires can adopt children?" Steve said rather worried
"Don't worry we do not feed on them they are way to young for
that, but my wife always wanted kids and now we are in a position to provide a wonderful life for them, it would be wasteful
not to help some poor disadvantaged children achieve a much
better life" he said smiling at the agent
"Ok well I shall go" he said hurriedly getting in his car the drive-

way was horseshoe style and he went in before the RV and SUV so he took off out the driveway.

"He's going to make trouble" Brutus said standing next to Julian "I think your right" Talon said coming up next to the boys "I shall make sure we are prepared for them"

Mary-Anne and I came out with the kids all changed and with bottles in their mouths.

"So let's go have a look at our new home" I said as Julian took Althea from me so I could be hands free

Brutus had the keys and we went to the first house.

He found the lights and the alarm pad and turned the alarm off.

It was a lovely house, and it was big, all the windows had special UV filtering in them, originally to protect furniture and human's from the harsh sun in summer, but now perfect for vampires living in the burbs if we felt like doing daytime.

The kitchen was massive and built to entertain with 6 ovens in total and 12 hotplates. I didn't like that they were gas and found a pen and paper to write down all the shit that would need changing, it was first on my list. Change ovens to normal electricity, followed by building big fences, and Solar power.

There were three living areas downstairs and two bedrooms with a full bathroom and two en-suites, and a huge laundry and mudroom, two dining rooms, one was formal and one was more a breakfast nook for a whole family and a huge entertainment room that opened out to a massive patio with a built in wood burning barbecue and pizza oven. There was also a massive infinity pool that was fenced off for safety.

Upstairs there were eight bedrooms, each with their own en-suite and a library that had wall to wall built in shelves.

It was very fresh and american yuppie styled

The place was partially furnished with very basic furnishings, a bed in each bedroom, a couch in one lounge, and a plastic outside table in the dining room.

Mary-Anne explained the furnishings were rented to sell the house but the agent had agreed to let us rent them till we got our own sorted.

We walked over to the other house, it was a good hundred meter walk.

The babies were behaving and looking around. Angelus was looking serious and concerned while Althea was open eyed with wonder and excitement.

The house looked just like all the others in the street from the outside.

Brutus opened the door and turned the alarm off.

This place was much more my style, it had been decorated dark, graceful and gothish.

"The agent said he had problems selling this place, because of the decor so he was very pleased we wanted both" Mary-Anne said

"This place is stunning" I exclaimed as we walked in the massive entry room, the staircase going up was curved and the banister was white black marble with white marble steps. It had very high ceilings

For the first time in a very long time I felt like I was home, even though I had never been here before.

I know people were babbling behind me but I was lost in the exquisite design and decor of the house, the kitchen was an entertainers dream again, and again there were several living areas, it had three bedrooms downstairs, and each had a semi ensuite (one that was shared by two bedrooms and the other room shared the main bathroom)

The entertainment room came with a full sized marble pool table, and a nice bar, it also led out to a patio and a covered pool. With the outdoor lights on I could see solar panels all over the pool roof, and the main house had solar tiles for roofing.

There was a conservatory shaped like octagon that sat in the direction of the other house, and a covered walkway to it that was heavy with Ivy.

"I will be staying here" Alipa said when she saw that "your boys chose well"

"I think I too will be staying here" I said "Once we have furniture"

Unlike the other house this house had nothing except the pool table and other things that would not have been able to be moved like the bar.

I raced to see upstairs.

Up here were 6 bedrooms and a walkway, I wandered down the walkway first.

Across here was a massive room with nothing to show what it

would have been used for, all the walls were black, it was over the garage and there was a spiral staircase going down to the garage, it had a toilet room as well. I went back to the house and looked at each bedroom, it was like each room had been decorated for the occupant at the time, they each had built in beds, one room was for a small boy, one for a teenage boy, one for a very girly girl I would guess around 10ish with a pink canopy bed, and one for a very gothy young lady with a black four poster bed, one room was very plain, they all had semi en-suites that they shared with the neighbouring room and the teen girls one was separate and then there was the master bedroom.

I opened the door and saw a built in super king sized four poster bed that was up on a platform and had steps up to the bed.

This is why they had high ceilings.

"You look like your home" Julian said coming up behind me and hugging me

"Are you ok with it?" I asked suddenly concerned he would not like it

"Oh darling I love it, it is so us" He smiled spinning me around to face him and kissing me

"We need to sort out who will be in which room" Mary-Anne said "If you guys want this house then I guess I will be down the hall."

"I think we should turn the space over the garage into a room for you guys, like a self contained unit thing" I suggested

"Cool but for now I just want somewhere to put the kids to bed" She said

"Ok um the blue room, I am against pink like that until it's her choice" I said

"Cool the containers will be arriving tomorrow there was some kind of delay caused by weather" She said as she headed down the hall holding Althea, she looked tired, and Mat followed behind her holding Angelus

I followed both of them.

Some of the guys had brought the kids bassinets up and were moving them into the blue room under the annoyed gaze of Mary-Anne.

"You can take whatever room you want hun" I said putting my

hand on her shoulder

"Thanks, I am feeling a bit tired" she said

"Go rest" I said "I can do this"

"Can you tell Brutus I'm in the goth room?" she said handing me Althea

"Do you think he will let you rest if I do that?" I said jokingly

"Actually you have a point, tell him he is not to come to bed till he wants to go to sleep and not to disturb me" she smiled

"I will hun" I said smiling

We said good night to the babies and put them to bed, Mary-Anne had the good sense to have a baby monitor with us so I set it up and we went downstairs to help unpack the shit we had with us.

I started making a list of what we needed to buy and what would need to be done to make the houses secure.

Most of the beasts went to bed around midnight the babies didn't wake again till 6 am, as the sun was rising, Julian and I took a drink of blood and went to go look after them till Mary-Anne woke up.

It was 7:30 when she came racing down the stairs in a panic.

"Silver the kids are gone," she said in a panic at me then she looked confused

"Sorry I let you sleep in" I said sheepishly "I wanted to spend some more time with them and you deserve a sleep in"

"Next time could you warn me" she said sitting down

Julian handed her a cup of coffee and went to get another as Brutus came down the stairs

"I told you they would be fine" He said to Mary-Anne sleepily

He gratefully accepted the coffee Julian had made him, he took a big gulp.

"How is it you vampires who do not drink coffee often make such a good cup?" he said

"Modern technology" Julian said laughing "there's a coffee machine in the kitchen that does all the work"

"I think I will like this place" he said sitting next to Mary-Anne

"You two should go to bed" Mary-Anne said looking at me "I can take care of things from here"

"Oh I have made a list of everything we need here and next door, can you get a couple of the wolves to go shopping, anyone you think will have the right sense of style for each place, and we need to find some builders to start on the fence, I want 6 foot stone wall around both houses not in between, I want a proper path put in between the two houses and the room above the garage to be made into a little unit for you two" I said starting to feel the tug of my bed

"I will take care of it" Brutus said taking the pile of lists "it will give me something to do"

 "I am quite capable of doing it dear" Mary-Anne said

"Yes I know but I thought you might like to go shopping too" He smiled at her

"Well I would but who would look after the babies?" Mary-Anne laughed

"I will," Mat said, bouncing in the door. "Or we could take them with us and both go shopping?"

"You could do that" I said , I knew the kids would be safe with both of them out there

"Ok well we shall bugger off, so you can do whatever" Julian said giving the babies a kiss on the forehead "Good night my angels" he whispered

I gave them both a kiss too

 "Be good for your aunty's" I whispered

We went to bed.

When we went downstairs the next evening the house was feeling excited, I know houses don't have feelings but this one felt excited and it was infectious.

Mary-Anne and Mat had taken Rain and Declan, who never left Rain's side, out shopping with the kids.

They had found places willing to deliver today and some were even delivering into the evening, Mary-Anne was holding Althea and feeding her while ordering people around and directing where things needed to go, Rain was holding Angelus and burping him.

"You look like a natural" I said coming in behind her Angelus head lifted when he heard me and he smiled, Rain turned around

"I was just helping Mary-Anne and Mat" she said suddenly as if she were in trouble but turning slowly so as not to disrupt the baby on her shoulder.

"Its ok" I said "I am grateful that she has more help, in our case it really will take a village to raise these kids"

"Do you find it hard having to sleep during the day?" she asked innocently

"I never used to but now, that is when the kids are awake and they will start doing things and we will miss it, good thing about these houses is we can be up during the day as long as we stay inside" I said "May I have a cuddle?" I said indicating I wanted to cuddle my son

Julian took Althea from Mary-Anne and Rain handed me Angelus.

"They really are great babies" Rain said "So peaceful and relaxing" she smiled at them

"I want to have a small gathering tomorrow evening when everyone is awake, like a welcome to our new home," I said as Angelus let out a huge burp.

Mary-Anne had vanished, I could hear her barking orders as to where to put furniture.

Brutus came in the front door.

"Everything next door is sorted, how's things here?" he asked

"We are nearly done" I heard Mary-Anne yell from one of the living rooms...I'm not sure which one, then she popped back in from the patio doors.

"I will get the artwork up tomorrow" she said smiling, "I think your going to love what I have done, well at least I hope you do" she bowed and waved her hand "After you"

I walked into the first living room, it was exquisite, all old furniture, like antiques but solid. None of the delicate frilly stuff in here. There was a huge tv and it felt a bit like where we would go to watch sports but more gothish, maybe some motor racing. We went to another one of the living areas and it was decked out to play with babies, comfy big dark couches but lots of colour around the room and on the floor was a road map of a town, the next living area was more delicate the furniture was classic gothic finary.

I absolutely loved it.

All the rooms had TV's, even the formal dining room.

I got excited and half hugged Mary-Anne, everything she had done in such a short time amazed me.

"Thank you" I said starting to leak from my eyes

"Oh no you don't" she said pointing her finger at me "Do not cry woman, you are ...Abigail Althea Giovanni and Giovanni do not cry" she laughed

"I am just so grateful to you Mary-Anne" I said then I turned to see all the others who there "All of you have done an amazing job"

There were lots of you're welcome and thank you miss. Julian and I swapped babies for cuddles

My phone rang, now I always carry it with me, I never use it except for taking photos and playing games, it hardly ever rings anymore.

I took it out and looked at it as if it were possessed and it stopped ringing.

I put it away with a sigh of relief.

Julians started ringing and he answered it.

"Hello" he said

"My lord what can I do for you?" Julian asked

"We are retired and parents now my lord our priorities have changed" He said looking annoyed

"Yes we have moved house" Julian said looking mad

"My lord you have no need to come to us, if we have to we will come to you" yup he is getting quite angry

I shooed everyone off to go back to what they were doing and Jualin and I went upstairs taking the kids to bed.

"My lord with all due respect I do not give a fuck what you have got yourself into, we have retired from that life" Julian was very careful not to get to volatile while he held our baby "and that is the end of the story" he said in a baby voice as he lay our son in his crib

He stood up straight and walked quickly out of the room.

I put Althea down and said a quick good night and raced after him, I caught up to him in our bedroom

"You wouldn't dare" Julian said looking furious "That will turn everything we have done on its fucking head"

Now I was wanting to be clued in. I gave Julian a look that we had started using as code for may I pop into your head. He nodded.

He wants to come and visit us and the kids to give us an assignment" he said fuming

"You just can't help yourself can you my lord" Julian seethed into the phone

"But here's the kicker if we don't do the assignment he is threatening to tell the world we mind fucked them all" Julian explained in our head

"What the fuck?" I said in shock

"I know right" Julian said back

"If we do not find this artifact" I heard Ivanovich through Julian "Someone else will and they will not protect humanity from it and everything we have worked for will be fucked as you say"

"Why not send someone else?" Julian asked

"Because I do not trust anyone else" he said

"You are aware we have two babies to look after, aren't you?" Julian said having calmed a tiny bit

"Yes" came back that thick accent "I am sorry that I have to ask this of you because of the babies, but this is just too important"

I got out of Julians head and went and sat down on the bed. I put my head in my hands and cried.

"Tell him where we are Julian" I said quietly

"Silver are you sure?" he said looking panicked

"If he goes into the public and lies like that we will all be fucked there will be no future for the babies" I said indicating for him to use speaker phone, he did "but we chose our team, we take our people, and that is non negotiable"

"Did you hear that my lord?" Julian sneered at the phone

"We will talk of this when I get there" I heard from the phone

"And my Lord, if anyone untoward finds this house I will be hunting you first" I said I pushed the end call button

"I wish you could slam the phone down like the old old days" I went back to the bed and flopped down

"We are never going to escape this shit" Julian said sitting next to me looking at the wall

"I was stupid to think we could" I said

He lay back and looked at me

"We can do this babe" he said "we can work out how to teach the kids to protect themselves, I am sure they will be better faster stronger than humans"

"They seem to grow faster, I am sure," I said, "I don't want them to grow up with absent parents though"

"Neither do I" Julian laughed

"Excuse me" we heard from the door of our room we both sat up and looked at a young man who had in his arms a very large mirror with a beautiful black ornate frame he was only holding one side "We were told to put this in here sorry to disturb you"

"Oh that's fine" I said getting up "wow that's an awesome mirror"

"It's one of a kind " The second delivery guy said "was part of the estate sale of some old reclouse up north somewhere"

"Did we get a lot of things from that sale?" I asked admiring it as they carefully put it against the wall

"Most of it" the first guy said "Mary-Anne was a very enthusiastic buyer"

"This comes with a dressing table that holds it up, it's quite big and will have to go against this wall if that is ok?" the second guy said pointing to the other big wall space we had

"Yes that is fine" I said still admiring the mirror

Julian came up beside me and put his arm around me

"That is one hell of a mirror" he said "Even with the bed up that high I could watch us going at it in that mirror"

I whacked his arm playfully

"You perv" I laughed

"But you love me anyway" he said snuggling me tighter

"I better go see what else Mary-Anne has found" I said wriggling out from under his grip

"You should check our account to, see how much all this cost us" he said

"Really when did we care about money?" I said turning back to face him

"Since we splashed out a few million on a couple of houses, and now all this" he waved his hand around as the delivery men came in with the center part of the dressing table.

"Wow that is a bit underwhelming for the mirror" Julian said looking at it

"This is just the middle bit, the sides are still downstairs" the first guy said

"Well then I might just give you guys a hand then" Julian smiled at them

"That is not necessary sir but thank you" the second guy said

"No I insist, I need something to do and I am a lot stronger than I look" Julian said

"Ok I'm going down to see what else there is" I left the room Julian and the delivery men were right behind me

"Hay Sil" Mary-Anne yelled when she saw me "I need you to come into the entertainment room I have something to show you"

I followed her over to one side and there was a huge frame much like the one on my mirror but it was mostly covered.

Mary-Anne curiously closed all the doors.

"I went to this auction to get some things you might like, but one of the things was this, I didn't want anyone else seeing it yet but I thought you should know about it," she took the sheet off the frame, it was a massive larger than life painting.

"The auction house said the old guy had this commissioned over 50 years ago," she explained

I was dumbfounded.

"How?" I asked, staring at myself with my wings and a baby in each arm, looking like an angel of death in the full moon light.

"I don't know" She said "I did some digging but the artist died not long after he finished this and well the old man is dead with no surviving relatives"

"It's not possible" I sort of fell down onto the couch. I was totally stunned looking at the painting of me with my wings and my baby's.

50 years ago no one knew any of this, not my wings not my baby's

"How?" I kept muttering

"Julian can you come to the entertaining room quickly and bring Talon if you can find him," I said to Jualin in my head

"Sure hun what's wrong?" he replied

"Just come" I said

"I mean I know not many people know about the wings and baby's, and over 50 years ago there's no way they would have known, but read the inscription on the back" she pointed out as we both moved the very heavy painting.

The mother
The moon
The hero
Our saviour

"Oh fuck off" I said rather pissed off as Jualin and Talon came in. Both of them were laughing when they opened the door and both stopped and stared mouths open in stunned silence.

"Where did you find this?" Julian asked

"The auction house where I got your dressing table, and some of the other more gothic items" Mary-Anne said

"It was done over 50 years ago" I said, still stunned. "I am not going crazy the woman is me isn't it?"

"Yes darling, it very much looks like you" Julian and Talon went over to have a closer look

"How is this even possible?" Talon asked staring at the painting "I mean even with the time thing there's no possible way"

"We need to hide this" I said "I don't want people thinking I am that person"

"And where do you suggest we put it?" Mary-Anne said

"A fire" I suggested

"Oh hell no" Julian said "I think though for now we should put it in ...the garage..till we can find somewhere to store it"

"No" I said "I don't want people to see this ever and think that is me"

Talon was looking at the back.

"It's not wrong though" he said

"It's not fucking right either" I said "We need to find out more about it"

"Or we could ignore it as some old man's dream woman who happens to look like you" Julian said "I mean it is a stunning piece of work"

"We need to see if it is...something else" I said remembering the art way back when we sorted out Chicago

"I'll go find Alipa" Talon said shaking his head

"Surely you could sense if there was something else?" Julian said

"Darling since getting pregnant and having babies my head is all messed up," I said, "Do you think Sin had something to do with this?"

"Do you?" he asked

"I don't know" I said "I hope not"

 Talon came back with Alipa

"My that is a big painting of you Silver" she said coming in the room

"Alipa could you tell us if it has any...other ..qualities please" Julian asked nicely

"Let me see" she said getting up close to it she was touching the paint and really investigating it. "No blood, no magic, just a painting" she said after a few minutes

"It was painted over 50 years ago" I said

"Well that is interesting" Alipa said "But there is nothing special about it"

"Maybe in the future you go back in time?" Talon suggested

"Well the babies there look like newborns" Julian said, "and our babies already look about 6 months old"

"Did I vanish when they were born?" I asked

"No" they all said I could tell they were thinking about it

"So shall we leave it to the old man or the artist to have a prophetic vision?" Alipa said smiling

"How do you know it was an old man's?" Mary-Anne asked her

"I can see them when I touch the painting" she said smiling, "he was young and handsome when he got this done"

"It is going away until I am sure that is all it is, also Ivanovich is coming he should not be allowed to know of it at all, so we need somewhere good to hide it" I said

"Is it wise that he come here? We are in hiding after all" Talon said

"He threatened to fuck us all over" Julian said

"Really?" Talon asked "I thought he had learnt not to do shit like that"

"He wants us to go on a mission to find some artifact, said if we don't and someone else does the world will be fucked anyway" I said, "I told him we take the team we pick, although I have no idea how we will do this with the babies"

"Oh yes about your babies" Alipa suddenly said "They are growing much faster than human babies, I think if you left them for a week they would be walking and talking"

"I am not leaving my babies, I may have never wanted to be a mum but I am now and I am going to be there for my kids" I said adamantly "It's bad enough I can't be a normal mum"

"Darling even when you were human you were not normal" Julian said coming over and hugging me

"You know what I mean" I said giving him a half evil look

"If you have to go on a mission why would you take the babies?" Mary-Anne asked

"I don't know but I do not want to leave them, not when they are so young," I said "cover that thing up and put it picture side against a wall in the garage for now please hun"

"Ok darling, but I think you are overreacting about it, Alipa says its fine and it is an amazing work of art" Julian said

"It's vile and ostentatious" I said "and the fact it looks so much like me is just creepy"

"Ok, well we will put this away for now" Julian said as he and Talon picked it up and moved towards the garage.

Mary-Anne and I went out to the main living area and entry way on our way to the kitchen, I needed a drink.

That was when I saw Lord Ivanovich standing in my front door.

"My lord you have arrived" I said not happy in the slightest

"I went to the address Julian gave me and they said you would be here" He said in his thick accent

"Yeah great, did they give you a room" I asked feeling annoyed

"I will not be staying that long" he said gruffly

"Right so you just turn up and expect us to drop everything we are doing to do what you want us to do?" I said

"I need you to do this" He said looking desperate

"Lounge is that way" I pointed to it "I am getting a drink before I speak with you" I stormed off to the kitchen, there were too many people around, I needed to breathe.

Mary-Anne came into the kitchen after seeing Lord Ivanovich to the main lounge.

"I need a minute" I said to her "I'm going up the backstairs to my room for a minute ok"

"Ok I will stall him" she smiled at me and rubbed my arm "It will be ok we will work something out"

"I need to know how exactly the artist died and how the old man died" I said "I don't trust that painting, not after all the devious things Sin has done"

"I understand, I will look into it" She smiled at me and she went back out to the main lounge I snuck upstairs to my room.

The whole dressing table was up now and the delivery guys were on their way back out. I went over to it, it was an amazing dressing table, the mirror was bolted to the wall because it was so big and heavy.

I went to my bathroom and splashed some water on my face.

I did not want to deal with Ivanovich, we were meant to be free of all the drama he comes with. Yet here he was dragging us back into his crap.

"Are you ok hun?" I heard Julian say in my head

"Yeah I just needed a moment, I'll be back down shortly" I said

"Ivanovich seems eager to leave, he is pacing in the lounge" Julian said

"Let him pace" I said

I straightened myself up, took a deep breath and headed back downstairs.

"Is there somewhere we can talk quietly?" Ivanovich said as soon as I got in the room

"Not really my lord, you see we only just moved in and things are still being sorted out, besides these three are part of my team so whatever it is you can say in front of them" I said

"Very well, your ex Jualin, Cleo is currently hunting down the trumpet the felled the walls of Jericho, the sword excalibur, and the holy grail, although I am not sure why but if she gets her hands on those, she will be able to wipe the planet clean"

"Excalibur will not let her use it, it only lets people of good intention kill those who are evil" Julian said as if this was a well known fact

"How would that work?" I asked

"The trumpet of Jericho sends out a sound wave that crumbles anything in its way, the longer it is blown the larger the area is flattened, the holy grail can give humans eternal life, but it is believed it can also make a vampire turn into a god, and Julian is right about the sword so I have no idea how she plans to use it, but you need to go and get these things and hide them before she finds them" Ivanovich said

"I thought you had the sword" Talon said

"I thought I had that sword as well but it is gone" he said looking very vexed about it

"Your a vamp lord, why don't you find these things" I said

"Because young lady I have other important concerns happening, there is a faction of rebels who want to wipe out vampires and I have been hunting them down, also I have the council to keep an eye on and if I am away to long things fall into chaos there" he explained

"Did you find any evidence as to where the sword might have vanished to?" Talon asked

"No it was strangely void of any evidence" Ivanovich said looking very angry "I am hoping with Silver's interesting talents she may be able to find out more"

"I can't do it" I said "I have kids to look after"

"Silver if we do not do this there will be no kids" Ivanovich said flatly

"So you propose that I leave my kids behind to chase artifacts that have been lost for centuries, and that managed to get stolen from you, I have seen your security on things that do not matter, when I find it very hard to believe that I will be of any use at all," I said

"Silver do not underestimate your abilities" Ivanovich said "You shall start in my secret vault, in Ireland, and go from there, since you insist on having a team I am sure your team will be able to find the clues and match them up as to where the other things could be"

"Do you know how many people have searched for these things over the millennia they have been around?" Talon asked

"Yes I do but they did not have the resources we have today" he said getting up

"I will expect you to drop in to London to update me, when you have checked out my vault." he added heading for the door

"I said no my lord" I stated firmly

"No is not an option, my dear, I must go if I am to catch my flight back" he said still heading to the door

I went to chase him down but Julian stopped me.

I looked at him as if I could kill him

"We are not doing his fucking bidding this time" I said

"Yes we are" Julian said quietly, "We will work out how to manage with the babies but I know Cleo and she will use these items to destroy everything"

"I knew we should have killed that bitch when we came back" I seethed

"I want to know why she is doing this now" Julian said

"I want to know how we find these things before her" Talon said

Ivanovich's car drove away

I took a deep breath

"First we need everyone," I said turning around and taking control.

I started towards the stairs "I want the twins, one of the wolves or two, I want Khan and Brutus, Talon your whole team, my family anyone who can make it, I understand if they don't, Julian I want your family too if they think they can help, I want all our people on standby, and I want 5 minutes with Julian"

"I think I can help" Rain said gliding through the door so gracefully "I think this is why I was sent to find the wolf, so I could be here for this"

She looked so elegant and godly I looked around all the open mouths of the stunned people in this room.

"You Silver should not go after the grail itself but work on the other two" she said coming over to me "I believe Talon should go for the grail with Mat"

"Do you have visions often?" I asked her

"Yes sometimes they are good" she smiled

"If you think you can help then welcome" I said "But I do not want you out there in the field ok"

"That suits me fine" Declan said smiling at her

"I can go wherever I am needed" She said "I can look after myself"

"Like when Ethan found you?" He asked

"I was commanded to walk into freezing wilderness, I had no choice" She snapped

"Ok guys take a breath" I suggested they both listened "Now lets deal with this other bullshit then you guys can sort out your relationship when you are in a room alone"

"Sorry " they both said quickly turning back to me

"I understand shit happens, it happens to me all the time ...ie we are doing a mission with a couple of baby's to consider, and the possibility they are ...something else. But it will pass and those who stay with you will be like family forever"

"How do you know?" they asked at the same time

"Because I have been there, more times than I like, except the baby part. You guys are part of my family, because you are Jay's family and Rain you are destined for so much more than you know" I said "I can just feel it"

"So are we saving the world again?" Julian said to me, grabbing me around the waist from behind and loud enough for everyone in the room to hear it.
Everyone was looking at me.
"Yes" I said then we heard a cry on the baby monitor just before everyone cheered
I took off up stairs Julian and Mary-Anne behind me.
I went into the baby's room and picked up Althea, Julian got Angelus and Mary-Anne sorted bottles, we had a mini kitchen set up in here just for this. Mary-Anne had really done an amazing job in such a short time.
"So do you still want me to look into that other thing?" Mary-Anne asked
"When you can, don't rush it, if you don't get the chance that's ok things are about to get hectic" I said
"What are we going to do about the babies?" Julian asked
"Well I figure we do what we can to find the things from here, a team goes to get the grail and another team can go get the sword and another the trumpet if we can find them" I said "we can try and work it so one of us is here"
"And you have me here and I think Rain would help if I needed it so any time you both had to be gone it would be ok" Mary-Anne said
"You do so much already Mary-Anne" I said smiling at her
"I don't think it will be any hassle after all, they sleep at night and I only need 4 hours" she smiled "and they do know me"
"Ok" I said "We can do this" I added in baby talk directed at Althea, she smiled at me
The baby's were so alert now, looking everywhere at everything.
Alipa was right, they were growing fast.
"I need to go see Alipa" I said, giving Althea to Mary-Anne.
I went to her room and the door was open.
"Come in Silver" I heard Alipa say from inside
"You knew I was coming to talk to you?" I asked her
"Ofcourse" she said
"Do you know why?" I asked her

"Yes dear" she said smiling "Come sit" she patted the bed beside her, she had chosen to stay in the girly pink room

"How will the fast rate of growth affect the babies?" I asked her

"Well aside from you will have to keep up with them, they should be ok" she said

"But they are growing too fast" I said

"Yes and I suspect they will till they reach full maturity around 8 or 9,"she said

"But a 9 year old in an 18 year olds body?" I exclaimed

"Yes dear you will have to make sure they keep up, so when they are 9 and look 18 they know how to be 18" she said

"Can that be done without destroying them emotionally, and mentally" I said

"I think you and your family will be able to pull it off" Alipa said, "but you could ask Rain to look into it" she suggested

"Do you know anything about the painting Mary-Anne bought?" I asked her quietly

"Not really but it is safe at this time" she said putting a hand on my knee

"Is it in any way connected to Sin?" I asked

"Not that I can tell my dear, I can tell you blood has been spilt over it, and it is safe now" she said smiling

"Do you know how it is me?" I queried

"Maybe the artist had a vision" she said "Maybe the man who commissioned it had one"

"Will we get through this mission alive?" I asked

"Most of you will" she said nodding her head but looking solemn

"What do you mean?" I asked

"You may lose one or two but most of you will be safe" she said "and it is not one of those close to you that will be lost"

"This will not stop till everyone believes I am dead will it?" I said

"No my child, it will continue long after your dead, but you must not die yet" she patted my knee again

"Gee thanks" I said

"I will keep an eye on the painting and on Rain, Mat is refusing to leave until it is done, you have the support and the love behind you, you can beat anything" Alipa said smiling

"Do you think I should listen to Rain's advice and not go after the grail myself?" I asked

"Oh yes" she nodded

"I sense it, if you go after the grail yourself, you will not come back as you" she said ominously

"Done deal I will go for the sword then" I said

"You my dear have already lived so many lives but you still have many to live" Alipa said

"Well after this mission and raising the kids maybe I will get to run away for a while" I said wistfully "Play dead a couple of centuries or something"

"I can see you need a break" Alipa said "Maybe enjoy the sights a bit where you are going, like a working holiday"

"I should get back, we have a lot to do before we gather everyone" I said getting up

"Do not worry yourself so much dear" Alipa said smiling again "things will work out"

"I hope so" I said walking out the door "and thank you"

I bumped into Julian and Mary-Anne coming out of the kids room

"We need to start making plans" I said "I take it they have gone back to sleep?"

"Yeah" Julian said "so Mary-Anne you go to bed, so you can get up before dawn and we can brief you on whatever is going to happen"

"When we are here I want as much time with the kids as we can" I said "without ruining their routine of course"

"Yup" Mary-Anne yawned "I will see you both before dawn"
She went off to her room and Jualin and I went downstairs

We had set up the entertainment room as a war room for now, someone covered the pool table with a large piece of wood so it was all flat. There were a couple of laptops on the bar, really we had minimal gear at the moment.

"Ok has everyone who needs to be called been called?" I asked Talon

"Yup and most have said yes" he replied "everyone should be here by midnight tomorrow"

"Awesome so we will have a meeting tomorrow at 1am then" I said

"I made a start on trying to find where we might find some of the relics" Ivory said "It looks like the grail will be the easiest, there's 10 possible locations, the sword may be harder to find since we know Ivanovich had it so everything I have found is useless, and the main trumpet of jericho I can't find anything on in the normal web, but I haven't yet looked deeper"

"Ok well I want 4 teams made up from who is coming, Talon I want you to lead the quest for the grail, Julian you take a team to go after the trumpet, a team to stay here and make sure we all get info we need as soon as it comes to hand, and I will lead the team going for the sword" I said "does that sound ok?" I looked around at everyone and they all nodded

"Silver if I may" Rain said quietly I nodded at her

"There is someone you should go and see, she will be able to help, she has an ability to find ancient things" Rain said

"Ok do you have a name and address?" I asked

"I have a name, but I do not know where to find her" she said "Her name is Etana, I believe she is a vampire from the middle eastern area in ancient times"

"Mmm yes she is, and she is a vampire lord" I said "I wonder if Ivanovich knows how to get in touch with her?"

"I will ring and ask him," Talon offered, I nodded.

"We should rest till tomorrow" Julian said looking at me concerned *"You are looking very pale my love have you eaten"* I heard in my head

"I'm feeling a bit weak actually, I will go and grab a bottle from the fridge" I said back

I got up and went to the kitchen Julian was right behind me I got a bottle and opened it, I skulled it back

"I think I will go lie down" I said looking at Julian

"I will come with you, we may not get too many nights together for a while" he smirked
We went upstairs and to our room, the mirror suited this room with the massive bed, and it was in the perfect place for it. I stood for a minute just looking at me in it. Julian came up behind me and put his arms around me.
"This mirror is amazing" he said looking at it as well "You looking amazing" he turned me around and kissed me. I felt like I wasn't really there for a minute and then suddenly I was and I kissed him right back.
"Lets just go to bed" I said letting him pick me up and walk me up the stairs to our bed he threw me on the bed and jumped on top of me.

Chapter 3

The next evening the whole house was in chaos, there were people everywhere, I wandered outside to see progress had been made on the fence, One of the builders walked past me carrying a large post on one shoulder.

"Excuse me, could you point out the boss to me?" I asked her

"Sure that would be Jim, he is over that way next to the truck" she sort of waved with a spare hand

"Thank you" I said heading that way

I found the truck and saw people lifting posts and wood off for part of the fence

There was one guy standing there ordering people around so I went to him

"Excuse me, I am looking for Jim" I said

"Thats me" he said looking down at me...the guy was at least 7 foot tall (maybe a bit shorter, he towers over me)

"Cool may I ask what exactly you are doing here, just so I know" I asked

"Our directions were to build a fence around both this and the next property but not between them, and I was asked to wait for Silver to see what she wanted done inside" he said

"Great well I am Silver and there's just a couple of things we need in this house" I said

"Well it is nice to meet the boss at last" He put out his hand and we shook "So what did you want done inside?"

I saw Mary-Anne come out of the garage and make a beeline for us.

"Well I want some work done above the garage" I said as Mary-Anne got to us

"Actually Silver" Mary-Anne said "I spoke to Bruno and he is happy to keep the room we have, I thought we could make up there, a boardroom"

"That would free up my entertainment room" I said "Are you sure? I don't mind turning it into an apartment for you guys you do so much you deserve you own space"

"It is ok Silver we will manage just fine and I really like our room" Mary-Anne said smiling a semi childish grin

"Ok well we will need a bathroom and mini kitchen above the garage and if you could build a table up there in the center of the room we need one too big to get in there" I said to Jim

"How big should this table be?" he asked looking concerned

"Let's go up and see" I suggested

We all went upstairs to the massive space above the garage.

I pointed things out and Jim measured them up.

"Now what sort of table?" he asked

"Something solid and big, if we put the kitchenette and bathroom over that side we could also make the table a T shape to go across and down the center facing that wall" I suggested

"May I ask why that wall?" Jim said

"So we can see the computer screens from the table, I want desks all the way round and computers at each one with a main large screen right there so we can see everything, like a security room crossed with a boardroom" I said

"What about storage for files?" he asked

"Ummm under the desks and in the garage" I said looking around. "Also I would like a deck off that wall so we can access outside quickly is we need to"

"Ok we will need to put a door in to access the deck but I don't see an issue with that," he said

"Wonderful" I said

"Now how soon did you want all this done?" he asked

"As soon as possible" I said "But the fence is still top priority"

"Yup we can do that and it could take us about 6 months in total," he said "I have recently hired some werewolves and vampires that are happy to work nights so this is great and I can give them some work"

"That's wonderful, I do not mind if we have workers here all day and night, we all sleep pretty solid" I said

"This will work out just right all round then" Jim smiled

"Great if I think of anything else I will let you know and if we build anything else you will be my first contact" I said as the baby monitor went off "Now I have to go see my babies" I went into the hallway and met Julian going into the kids room. We got them changed and fed then had some cuddle time before they were going back to bed.

"What are we going to do if these two really do grow at double the speed, how the hell will we keep up, I mean having a 10 year old with the body of a 20 year old is not a healthy thing for anyone" I said snuggling into Julian as we watched the babies sleeping

"We will have to educate them twice as fast I guess" he said looking concerned

"But emotionally?" I said

"Pray?" he suggested "I don't know we can only do the best we can and hope it is enough"

"That is what most parents do" Mary-Anne said from behind us "only most parents do not have the support you guys have"

"Yes we have the best support" I smiled at her

"Well they are asleep again, you two should go get ready for the meeting" She said smiling at us

"Ok so we need to make sure we have the right teams" Julian said as we walked down the stairs

"That shouldn't be hard, I'm sure Talon will take his enforcer team, mind you I have no idea who you want, and I will take whoever is left" I said

"No" He said "I will pick your team, I want people I trust looking after you"

"I can look after me hun" I said

"There is someone here to see the owner" some guy yelled out from the front door

I walked to the front door

"What can I do for you?" I asked the suited man and woman at my door

"We are here to ensure you got the list of rules we have in our community for people like yourself…"The woman said handing me a piece of paper "Are they building a fence?" she asked looking at the builders hard at work.

"Yes" I said looking at her papers "We checked the bylaws and we can build a fence 7 foot as long as it encompasses two or more properties"

"So you are just fencing your neighbours in?" the man said

"What kind of daft ass are you?" Julian said looking at the man as if the smell of his stupid offended

"You do know this area is being advertised as welcoming to our kind ah?" I asked them tossing away the papers that really gave us no new rules

"Yes as long as you play by the rules you are welcome," the woman said

"Well I own these two neighbouring properties so I am entitled to fence them as high as 7 foot and I intend to do so" I said

"Oh you own next door?" The man said "But that little albino girl was there"

"That little albino girl is a lot older than you realize and she is in my care" I said

"And the old woman?" the woman asked

"She is younger than you think and also in my care, in fact everyone in these two houses falls under my care" I said "Now thank you for the most unwelcome welcome I have ever had you may leave"

"Are you sure you read all the rules?" the man said trying to stall

"Yes I am sure I know the legal rules of being a vampire living in a city as I helped write the fucking things, and I also know your rule 7 and 19 are illegal, you cannot limit what we do within our property lines as states the rules of vampires living with humans, and it is entirely illegal to tell us we cannot have children here as many of my people have children and they are welcome here anytime"

"We are just looking out for our community," the woman said

trying to be stanuch

"We are just trying to live, in the homes we bought with our own money, we will not be breaking any laws when I have the head enforcer living with us" I said stepping up to her, I hate being so short this woman was a good 6 inches taller than me "And don't worry about your community we may be living here but we have no interest at this stage in being a part of it"

"You do know living in this street you are expected to do certain things?" the man said

"Like?" Julian asked

"Christmas time every house must be decorated appropriately, as the same for Halloween, Easter and July the 4th" the woman said

"Really?" I asked "Why the fuck do you make people do that?"

"It is part of our community spirit" she replied

"Fine we will decorate for your silly holidays" I said "Now I think you should leave I am getting very hungry"

The pair of them looked terrified

"You can't feed on us we are not willing," the man said slowly backing up

"I didn't say I would feed on you, you have a bad coke addiction and she is rittilined up the ass, I don't drink druggies blood"

"How dare you" the woman screeched

"I would suggest you leave quietly or we will call the police on you and have you removed" Julian said "We are not a big fan of human drug addicts, no matter what mask they wear in public"

The pair of them scurried off

"God I can't wait till we are fenced and gated so people can't just wander on up the driveway" I said

"I see the builders are working on the entryway" Julian said hugging me

"Yup, they are building a wooden frame for the stones to be stuck to later" I said

"Lets go inside and get a drink before we meet with everyone" he suggested guiding me in the general direction of the kitchen

"Why would those people be so...arhhh" I said grabbing a bottle

"You know hun some people are just born arh" he laughed

"Oh and I want to decorate for some other holidays too" I smiled

"Oh what ones?" Julian asked looking at me suspiciously

"I think we will have to do all the pagan holidays and make up some vampire ones" I laughed

"How about we do every full moon,a shifter party?" Julian suggested as Mary-Anne came in

"No" she said

"I agree it would be to much unless some full moons we don't have something to celebrate then we can decorate the fence for shifters" I said

"Wait why would we do that?" Mary-Anne said

"We had some friendly neighbours come over and try to force rules on us..this neighbourhood decorate for xmas, halloween and july the 4th and we must comply" I laughed

"You're fucking kidding?" Mary-Anne said, we were both not really into holidays and decorating

"No they also tried to tell us we are not allowed children here, and if we want to do landscaping we have to get permission" I said

"They can't do that" She said

"Yes I know" I said smirking "so I am going overboard, we will decorate the fence for those times and every pagan holiday and we need a vampire holiday"

"You know all hallows eve is next month?" she said

"Yes, I don't think the fence will be done in time" I said frowning

"Don't worry I will find someone to decorate around the fence work" Mary-Anne said

"Oh no hun you have more than enough to do" I said "give that task to someone else in fact hire yourself a P.A"

"What? Who ever heard of a P.A hiring a P.A?" she said

"When the P.A is doing way more than her share and constantly going above and beyond" I said "I don't want you to be overloaded hun and with the twins and everything going on I just think it would help you to have a assistant"

"I will think about it" she said "Anyway everyone is here, well next door"

"Why are they next door?" I asked

"Because they have more room in their entertaining area than we do" Mary-Anne said

"Ok so we shall head over there then" I said rinsing out the bottle and throwing it in the recycle bin

"Wait this means you aren't coming?" I said remembering the babies

"Yup I am staying here to make sure the babies are safe" she said

"If you need me Ivory gave me this phone so I can video chat with you guys over there if I need to"

"Ok cool" I said heading towards the door

"Oh and I found something out about the old man who had the cool furnishings" she said

"Oh what " I said waiting

"He died of old age, a heart attack, he was in his 80's," she said, "but the artist he died mysteriously"

"Ok thanks hun" I said and Julian and I went next door

It was a bit like one of our family vacations, walking in the door and seeing everyone, everyone stopped when I walked in.

"Well since we seem to all be here shall we go hash out our new mission?" I suggested

"I thought you had retired?" Colin laughed

"Yeah so did I" I said

We all gathered in the entertainment room.

"Ok first thank you all so much for coming, I figure the more people we have the quicker I can get back to being retired" I said smiling

"So what's up?" Jackson said

"Ok we need to find some old artifacts, I have to go to London and investigate where Excalibur was and how it vanished then find it, I am sending Talon to find the trumpet of Jericho, and Julian will be finding the holy grail"

"Gee ye don't ask much do ye lass" Toby said laughing

"OK what we know is Excalibur was stolen from Ivanovich, Ivory and Ebony have a list of possible places the grail could be, and we have no idea where the trumpet is at all" I said

"OK" Talon said "Alexa, Colin, Hex, Jake, Kerry, Mat and Sombra your with me, we will find this trumpet" they all looked at him as if he were crazy

"Bastian, Aaron, Jackson, Bruno, Tiny, Khan, Lena and Angel you're with me" Julian said and they moved over to stand with him, Talons team were already standing near him

"That leaves you with a rather large team Silver" Dominic said

"No I will be taking Rift, Hemi, Thunder, Ana, James, Toby, Brutus and Silvia" I said "The rest of you I need here with the Ebony and Ivory and next door with Mary-Anne"

"Oh that reminds me," Dominic said grinning like a Cheshire cat. He left the room for a minute and came back with a huge basket of baby stuff.

"Congratulations on your twins," he said, handing it to me, everyone started cheering and clapping. I was so embarrassed.

"I must say you look damn fine for a woman who only gave birth a month ago" Bastian smirked

"What can I say I bounce back quickly" I said shyly

"No need to be shy sister dear" Angel said "we are all family here"

"Yeah I just ...Mary-Anne deserves the attention she does all the hard work in that department" I said

"You are still the first vampire to ever give birth sis" Angel said "That's a pretty big achievement in itself"

"Are ye not worried lass that the twins will be lost without their ma" Toby asked

"They are used to Mary-Anne looking after them and I will not stay away too long, I am hoping while I am in London Julian's team will be here doing research, then I will come back so they can go, well that is what I am hoping, but you know how shit happens, and that is why Mary-Anne will be looking after the twins, and once this is done she will be going on an extended vacation" I said

"She won't go" Brutus said laughing "she is loving her life right now, and what makes her happy makes me happy"

"Well take her on a honeymoon then" I said raising both my eyebrows at him

"Oh burn brother" Ebony said laughing

"Ok back to the mission, My team will be leaving near dawn for London. Ivory I need you to tell me the minute we get a location on Etana or a meeting" I said "I want everyone to stay in contact as much as possible"

"We will be waiting more than a normal day when we get there we will basically be following dawn" Hemi said looking concerned

"That's fine, means it will still be day when I wake up and we can get ready before it gets dark and be done hopefully to get home in time for breakfast so to speak, I'm sure you can get us home by dusk" I smiled at Hemi

"Rain if you find out about anything that might help, in the way you do, no matter how silly it might seem please tell Ebony" I said smiling at her

"Yes Silver I will" she said looking proud

"Remember we all work as a team, if you have to make a decision in the moment to save the team do it, none of these artifacts are worth any of our lives" I said

"Are you sure Ivanovich will like that?" Dominic said

"I don't give a fuck what he thinks, and besides chances are with how well skilled we all are now, not getting the artifacts seems like the impossible, but shit happens" I said

"So how is retirement treating you sister?" Angel smirked

"Not even funny Angel and not very original" I smiled at her and we both cracked up laughing

"Ok guys we all have work to do, we need to prepare for anything" Julian said moving closer to me, I felt his arm around me and I felt him pull me closer to him , I turned to face him.

"Colour me crazy, but I swear I can taste the way you are looking at me" I said smiling at him

"Must be the same way you are looking at me" He smiled

"For christ sake you two, go to your room" Dominic laughed

It still seemed weird to me that we are all good friends

"How is Tatiana?" I said not turning away from Julians face

"She said hurry the fuck up and get over there" He said "She is not the world's most subtle woman, especially when it comes to you two"

"So are you going to narc on me to her boss?" I asked turning to look at him

"Hell no" he said smiling "I owe Ivanovich nothing, he just happens to be her sire, but you are family, and you both freed me in a way"

"Thanks Dom" Julian said

"Oh and if you guys really want to disappear after this mission, I can help" he said very close and quietly "I recently acquired a property off the grid, it has power, heating, water. Lots of room, great place to raise kids"

"Why would you have a place like that brother?" I asked

"I will tell you later" he smirked and indicated with his eyes he didn't want everyone knowing

"Ok I am going to go pack…" I started to say "where is our armory?

"Still in transit, they sent it later so as to not seem suspect" Ivory said

"It's ok we have plenty" Talon said he nodded at Colin

"We have everything we will need in our vehicles in the garages" Colin smiled "Possibly even a little something the boss lady might like" he winked at me

"We have 3 sets of gear for 9 in each team" Alexa said grinning "We never travel light"

"We also have the latest in military communications, thanks to Julian" Hex said giving him a nod

"Why thanks to me?" He said looking confused

"You own the company that we got our tech from, you have a few military contracts" She said "I traced it back through a lot of shell companies and many false leads"

Ivory looked panicked and started tapping away on his keyboard frantically.

"How?" he said looking at her with a hint of desperation

"Don't worry Ivory, I won't tell anyone" She smiled a cruel smile at Ivory

"I need to know how you did it so I can fix it because if you can find it anyone can" He said

Now if looks could kill Ivory would have been dust

"Why can't you just admit I am slightly better than you?" Hex said backing off

"You are obviously, now how did you do it?" Ivory said trying to calm himself

She handed him a flash drive

"It's all on there" She smiled "the program I used to crack the path, my own design"

"You are a goddess" Ivory said smiling at her "If I wasn't gay I would take you right now"

"I'll take that as a compliment then" she said

"Hold on" Julian said confused "Since when did I own a tech company that handles military contracts"

"Just after we found out Silver was pregnant, I told you it looked like a good investment and you said to go for it" Ivory said "I did and it took off"

"Oh right" he said looking less confused "I think I do remember telling you that, but I did have a lot on my mind"

"I think we need to catch up on where all our money is and is coming from" I said looking at Ivory

"I made sure all the investments and products that come from it cannot harm anyone," he said "that company does communications, but we are about 5 years ahead of the public communications"

"That is pretty good" I said "But military contracts?"

"Yeah they pay the best, and we still maintain control over everything, with the contract I managed to get us" he smiled

"Ok, so how are we financially?" I asked

"You could buy and alter houses every year for the next 20 years, and not have to sell off any" he said "But shit can happen, so I also have a number of high interest accounts just gaining interest for you"

"You know in all the time I have been a vampire I have once thought shit can I afford this, yet 90% of the time as a human I normally said shit I can't afford that" I said
Now everyone except me Dom Julian and Ivory were in the room, the rest had filtered out to get ready.
"So Dom spill" Julian said suddenly
"What about him?" Dom said looking at Ivory
"He's fine" I said
"Ok a couple of weeks ago I overheard Ivanovich and Tat talking about someone, and wanting to keep them in the game for now" he said "Then the other night when Excalibur disappeared, I heard him tell her, This was the perfect thing to get them back in, then you call asking for help, anyway back then I suspected it was you he was talking about and I found this cool place already built , but never been lived in, I went and checked it out, it's pretty remote, but we are vampires so that's no issue"
"We need blood too" Julian said
"Yup and there is a town nearby, or room for a couple of humans at the homestead" he said
"Why has it not been lived in?" I asked
"The owner sadly got cancer and passed away, his wife didn't want to live out there alone so she sold it" Dom said "They were going to move out there together once it was finished"
"Thank you Dom" I said "Your not a bad brother"
"Also he has a mole in your midst" he said
"What?" I said "who?"
"I have no idea" Dom said "But he knew when the babies had been born and Sin's visit and He knew you had moved here before he rang you"
"Shit" Julian said
"Oh well I think I shall trash him more when we gather" I said not really phased by it
"Sounds like a plan to me" we heard at the door
We turned to see Lucian standing there.
"I got ya call, sorry I am a bit late" he smiled
I ran over and gave him a hug

"How are you?" I said excitedly

"What the hell? I didn't get a hug" Dom said pretending to pout

"Well I heard some shit was happening and I was bored, so Jay is running shit and I am here to help" Lucian said smiling and heading over to Julian "Damn it's good to see you two again" he hugged Julian

"You too brother" Julian said smiling and hugging back

"Sorry I don't know you" he pointed to Ivory "and Dom well how's that shrew of yours?"

Lucian and Tatiana had a huge argument about 10 years ago at a family holiday and neither had forgotten it, even though no one else remembers it

"Tatiana is just fine thanks Luci" Dom said with a bit of bite

"That is wonderful to hear" he said sarcastically

"Ok well Lucian can you go with my wife" Julian said "because I trust you to watch her back around Ivanovich"

"It would be my pleasure" Lucian said bowing like in medieval times. "Oh and I have a gift for you Silver, I had forgotten about them but for some reason I came across them last week" he ducked out the door and came back in with a case putting on the table in front of me

"I cannot touch them, but I have a feeling you might be able to" he said He opened the case

It was the daggers he had given me another time.

I was so excited my face lit up like a christmas tree I carefully reached for one of them.

I felt it, the same feeling I had once before, these daggers had power and I could wield them. I picked up the other one, perfectly balanced. Oh I had missed these.

Julian smiled *"Now I know you will be fine,"* he said in my head

"That reminds me we should feed before I leave" I said back

"Thank you so much Lucian, these mean more to me than you will ever know" I said hugging him again "And now I must go get my ass ready since I am in the first team leaving"

"Talon has packed gear for everyone" Julian said

"Well we will be prepared for everything then, I too, brought my own gear" he smiled pulling out one of his daggers and giv-

ing it a twirl and putting it back
"I will see you next door. We will be meeting in the entry hall at about 4" I said carefully putting my daggers in my boots.
We all went to get ready Julian and I went up to our room and fed on each other, just to make sure our connection was solid.
"Are you sure about this?" Julian said as we went to go downstairs "I mean someone else could lead my team and I can come with you"
"The babies?" I reminded him
"Oh yeah that is going to take a while to get used to" Julian said "How do humans do it, go from free awesome life to being chained to two kids?"
"Still an awesome life we just have to consider them like we do the rest of our family, it's just different, and because we will have to teach them everything and they are growing to fast they just need a bit of extra attention for now, like when any member of our family fall down and we put everything on hold to help them" I explained hugging him
"I will miss you my phoenix" he said in my head
"I will miss you too sexy so let's get this done" I said back
We walked downstairs
"Please be careful," he said in my head
"Hun I am always careful" I said
"No you are headstrong and passionate" he laughed
"Only if someone crosses me, not sure what to do about Ivanovich trying to drag us back into his shit" I said
"Don't worry, we will work something out" he nudged me and then put his arms around me as we waited for the rest of my team

Chapter 4

I woke a couple of hours before dusk everyone else was up and chilling in the main seating area.

"Morning boss lady" Toby said smiling at me

"Don't be cheerful, I have not fed yet" I said going to the fridge and grabbing a bottle

"Ivanovich is sending cars so they should arrive at dusk" Rift said

"Great" I said skulling a second bottle

"Are you planning on working hard?" Rift asked

"Just being prepared brother" I said

"Good point, we are going to Ivanovich after all" he said getting up and grabbing himself another bottle

"Maybe I should too then?" Silvia asked

"It would be advisable" I said

"I have already had two" Ana said laughing

"Ok well I am basically ready to go, so the plan is at this point ...go to the place Excalibur was and see what we can see, smell anything that might tell us who stole it."

"Sweet so we should be done in what an hour after we get in?" Lucian said

"Why do you have somewhere to go?" Rift asked

"Well there's this club here I want to check out" he said "since we are in the neighbourhood"

"Do you really think that's a good idea?" Rift asked him

"It's a club for our kind, it may be a useful spot to gain some info" Lucian said

"Let's see what we find first guys then we will see" I said

Ivanovich had emailed us very detailed plans and descriptions of what he thinks happened and we were going over it when the cars pulled up, 5 minutes before dusk, with Ivanovich's emblem on them.

Thunder and Lucian went out to greet them.

The drivers looked very nervous and that concerned me.

Finally the sun vanished and we could all step out of the plane.

James had decided to stay with the plane. The rest of us stayed on high alert

We got into the 2 SUV's and they took off.

"So where exactly are we headed?" Hemi asked the driver

"Lord Ivanovich's house" the driver said

Rift nudged my arm and nodded at me to look out the window

There was a lot of anti-vampire graffiti everywhere, I had no idea this was even a problem.

"What's with all the graffitti?" Rift asked

"Something happened a few months ago and people here started getting mad with vampires I do not know why but I am sure if you ask Ivanovich he will tell you" the driver said

"I'm sure you do know why" I said "Is that why you and the other driver are so scared?" I asked

"If we get attacked and any of you die we will pay for it" the driver mumbled

"That's not right" Rift said "If we die it will be on us, we know how to defend ourselves"

We drove out to a semi rural area and down a nice narrow country road to a huge gated driveway.

The gates opened automatically and we drove through, down a long driveway with trees growing over it. When we came out the other side of the trees we saw a huge mansion, that did not surprise me. The driver pulled straight into the garage with the other SUV parking next to us. They closed the door as soon as they were both in and we got out.

Ivanovich was standing in the doorway to his house.

"So what the hell is going here Ivanovich?" I said stalking up to him "Why so much vamp hate?, and I thought you wanted us in Ireland"

"All I know is that someone is breaking all the rules and doing as they please and I cannot get a hold of them" he said seeming pissed off "and I lied just in case"

"Well you need to get your people to put a stop to it" I said "anyway I am only here to look at where you kept the sword"

"Will you not be staying while you investigate?" Tatiana said coming up behind Ivanovich

"No" I said a bit bluntly "so where was it?"

Ivanovich nodded to Tatiana and she led the way through the back of the garage down the back lawn to a small shack.

She went in the shack and we followed. She waited for us all to get in and closed the door.

"You cannot open the door if this door is open" she explained

I didn't like this, I looked around my team and saw they didn't either. She went to another door and pushed some buttons on a panel, then she went through the door and down some stairs, we followed carefully.

"This hallway is rigged with boobie traps and camera's, Ivanovich will be watching us now," she stated firmly as we got to a door at the bottom of the stairs

"Then he should have footage of whoever stole the sword" Rift said

"They did not show up on camera, or set off a single trap" she said looking pissed

"So it was an inside job?" Lucian asked

"No only myself and Ivanovich know how to get down here," she said

We went through more doors and stairs that all headed down. We finally got to a large vault room.

"So there's traps all the way here?" I asked "And the thief didn't set a single one off?"

"Yes, it is like they ghosted in and ghosted out" she said

"How did you know the sword was gone?" Rift asked looking around the pedestal the sword had obviously been placed on.

"The sword was alarmed as well and when it was moved it went off and Ivanovich came down with me to find out what the hell had happened" She said

"Did they take anything else?" I said looking around with my special sight. I could see so much magic in here every single item down here shone with a magical aura.

"No nothing else was removed," she said

"But if someone could ghost in and take the sword why would they not take half this other stuff?" Rift said confused

"I do not know" Tatiana said

"I do" Lucian said "they took what they came for and took a quick inventory of what else was here so they can pop back later"

"How do you know?" Tatiana said looking suspiciously at him

"Because it is what I would have done, if I was time limited," he said

"FUCK!" I exclaimed suddenly as everyone looked at me. I had been scanning the room using all the abilities I could, and one thing that kept coming back to me.

"What?" Tatiana said

"The only thing I can pick up is Sin, he has been here probably the guy who stole the sword" I said "So I guess now you and your boss can hunt him down and kill him"

"We do not have the time for that" Tatiana said brashly "This is why my lord asked you to do it"

"Why what is he working on?" I asked

"Finding the vampire who is causing strife" she said

"I think you will find whoever is working with Sin is the one causing issues" Lucian said

"If it were Sin we would know" Tatiana said

"Ok so how many supers can walk anywhere without setting of alarms made for supers" I asked

"None can pass our security" she insisted

"Yet here we are" I said

"Why is Dominic not on your team?" she asked

"Because he is better placed at home for now" I said

"He should be with you, he is head of the family he should pro-tect you" she said

"He is weaker than me and dating you, so no thanks" I said "and we are not here to discuss your boyfriend"

"He is not weaker than you," she insisted, "Are we done here?"

"Yes we are done here" I said looking at Lucian who was sniffing with his alpha nose he smiled and winked at me
"Ok we go back to house now you tell my lord what you found" she snapped walking out
"There was a vampire here with Sin" Lucian said quietly to me as we went back up all the stairs
"I know I smelled her too" I said none too impressed "but shh" we smiled at each other and continued

Back in the house we had to wait for Lord Ivanovich who was yelling at someone on the phone in possibly russian. He was not very quiet about it. He hung up the phone and screamed for Tatiana she went rushing into the room closing the door behind her.
When she opened it again she was very angry.
"He will see you now" she snapped as she went off to do something
We walked in.
"So Tatiana says you think it was Sin" he said before we even sat down
"Yes, I believe he could be causing you issues because he cannot interfere in my life" I said
"I want my sword back" he said
"My lord what is bothering you aside from the sword thing?" I asked
"You are retired remember" he said to me
"Yes and yet here I am" I said "if you don't tell me what is going on I will find out"
"Very well" he said "but the rest of you can go away"
Rift went to leave
"Lucian and Rift can stay" I said
Rift rolled his eyes and sat back down. The others left Lucian just stayed where he was leaning on the wall
"Some of the council have been persuaded that we are wrong and that humans should be above the undead" he said "They have started trying to make waves and they have people running around trying to disrupt everything we have worked for,

and not just in England. Humans for Humanity have started up and are spreading their vile word everywhere"
"So kick the humans out and replace them with better humans" I said
"This is no longer possible as we made the council a democracy and people get voted in and out" he said "The only way to end them is to get them replaced by voters or kill them"
"Are they being led by a vampire again?" I asked
"No I do not think so" he said
"I think you will find your sire could be behind it" I suggested
"NO he is not" Ivanovich said very confidently
"How do you know?" I asked him
"Because not long after we came back I took him off the table for good" Ivanovich smiled
"Well then what about Salamoanious?" I said
"He has also been dispatched" Ivanovich said
"And Cleo?" I asked
"She has been keeping a very low profile and she has been behaving" he said
"So you are keeping tabs on her too?" I said
"Yes and making sure she remains somewhat less powerful than she was" he said
"Yeah well she doesn't have my blood to boost her ass does she" I said
"No but she has also been suffering a little" Ivanovich said
"Why?" I asked
"She tried to get Miss Bathory to come after you, I stopped her and it somehow weakened Cleo, then she went a little crazy" Ivanovich said "She is in protective custody, for her own safety"
"So she is only behaving because she is locked up and can't start trouble" Lucian laughed
"You could say that" Ivanovich said
"My lord" I said "this is not the thing vexing you I can tell you are hiding something from me"
"I am hiding nothing that is important to you" he said sounding a bit hurt

"At least that's the truth for now," I said, "Look , I don't want to get involved with your politics and I am not going to, but you should know when you act cagey around me, I start overthinking and that's no good for anyone"

"I understand" he said looking thoughtful

"Ok let's go see if we can find out anything about the sword aside from Sin may have taken it" I said

"You should go to The Pit in piccadilly, you may hear something, it is a club for our kind, many strange beings hang out there maybe you can glean some information about the sword" He suggested

"That is a great Idea Lord Ivanovich" Lucian said smiling

"Let me guess that is the club you wanted to visit?" I said to Lucian

"Yes it is" he smiled

"Ok so we will go to this club and see what we can find however I think we will not find answers there, if it was Sin he is a god, why would he go to a nightclub" Rift said

"Everyone likes to let loose sometimes bro" Lucian said

"Look my lord we are going to go get ready to go clubbing, have a good evening and I shall contact you if we have any questions or answers" I said getting up

"Silver" Ivanovich said as the boys walked out the door

"Yes my lord" I said

"Please try and keep low key, I do not want to have to send you before the council" Ivanovich said looking at me as if it were a threat not a suggestion

"My lord in the past 35 years you know damn well I have become an expert at low key" I smiled at him and walked out.
Tatiana showed us the door and we got back in the cars that had picked us up.

"Where to, my lady?" My driver asked

"Back to the plane we have to get dressed before we go out" I said

"And where are you going once you are dressed" he asked

"Dru's pit " I said

An hour later we were headed back into London proper.

Dru's pit was an interesting club. It had been recently refurbished to its original state and the sign on the wall said the dance floor consisted of 3 circles, two smaller ones were slightly higher than the large one. There were booths all around and everything was black or silver. I liked it.

The music was loud and trendy.

There were plenty of people here, we even had to wait in line, then a woman came out and asked for me and let us in, her name was Druantia, she owned Dru's pit and she was very proud of it, it had even been destroyed at some point but she had rebuilt it and it had become the most popular supernatural hang out in London. She showed us around a bit and then had to run off to do something else.

"She seems nice" Rift said watching her go as if he was a lion and she was diner

"Maybe she will be into you too, you should ask her out" I said not really paying attention to him

"Oh yeah how's that gunna work sis" he said looking at me as if I were crazy

"Easy you come back to London on your way home, and invite her out" I said

"And when are we going to be able to go home?" he asked

"Good point ask her now before we go back to the states explain you have work to do and will ring her in a couple of months" I suggested "Anyway we need to mingle and keep an ear out" I said moving away from him

Angel and I went to dance and listen, I looked around regularly to see where everyone else was. At one point Rift was chatting with Druantia and she was laughing, that's a good sign.

We had been there for about two hours and I was bored. The only thing I had heard was superficial blah blah and some concerns about HFH, but nothing relating to our current mission.

I heard something outside like a truck revving the engine.

I saw Druantia run to the main door and slip out

"No Cleo don't do it, I just rebuilt the place" I heard Druantia yell
The sound of trucks went away, and Druantia came back inside. She looked relieved. She should not have been.

I heard it coming, my whole team did, Rift ran for Druantia, the rest of my team tried to quickly move everyone back from the front wall. We were not fast enough to clear everyone out of the way.

Two trucks crashed through the front wall of the building, Cleo was not driving. I went outside. I saw some motorbikes ride off in the distance and I knew Cleo was one of them. The bikes stopped and turned half back, that was when I heard the ticking.

Someone else must have too because I heard people yelling "BOMB" and vampires and were beasts were running everywhere to get away.

Some grabbing slower friends along the way, Rift came by me with Druantia still in his arms

"Move sis" he yelled and we all bolted away from the club, we had got far enough to avoid harm but we were still knocked over by the blast.

Rift landed on top of Druantia protecting her from falling debris, not that any fell where we were.

I had ended up against a wall , I looked around and saw my team scattered in amongst others who made it out, and my team were all accounted for. I got up, I saw Rift carefully get off Druantia, she sat there looking at what used to be her club and she cried a lot, Rift tried to comfort her. I went over to her and sat next to her.

"You will be ok Druantia, I am sure you have survived worse" I said to her

"But this club was my baby, Cleo knew that, she knew how much it meant to me" Druantia sobbed

"Are you friends with Cleo?" Rift asked

"Sort of, well I thought we were at least on good terms where we would not ruin each others lives" Dru said "I will kill her for this, that fucking bitch"

I looked where the bikes had stopped but they were gone.

"Do you happen to have a vault of artifacts here?" Silvia asked coming over

"Yeah but there's not really anything in there, we cleared it out a few years back, why do you think she is after what's in my vault?" Dru asked

"It is a possibility" I said "What exactly is in there?"
"Some old swords, an old jewelry box, some really old book, not a lot really" She said
"Ok well I am guessing Excalibur is not there?" I said
"No Ivanovich has that stored somewhere else" Druantia said confidently
"Do you by chance have a goblet and a trumpet in there?" Rift asked
"Yes there is a goblet, oh and a cool opal stone and a cloak" she said as if she always gave out this info
"May we see the goblet?" I asked
"No" she said "No One goes down there without explicit permission of Ivanovich" she smiled
"I'm sure if it were the one we are after Ivanovich would have told us" Rift said
"Oh" Dru said as if she just clicked "You're the ones he is sending after the grail and the trumpet?"
"Yes" I said "But please don't give that information to anyone who asks"
"Come into my..."she looked at what was left of the burning mass of rubble...fire trucks were just arriving. "Look I can't get in there right now, but the stone and the goblet may be of use to you, I just can't tell you out here"
"We could go back to the plane" Rift suggested "Or maybe just in the car?"
"That will do," Druantia said getting up.
One of her men came running over and she waved him away
"I'm ok go check on everyone else" she said
We got to the SUV's and some of us got in
"Ok the goblet lets you see everything, you just have to put the right liquid in, I don't know what that is but if you find it then it may be useful for finding what it is your looking for and the cloak is Freyja's falcon cloak" she said as if we would know what that meant
"You mean the one from norse mythology?" Rift asked
"Yes it will turn the wearer into a falcon, again I don't know

from experience I just know what Ivanovich told me" Dru said
"What's the old book?" I asked out of curiosity after all some goblet and some old cloak seem pretty special
"Book of twot or something, all I know is it's cursed" she said
"Do you know anything about the things you hold in your vault?" Lucian asked
"Yes, I know a bit about each, just enough so I know not to freaking use them" She said
"There's a viking king sword, a demon killing sword, King Charlemagne's sword, the sword of Muhammad's son in law ha, I'm not sure what the jewelry box is but Ivanovich said it should never be opened, the opal looking stone heals and purifies water, the hand of a thief which can help you steal shit, works well that one" she laughed "In saying that I won't be able to get to them till this mess is cleared
"That may be useful too" Lucian suggested "We may have to stay a while Sil"
"Or we could come back later to get the items once Druantia has retrieved them" Rift suggested
"We may have to" I said
"Or I could stay till she can get them and bring them to you?" Rift suggested winking at me
I laughed a little
"Sure Rift hun you stay and help Druantia and then you can bring them, that way if Ivanovich decides he has shit in his vault that might help you can get that too" I said pulling out my phone
I went to dial Ivanovich but it rang
"Hay Talon what's up" I said answering Dru gave me a funny look
"I'm about to take off, we found the trumpet maybe so we might be headed to Jerusalem, Julian is upstairs playing with the kids, and Ivory found Etana, she is in Medford Oregon at the Crater lake" he said
"Ok so we need to go to Oregon on the way home?" I asked
"No I am going to get her, just in case I am going the wrong way, but I will be asking her about the sword and grail too" he said
"Good idea" I said "Well we have found out Cleo is behind some

shit, not sure how Sin did it but he got her into Ivanovich's vault and she took the sword then he got her out, the place reeked of them I don't know how Ivanovich didn't smell her right away at least, but she just blew up the nightclub we were in, don't worry, our team is fine"

"God damn it I knew we should have taken her out when we came back," he said

"To be fair we had bigger fish to fry" I said thinking of the vampire lords we killed

"I have to ring Ivanovich and tell him what's going on, Rift is going to stay here and help Driantia get some items we may be able to use from her vault and hopefully Ivanovich will remember anything he has that may help" I said

"Oh god you were at Dru's pit" he said shocked

"You know this place?" I asked

"Yeah, don't tell Dru you know me" he suggested

"To late" I said looking at her face "She is here with me"

"Tell her I say hi then and tell her I am sorry" he said sheepishly

"Ok now I want to know what's going on" I said

"He freaking used me and dumped me thats what was going on, but it's ok , I get why" she said I could tell she was a little hurt but not so much she would hold a grudge

"I am guessing this is before you meet Mat?" I asked Talon on the phone

"Sort of" he admitted "I knew Mat was coming but I was infiltrating what we thought was a group of bad vamps, turned out they were just party animals, it's how Ivanovich found Dru"

"Oh right" I said "Anyway I will be shooting home to do some research before we go anywhere else, Cleo is in London now, do you think you can have some enforcers keep an eye on her? Ivanovich thought she was locked up"

"Yeah already on it" he said sounding happy "Anyway I will miss you when you get in so kia kaha"

"You too brother" I smiled hanging up.

We had started using Kia kaha which is stay strong in maori to let the others know everything was ok

I looked at Druantia very seriously

"So you dated my big brother?" I asked her

"Sort of" she said timidly "But he broke up with me when he found out who Ivanovich was"

"Oh he's known Ivanovich for a very long time," I said

"Yeah but Ivanovich kind of raised me, then I got free and ran into some other vampires who decided turning me was a good idea, and I lived such an awesome fun life, then Talon came to town" she explained

"My brother is not fun" I laughed

"No he was and soo sexy" she smiled "But then I found out he was using me to infiltrate the Angels here and he took me back to Ivanovich"

"Great" Rift said sulking "yet again some members of my family beat me to the punch"

"You were not serious about Talon ah Dru?" Lucian said

"Not really" she laughed "we had fun but it was a long time ago, I had just opened this place for the first time" she looked longingly out the window at her burnt down club

"Ok well I need to get going, I want to be home before dark over there" I said

"All good can you drop me at home though" Dru asked "Ivanovich might want to know what happened"

"Do you have a car?" Lucian asked

"Yeah but it's that burning pile of shit over there, Tatiana will not be happy, I borrowed her car to get to work tonight"

"How do you know Cleo?" I asked

"She used to come here often, then about a week ago she stopped coming, when I saw her tonight she told me to get my people out fast and then she left to go stand over by some seriously scary dude, then well you saw the rest" Dru said

"You know she is Ivanovich's grandsire?" I asked

"NO WAY" Dru exclaimed "she is way cooler than he is"

"Actually she is a psychotic bitch" I laughed "and my man's ex"

"No Cleo is cool" Dru insisted

"So cool she just blew up your club" Lucian said "Trust me, she is not a good person, I can smell it"

"Well you guys can take this car we will go in the other SUV back to the plane" I said

I didn't have time to explain why we knew Cleo was a bad egg, it was another timeline as well and that just gets super complicated

"So are you into me or are you into the artifacts I have in my vault?" I heard Dru ask Rift as we got out

"Well I was interested before I knew who you were and what you had, now I am not so sure, I don't know I want another brothers seconds" Rift said

"Oh I never had sex with him" she said all defensive and innocent

We got over to our SUV, I noticed there were emergency services everywhere, a couple of humans had been injured, some vampires totally ashed, I saw a team of Vampire enforcers dealing with all that so I knew I could just go. We squeezed into the SUV I sat on Lucians knee.

"This is most improper" the driver complained

"Just take us to the plane thanks" I said

We got back to Ivanovic's private airfield, there were Human police blocking the entrance.

The driver stopped and rolled down the window.

"Evening officer may I help you?" the driver said

"Where are you headed?" the officer said gruffly

"To drop my passengers at their plane officer" he said

"Where did you pick them up from?" he asked as if it were routine

"A nightclub in town that just exploded," the driver said honestly

"The officer quickly pulled his gun which startled the other 4 police there and they did the same as they were yelling to step out of the car with your hands up.

We all carefully got out with our hands in the air

"Since when did cops in England act like american cops?" Lucian asked me quietly as we got out I just shrugged

"Who's in charge here?" the first officer yelled

"That would be me sir" I said stepping forward and raising my hand

"What were you doing at the club and why are you trying to escape?" he said

"Ok we were having a good time and the club was attacked so we stayed around a bit and waited for clearance to leave so we can go back to the states" I said

One of the other cops walked off talking on his radio.

"You are all under arrest for terrorism" the first cop said

"Wait" the cop on the radio said walking back over he whispered something to the first cop who lowered his gun, at that the others lowered theirs too

"Seems you do have clearance to leave" the first cop said to me

"So why are you in London?" the radio cop asked

"We came to visit an old friend, he suggested we check out the club before we go home, so we did, poor Druantia was so distraught my brother stayed with her" I said

"So you are friends with the owner?" he asked

"Not really we only met her tonight" I said

"Why would your brother stay then?" he asked

"Well he took a fancy to Dru and she took a fancy to him, then shit happened" I said

"Right" he said not believing me

"Look officer I can tell from what I have seen in London that things are not going well, but I can assure you we are not responsible" Lucian said looking as innocent as he could

One of the other cops was moving one of the cars out of our way.

"Excuse me officer" the driver said "It is just on the news Humans for humanity have taken responsibility for the nightclub bombing"

He looked over at the cop in the car who got out and walked over to whisper in his ear

"Ok you are free to go" the cop said not looking happy

"By the way officer" I said "When you go looking for HFH, keep in mind they are run by vampires and your pea shooters will not do shit to them"

"How do you know?" he said looking at me again with suspicion
"Because my other brother Talon, he is the head of the enforcers and he called me after the club was bombed to tell me" I said "wanted me out of harm's way ASAP"
"Oh" the cop said "well you best go then"
We got back in the SUV and drove to the plane. James was waiting at the door.
"Did they come talk to you?" I asked going up the stairs
"NO they just blocked the road and waited" he said watching them as they left
"I wonder why they were here, who could have told them about this airfield" he said
"I think it may have been a tip off from possibly Cleo" I said
"They told the Airport security that they had a report that the bombers were trying to escape here" James said "So what happened?"
"Cleo happened" I said she was on the enforcers watchlist, just in case but it wasn't really one hundred percent accurate, then she was under 24/7 surveillance, and locked down but well that wasn't so true"
"I am glad I did not see her" Silvia said seething
"You knew her too" I said nodding it made sense
"She fucked up my sire, he made sure we knew about her" She said
"Fair enough" I said
"Ok we need to go home, I want to see my babies" I said going and sitting down
"What about Cleo and the sword?" James asked
"Rift is staying to help Drunatia, she is going to let us borrow some artifacts and I want to meet with Etana and see if she can help" I said "The enforcers are tracking down Cleo"
"Ok home it is" James said Hemi and him went to the cockpit and they got the plane ready for takeoff

Chapter 5

I was grateful to be home. We pulled in the driveway and the fence and gate were coming along nicely.

 I walked up to the door and opened it to see my man and his team standing there getting ready to go.

"Thank the gods you made it" Julian said hugging me tight "*I wish I could stay longer and enjoy all of you but we have a positive lead,*" *he said in my head*

"I'm am glad I caught you" I said kissing him "*I missed you*"

"Talon met with Etana, she is on her way here now to see you, she told him where the grail actually is, everyone was way off" he said "and the trumpet we need is in the vatican vault"

"Oh fuck" I said the one place in the world no vampire could get into. Well that is what we were led to believe no one had tried in recent years.

"Maybe Ivanovich can go in and get it" Julian laughed

"Yeah he has bigger issues right now," I said "humans for humanity have started up and started causing grief in London"

"But Caligula is not around" Julian said

"But Cleo is" I said "anyway she is the councils problem not ours"

"Nice job staying focused" Hemi said "Rift is trying to hook up with Druantia and get us some artifacts"

"Who is Druantia?" Julian asked

"She is a girl who Ivanovich seems to have adopted or held prisoner, she looks to him like a father anyway, but she ended up going her own way and becoming a vampire anyway" I said

"Right" Julian said "that man keeps too many secrets"

"Agreed" I said

"So does she have a god killing weapon?" Julian asked looking hopeful

"No but she does have a demon killing one" I laughed

"So do we" Julian said hugging me tighter "Anyway we best get going we have a flight to catch" he kissed me and let go

"Where exactly are you going?" I asked

"Syria" he said "Then to a place in the north where an old christian ruin was found"

"I take it you have all the paperwork you need?" I asked

"Yes my love Ivory and Eb's took care of it" he smiled

"Ok well you lot stay safe, kia kaha" I said "and bring my man home"

"We will" Bruno said he seemed very happy, actually they all did

I headed upstairs

Mary-Anne was coming down

"The babies have just settled again, they seem anxious tonight" she said

"I will just pop my head in and give them a kiss" I said

"Don't forget you need to debrief the team" she smiled

"How's the renovations going?" I asked

"Pretty good, that builder you got has some awesome hard workers, the boardroom will be done by the end of the week, the fence is getting there" she replied

"Any more issues with neighbours?" I asked

"Nope not a peep" she said

"Ok I will be down shortly" I smiled and continued up the stairs to see my babies

They were asleep so I snuck in and just looked at them, there is a certain kind of peace in watching baby's sleeping, it made me anxious. We had to do the right thing by them, we had to make sure this world would be a place they could live in and not constantly be on edge waiting for the next fight.

I left and went to my room...it felt dark and cold without Julian here so I went back downstairs

All the vampires had gathered in the kitchen, most of the were's had gone to bed to get some rest.

"So I hear you were in a bombing?" Ivory said

"Yeah but it's ok all ours got out alive" I said

"Reports came in earlier that 4 humans were killed 2 were seriously injured, hard to tell how many vampire were ash, but 7 have been reported missing and 3 beasts were injured but they switched and are fine now" Ebony said reading out the report

"Yeah good thing is we may be able to get some artifacts ourselves which if we are allowed to keep them I will send to the castle for safe keeping once we have used them, if we use them. When is Lady Etana arriving?" I said

"She will be here in the evening, she gets in just before dawn" Ivory said

"Is Rain resting?" I asked

"Yeah she is" Dominic said "there is something very strange about that girl"

"I have noticed she is very paranoid around you Dom" Ivory said "maybe she saw your past and it freaked her out"

"May be she saw Tatiana and that freaked her out, I swear that woman freaks me out every time I see her" Ana said

"Well get used to it because she may be family soon" Dominic said smiling

"You asked her?" I said

"Not yet but when I go home I will be" he smiled a goofy smile

"Anyway, since we can't really do much right now lets just chill and wait" I said

"I was thinking it might be best to have Etana met us over at the other house, away from the children" Ivory said

"That sounds like a good idea after all we don't know her, she is ancient and she may think my babies are abominations to be killed which would mean we would have to kill her and that's not how I want this to go" I laughed

"How ancient is she?" Ebony asked

"Older than dirt" Dominic said "Isn't she a lord as well"

"She could even be the oldest living vampire lord" Silvia said "she is not to be messed with however and killing her would be very difficult"

"Silver knows how to handle old vampy lords don't you Sil" Dominic laughed

"Yeah well having 3 living under my roof makes it not so special" I laughed

"There is not 3 vampire lords here" Ivory laughed

"Yes there is" Dominic said "Silver here is one, possibly the youngest of them all, then there is Julian, and Talon"

"And we know they are old as dirt" Ana laughed

"But we also have wolf leaders and tigers and they are much more of a challenge," I said

"We should go do a work out, you will be rusty Silver and if you die on this mission Julian will kill us" Silvia said

"I am not rusty, I have been training sort of" I said

"When?" Ivory said "Not since you moved out to the woods, I would know"

"Shhh" I said "I train in my head when I sleep" I laughed while the others did too.

"OK nerf guns in the backyard in 20 minutes" Dominic yelled

"Do you know where the nerf guns are?" I asked everyone looked blank "Maybe tomorrow night then we can find the nurf's tonight and do a full training thing between the two houses after Etana is gone or we can suss her out more at least"

"So the beasts can get in to train as well" Ana said smiling a huge smile

"Yes do you have your eyes on any beast in particular?" I said with a cheeky grin

"No I just love training with things that can kill me" she laughed
We all went off in search of the nerf guns we often used in training.

By dawn we had found some of them, and enough chargers to charge them up before tomorrow evening.

The beasts all got up before we went to bed, and they loved the idea too.

I went upstairs to poke my head in at the babies before going to bed. I got to the top of the stairs and heard one of them cry out, I decided I was going to stay up a bit, Mary- anne came flying out of her room.

"Oh morning Silver" she said "Did you want to help me?"

"Of course" I said happily "I'll just grab a drink and be right there, I'd like to spend some extra time with them"

"I had a small fridge put in their room so there is some blood in there" she said

"Awesome lets go" I said as the second one started

We went in and they were both standing up holding the sides of their cots. Both Mary-Anne and I were stunned. They had somewhat of a growth spurt, this could be bad, very very bad. I looked at Mary-Anne and she looked at me and shrugged.

"I ...they were not this big when they went to bed I swear" she said shocked

They had both stopped crying and were trying to get to us with big smiles. We tended to them, they were crawling, everywhere all at once. By 7 am we were both knackered.

"How the fuck does one human woman do this?" I said exasperated "I have a team and I can't keep up"

"I have no idea, but I guess they grow into it, this is a big leap" Mary-Anne said

"We need to get more professional baby help I think, I mean you do great but at this rate we will kill ourselves keeping up" I said

"I think you're right and I will hire a PA as well," she said as Angelus crawled at vampire speed past us. I reached down and grabbed him. I became a jungle gym for the 30th time this morning. Althea came racing over.

"I thought they were not meant to get powers till they were 18?" I said looking at Alipa who had just walked in

"It is a very interesting problem we have" Alipa said looking concerned

"The fence needs to be done now" I said "At this speed they could be out the gate in a second and ..."I started hyperventilating, which is very scary for someone who doesn't have to breath Mary-Anne helped guide me back to breath normal and then not at all.

 Alipa looked shocked

"I have never seen a vampire do that before" she said looking vaguely amused

"Happy to entertain" I said "Is there any way we can slow them down?"

"Maybe" she said "But I do not think I can stop their growth, just slow their abilities"

"That would be good, will it have any negative side effects?" I asked

"No they should develop just fine" She said "But both you and Julian will have to be here for it"

"Fine, we will do it when he gets back, I don't plan on going any-where till then, not now" I said

"You should get some rest Silver" Mary-Anne said looking at me

"I can't make you look after these two like this" I said

"It's ok, we will manage, I will make everyone who is not busy help me with them, I am sure a group of were's can keep an eye on them while you rest" She said as Brutus walked in

Angelus went crawling over to him at vampire speed and raised his arms as if he wanted to be picked up.

Althea was snuggling into my shoulder.

"Ma," she said smiling at me. I swear I melted right there she knows who I am

"Ma, ma, ma" Angelus said looking at me smiling then he turned to Brutus

"Uncy" he said

Even Alipas jaw dropped with that one.

"ANNNNNNNE!!" Althea suddenly exclaimed and jumped over to Mary-Anne, it was a good 4 foot jump from the chair I was on to her but she landed perfectly in Mary-Annes lap.

"No no no no no no no" I said "This is too much to fast" I got up and Angelus jumped over to me, from the other side of the room in Brutus's arms, I only just caught him and ended up back in my seat

"Oh my god Angelus please don't do that to mummy" I said looking him in the eye he smiled and I saw mischief, just like I had seen in Julian's eye before. "No Angelus Jax, you behave"

He pretended to go shy and snuggled into my shoulder then he looked up at me and looked so sweet and innocent

"Mama" he said quietly I hugged him till he started to wriggle and he was off, and Althea bolted after him ...crawling at vampire speed

"I am going to go to bed now," I said, "Good luck, I will ring Julian when I wake up and tell him what happened, or if one of you could depending on timezone things"

"I'll get Hemi to do it hun go to bed" Mary-Anne said

I got up and went to my room I climbed on the bed and was asleep in seconds

I woke late the next evening, I had a quick shower and got dressed in jeans and a nice shirt with my favorite boots and went out to check on the kids.

They were downstairs playing with Rain and Declan as soon as I walked in the room they crawled over to me going "mama mama" while Mary-Anne was making them some food. I picked one up in each arm, lucky I am a vampire these two were not light.

"I am so sorry I overslept" I said "Is it normal for them to be awake now?"

"Yeah they are about 6-8 months old so its baby food time" Mary-Anne said She had got fresh veggies and made the baby food herself "Do you want to help me feed them?" she looked hopeful

"Sure" I said "Do I have time before I meet with Etana?"

"Yes she is on her way but they are driving in a convoy so they are a good 2 hours away" Mary-Anne said

"Where are all the vampires?" I asked quietly

"Next door making sure everything is set and on guard duty in case we get an escapee" she looked at the kids

"How many times did they get out?" I asked

"Twice they got out of the house, once they nearly made the pool gate, the second time they went towards the other house" she said

"Great, can we fortify the pool fence?" I asked

"It's a pretty good fence, I had the builder guy check it out after they took off and he thinks it will be fine, we had Khan try to crash through it and it stayed up" she said

"Awesome, but can they jump it?" I asked

"Probably" Mary-Anne admitted "I mean if what we have seen today is anything to go by they may be able to jump a 3 foot high fence, but I honestly don't know their limits"

"Did Hemi get hold of Julian?" I asked

"Yes he did and Julian is on his way home alone, the rest of the team will stay and find the grail" she said then she nodded behind me

Rain was standing there just waiting

"What's up Rain?" I asked her

"Sorry to interrupt" she said timidly

"Your not interrupting dear" I said

"You are doing the right thing not going after Cleopatra" she said nervously "She is not well in the head, and she hates you a lot"

"Is she the one hunting me?" I asked

"No" she said "that was a scary man" she looked scared

"It's ok Rain" I said "When you tell us things, we believe you, I understand what it's like to be different"

"There is a man looking for me" she said "he is bad, I know he cannot find me here, I have seen it"

"If we ..if you want us to we can take this man out of the picture" I said

"He is not..." she started and thought for a second "a problem at the moment"

"If you feel trapped here that is a problem for me," I said, "You should be allowed to live"

"He is scared of Declan so I am safe" she smiled "I wanted you to know though"

"Thank you for trusting me enough to tell me" I said smiling

The twins started to wriggle as Mary-Anne had finished making their food "Time to feed you two I guess" I said laughing

We all went into the dining area, two highchairs had been set up for them at the dining table. Mary-Anne put the food down and took Althea who was closest to her; we put them in the highchairs.

"I had to get a couple of the boys to shoot out and grab these today along with some new clothes" Mary-Anne said "we were lucky enough to have some nappies their size"
We started feeding the kids.
"I had no idea it would be like this hun I am so sorry" I said
"It's ok Silver" She laughed "It's what family does, and it takes a village to raise a kid I heard"
"Takes an army to raise these two" I said laughing and pulling faces at Angelus
He was laughing too and Althea started laughing with a mouthful of food that ended up all over Mary-Anne.
We were all laughing then. We finished feeding the kids and bathed them and got them ready for bed and said good night to them.
We headed back downstairs
"Where's Alipa?" I asked
"In that greenhouse thing" Mary-Anne said "She said she would prepare the necessary things for slowing the kids abilities down"
"She knows Julian is on his way?" I asked
"Yup, and I think she wanted to escape the kids they started calling her nana next thing she was scurrying off to her greenhouse" Mary-Anne laughed
"Well I best go next door" I said
"Not like that" Mary-Anne said looking at me
Feeding the kids had been messy, and even though I had cleaned off the bulk of it, this outfit was not suitable for meeting a vampire lord.
I shot back upstairs and changed at vampire speed and was back in the kitchen as Mary-Anne handed me a bottle.
"Thanks" I said grabbing it and sculling it back
I noticed Rain standing at the front door looking over at the other place I went over to her
"What is it?" I heard Declan ask her before I got there
"She is very very powerful" Rain said opening her eyes wide she grabbed my arm "Be very careful Silver, if she doesn't like you she could snap you like a twig"

"I have no intention of pissing her off" I reassured her "I am also not taking any weapons, to show her I have no quarrel with her"
"Good idea" Rain said "she is not someone who will think twice about killing"
"Good to know" I said
"I think Rain should come and help me" Alipa said coming in from the back
"Good idea," I said nodding and looking out the door towards the other house.
"You can do this Silver" Declan said patting me on the shoulder before following Rain
"Are you ready?" Hemi said coming over to me with my whole team, the home team were already over there
"Yup" I said taking a deep breath
"Man it is so creepy when you breath" Hemi laughed
"Shut up it helps calm my nerves" I said playfully smacking him
We headed next door. There were two gypsy house trucks in the driveway.
Etana was in the lounge area with Khan and his girlfriend guarding her, she also had guards, but I could not pick what they were which made me nervous all over again.
She was a beautiful strong young looking woman with the most amazing dark skin you have ever seen and silver eyes
"Lady Etana" I said walking in holding out my hand to shake hers
She took my hand and shook it but did not try to read me.
She smiled
"You did not peek" She said still holding my hand
"Neither did you" I said smiling, "I am here asking for your help, it would not be right to try and probe your mind without permission"
"I like you" she said letting go and sitting down "Now I can tell I am not dealing with an everyday vampire, tell me, is it true that you are part fae?"
I sat down opposite her.
"Yes I am" I said
She smiled a very scary large smile

"I remember the taste of fae" she said almost drooling then she regained her composure "I am sorry it has been a long time since I was given the taste of fae blood, and as much as I enjoyed it, it was more than enough" her eyes went wide "Your brother has told me you need help finding Excalibur, I have already told him and your partner where to get their items"

"Yes" I said "It was stolen from an old associate of mine and he asked me to retrieve it"

"Yes Lord god damn Ivanovich" She said "You know I gave it to him to keep safe"

"Well he failed" I said

"Yes I am aware" she said, "and when you find it you will not give it back to him, he is also not have the other items you are acquiring for him"

"Ok why?" I said

"The grail will give him the power to walk in daylight, and never die" she explained "The trumpet and sword are weapons of war"

"He wouldn't dare" I said

"Are you sure?" she said "I have never trusted him"

"I can tell by the tone of your voice that's not true" I said

"Must you have all these people here?" she said looking around the room

"It just makes it easier because I have to tell them everything later anyway" I said "I keep no secrets from my family"

"Except time travel" she laughed

"It's not a secret to anyone in this room about what happened," I said. That wasn't really a lie, as such, in that not many knew what happened and the others hadn't asked.

"How did you become a vampire lord?" she asked

"I ate the heart of a vampire lord" I said I knew that would be a shock to some in the room, but not one let it slip

"And what of my stupid brethren?" She asked

"The ones who did the time spell thing, we destroyed their hearts" I said "they fucked me over, I got revenge, then Sin fucked me over"

She hissed when I mentioned his name

"You know him," I said smiling "and I am guessing you are not friendly?"

"That freak had me buried for 2000 years and it destroyed my home" She said still very angry about this

"That would be the kush empire?" I asked

"Yes" she said tipping her head to the side as if she wasn't sure she really heard that

"We did a lot of research into the vampire lords, and I thought you were very interesting so I looked into your background and where you came from, I have to say it must have been an amazing time" I said

"If you like human sacrifice and slavery" she said looking at me weird

"Oh I didn't know that" I said

"It is ok, even the archaeologists haven't worked that out yet" she laughed, "I was lucky, I was rather well born, so I was trained as a warrior and I was to be married to the second son of the king. It did not happen as planned"

"Nothing ever does" Alipa said stalking over

"Good gods is that you Alipa?" Etana said in shock

"Yes of course it is, who else would want this thin old useless body?" Alipa snapped at her "I just came over to get some hair and some blood and I will go back to what I was doing"

"You are working a spell?" Etana asked

"Yes, someone needs their abilities messed with" She said I was terrified she would mention the kids

"Oh" Etana said smiling "you know I have things that will stop abilities working"

"What sort of things?" I asked

"Collars, ankle things, cut it right off, I saw some when I was in Russia recently seems to stop people using their abilities pretty quickly," she said

"Oh hell no" I said *"Julian how close are you?"*

"15 minutes" he replied in my head

"Hurry" I said

"Not that it is not a pretty good idea for some, we kind of want

the people left unharmed at all" I said *"someone has made those damn collars from the boat"* I said to Julian in my head
"You are very attached to these people who need their abilities slowed, why is that?" she asked
"They are family, like the people here, but they are struggling with their abilities" I said not really lying
"There was once a rumour of ring that could stop a supernaturals abilities and if you wanted to use them just take the ring off," she said
"Could it be made into earrings?" Alipa said as she cut my wrist and took some blood and yanked a strand of my hair out as casual as one taking a sip of coffee
"If it does indeed exist I am sure it probably could" she said
"Well you are the one who finds artifacts" I said "what would it take for you to find it?"
"I don't think you will pay the price" she said looking serious
"How do I know if you just play games and don't tell me" I said getting annoyed
"You really are very passionate about this aren't you" she said leaning forward "The price is you let me in" she nodded at me
I knew she meant in my head
"I don't think that's a good idea Etana" Julian said coming storming in
"Oh look the other new Lord" She said looking over at him.
"Wait" I said suddenly, "What was the price we had to pay for the help you have already given?"
"There was none" she said "I wanted to meet you, find out why Sin is so scared of you and see if I could use that to end him"
She opened her mind and sent me images of things he had done to her when she was a young vampire.
Her sire was a lord, and he sold her to Sin , who in turn experimented on her and then buried her for 2000 years of utter darkness and hunger.
When she came out she slaughtered an entire village, Ivanovich covered it up. She lived her life in private and refused to be part of our world till now.
"You see" she said

"Yes I see, so how do we do it?" and why is he scared of me?" I asked her

"I do not know yet" she said

"It will be the kids" Julian said he saw it too with our connection "I am sorry Etana but no one jumps my wife's mind without me there"

"Fair enough" she said "What do you mean the kids?"

"We had twins just over a month ago, Sin made it happen and wants them once they are out of baby phase, we convinced him to wait till they are 18" I said

"He used your own husband to get you pregnant?" she asked as if she knew exactly what happened

"Yes" I said, "But they are such wonderful kids and they don't have the thirst for blood"

"He was never able to impregnate me, not that he did not try" she said looking sad "But that was another time and place" she shook it off like a chill had crept down her spine

"How do you, we kill him?" I asked

"We don't" She said "His kids will"

"NO" both Julian and I said at the same time

"He fears you will teach them to be kind but strong, and to fight, and that he is evil, which he is" she said "I was hoping you would be the one I had seen, A long time ago my sire gave me a gift, I found out he gave each of his Childe one, so we could be superior to other vampires, I have collected 5 of these rings, I am to give them to you to decide what to do with."

"What do they do?" Julian asked as she placed 4 rings one at a time on the table they were very shiny and black.

"The obsidian draws the sun's effect from you so you can walk in the day like any human" she said "This effect has the added bonus of being able to form an energy shield or blast, it is not fatal to humans but something in it hurts vampires an awful lot, I have given your brother one"

"So you came out of your beautiful quiet life to help us?" I asked her

"Yes, but I had to be sure you were genuine, about 100 years ago

an imposter tried to draw me out" she said "But still if you want my further help you must let me into your mind"
I looked at Julian hoping for an answer
"He may come too if you wish" she said
"OK then" I said and I opened my mind to her
When she was done she fell back on the couch exhausted, even though I felt a little uncomfortable, Julian seemed fine.
"I need blood" She said weakly
Someone ran off and got her a bottle
"How is it you two look tired and I am fine" Julian said
"Because you were just a passenger, we were the driver" Etana explained sculling the bottle back "Another two please"
She drank those just as fast
"Excalibur is hidden in a church in London, the big over dramatic one, it is under a pew near the front" she said seeming to feel better "You should drink my dear, there is no need for you to be weakened this long"
"I am fine" I said not feeling the best but good enough "So St Paul's or Westminster?"
"St Paul's, Cleopatra could not enter Westminster" Etana said
"Why?" I asked
"Because they have true faith and she has none" She said
"But isn't that catholic faith?" I said "Like the vatican?"
"Yes it is, however, unlike the Vatican, Westminster still holds their faith and it is blessed every year" she explained, "Your brother should not have any issue getting in with his team"
"Thank the gods for that I suppose" I said she looked at me funny
"You still thank gods after what Sin did to you, after all your life of terror and violence" Etana said
"I do not blame all gods for the sin of one, and I do not blame the gods for the actions of evil people" I said
"But you still wish for Sin to be dead?" she asked confused
"Of course, he wronged me and my husband, and threatens my children, my family means everything to me," I said
"Yes I did see that" she said
"And you would have seen that I too am capable of great vio-

lence" I said not feeling so proud of some of the things I had done as a young vampire

"I have seen" she nodded "But as gods do not force people to commit evil, you cannot be blamed for a moment when you were possessed"

"It is true I was not myself, but still I feel the guilt and everytime someone innocent was harmed in any fight we had, I feel the guilt." I said "But I also try to do my best to be a decent person"

"And you are, you care way too much about lives that are fleeting anyway" she said

"I must say I am surprised you did not want my blood as well" I commented "it's what most want from me"

"No if I were to take your blood I would become addicted only this time I do not think I would be able to restrain myself," she said

"I want to thank you" I said picking up a ring "you have helped so much with your gift and your information"

"I shall be staying a while, in case you have further need of me" she said smiling

"Oh and I will try to locate the ring I was telling you about, if it can be altered or duplicated Alipa may be able to do it" She said

"Thank you, I am not sure if we have room for another guest" I said "I will have to talk to Mary-Anne, so funny we thought we had more than enough room here and boom shit happened"

"I do not mind sharing with my people," she said, "We also have our own accommodation" she smiled "we just require somewhere to park"

"Ok well park where you can fit, just please try to leave room for people to get out" I said

Over the next week our spacious yard became filled with RVs and caravans. I walked over to the other house admiring the ring she had given me, I had always loved obsidian now it seems I have a good reason to.

Julian had put his on to.

"So what are we going to do about the kids?" he asked

"Well Alipa is trying a spell or something to slow their abilities, and Etana is going to look for a ring she once heard of that can do the same, I am hoping we could get the ring turn it into earrings so the kids can safely wear them" I said

"That sounds good, or maybe Alipa and Etana can turn some earrings into ability blockers" he suggested "So what were you telling me about the collars from the boat?"

"Ok Etana mentioned she had seen them recently being used to stop vampires doing their thing, we know that was something used in hell, and it could mean someone out there is trapping and holding vampires against their will" I said

"Which means we should tell Talon, and get him to get his enforcers on to it" Julian said

"Yeah we should" I said "he may know of some vampires who have disappeared or something"

"You want to find out yourself don't you?" Julian laughed

"Sort of but if I do Ivanovich will get his wish" I wrinkled my nose

"Lets just do this thing first then, tell Talon and see what happens after" he suggested

"I have to go back to London" I said "Or I could see if Rift will fetch it for me, but I would rather do it, since he has taken a fancy to Ivanovich's adopted daughter, he might not bring it home"

"Do you trust your brother?" Julian said

"Yes?" I more asked than said

"Then go" he said "my team got hands on the grail just before I landed, so they are on their way home, take your team back to London and I will look after the kids" he hugged me at the bottom of the stairs

"I want to see if Alipa got that spell thing to work" I said "Then I will go" we kissed

"Get a fucking room" Dominic said laughing

"This is our house " I laughed "we will smooch in hallways, we will smooch in the lounge we will smooch anywhere we want" I poked my tounge out at him

"Have you seen how many people Etana brought with her?"

Dom said nodding out the door
"Yeah a bit much really" I said "I am sure the neighbours will have issue with it, all these caravans and trucks"
"So who are you going to give the daylight rings to?" Dom said nudging me and winking
"Talon has one, we two have one, but we need it for the kids, I'm not sure yet who else" I said
"Could I borrow one till you do decide?" he asked looking a little sad "I miss the sun"
"Sure, you can borrow one till we need it" I smiled "Or until you go home"
"Thanks sis" he said as I handed him one "I will just use it for a day then you can have it back"
"Sweet as" I said, " Can you get Ivory to call my team together we leave in two hours"
"Sure sis" Dom said
"Well let's go see our baby's" Julian said smiling
We went upstairs to the kids room, Mary-Anne and Alipa were just coming out of the room
"Did it work?" I asked poking my head in the door
"We won't know till they wake" Alipa said "so what did the witch say?"
"She gave us daylight rings, and told us where to find excalibur, and now she is staying in case we need more help, but she also said she may be able to find a ring that can halt the kids a little, stop their abilities, slow their grow, but it is one ring, she also said you may be able to duplicate it or make 2 earrings from it" I said
"Mmmm" she said "And the price?"
"She wanted to see into my mind" I said
"Just be careful, I know she was lost for a long time and I cannot see her" she said "not like I see you, which means she is guarded and hiding something"
"Aren't we all" Julian said "if you guys don't mind I would like to steal some alone time with my wife"
"God you were only apart a day" Mary-Anne said

"Believe me we have spent enough time apart to be grateful for every second we get alone" Julian said smiling a very cheeky smile

Alipa snickered as she went downstairs Mary-Anne followed her with a look of disgust at Julian and a sly wink to me

We went to our room.

I stood in front of the mirror again just staring at it

"Are you waiting for something to pop out?" He said coming up behind me

"Maybe" I shrugged "I mean I know its been cleared but ...there's just something about it, not a bad something, just something"

"Maybe it is trying to show you there's nothing wrong right now" he smiled

I looked at our reflection in the mirror, really looked at it.

I saw a loving couple who almost seemed human, Julian started nibbling on my neck. I turned to face him and he kissed me. So deep and passionate I didn't notice him pick me up and place me on the dressing table, He started to pull my jeans off and I let him

He went down between my legs, I leant back against the mirror as he started lciking and flicking my clitorus with his tongue.

He pulled me closer to him licking and sucking until I couldn't take anymore

"Fuck me" I screamed

He looked up at me and grinned and went back to what he was doing. I was wriggling and writhing all over the dressing table then he suddenly stood up but kept his fingers working my clit

I could see in his jeans was a massive lump.

"Are you sure you are ready for me?" he said in my head jokingly

"Fuck me now or I will kill you" I screamed

He dropped his jeans and rammed himself into me.

It felt so good

He started pounding me hard and fast like I liked and I came screaming like a banshee

He too released and while he was still in me he lifted me up and took us to the bed where we collapsed in a heap together.

"God I love you" he said smiling at me

"I love you too darling" I said reaching up and kissing him

Chapter 6

The trip to London was a bit rocky, there was a storm rolling in across our flight path.
It was raining when we landed, we were instructed to go directly to a hanger that had its doors open. Rift and Druantia were waiting for us.
"That was quick" Rift said as I got out of the plane
"Yeah well we got a location, but we need to move fast" I said "Is St pauls open at night?"
"Yes they are open for vampires who still believe in myths" Druantia said "is that where she's hiding?"
"No she is not there, but I need to go there" I said
"I'll drive" Druantia said
Rift looked scared
"How about I drive?" he suggested
"Fine" she said sulkily
"I don't care who drives just get me there fast" I said
Silvia, Hemi and myself went with Dru and Rift and we got to the church fine.
I went in confidently with Hemi and Silvia behind me Riift and Dru stayed in the car.
There was some kind of meeting going on and a group were gathered at the altar thing
"Oh , we have some new people" the man I decided was the preacher said looking at us
"Oh no we are just here to sit a while thanks" I said going to the pew Etana had shown me
"So you are not here to join our choir?" he said walking over as the rest of the group waited
"No we are just visiting London and I really wanted to see this

place I have heard so much about, and to pray of course" I said smiling at him
I noticed right away he had a ring like mine. I turned mine around so he could not see the obsidian.
"Of course, but I must ask, as we have had some issues of late, if you could please not start any fights here" he said trying to touch my hand.
"I promise we not here to start a fight" Hemi said taking his hand and shaking it
"It is not often we see vampires with wolves" he said
"We have been friends a long time, we recently lost some friends and one is in a life threatening situation, we would like to pray if that's ok" Silvia said being a bit brisk
"Oh very well please pray we will just be over here singing" he went back to his choir
"Ever wonder why true faith doesn't work for everyone?" Hemi said whispering "to many branches"
"And they level of depravity" Silvia whispered back
"Would you two be quiet, how do we get this out of here" I said having felt where it was
"Kneel to pray" Hemi said "yanked it out and hide it in my coat"
We all knelt down and pretended to pray.
When the people were not looking I reached under the seat and yanked it, it was solidly put in place.
I ducked down a bit further and made quiet sobbing noises. I looked under the seat and it was there, duck taped to the pew really well, I yanked harder and it came off. I got back into my upright position on my knees, I carefully passed the sword to Hemi behind us and he leant down to "cough" and hid it under his coat, and we stayed there for 20 more minutes, pretending to pray.
We got up and went to leave, my phone went off it was a text from Julian

This new cup is weird
How are things there

I smiled and turned around
"Sorry, but praise the lord my friend is out of danger and stable"
I smiled and we left saying thank you

I dropped 200 pounds in the donation box, I know it's not a lot for me but we were not carrying a lot of cash.

We got in the SUV and Druantia was in the driver's seat and Rift was in the passenger seat

Hemi slid the sword under the seat. I sat down and text Julian

Got the trinket

See you soon as we can

"Who was that really?" Hemi asked

"Julian" I said "He has the grail, I have the sword"

"So just the trumpet to go?" Dru said excited

"Yeah just the trumpet to go" I said knowing Talon was on it.

A car pulled up in front of us.

"Get us out of here now" Rift said quickly to Dru

She was already turning on the car and getting ready to get out of there.

4 people dressed head to toe in black got out of the car as Dru backed up to go, They pulled out guns and I saw Dru smile.

Next thing she floored it, one arm out the window shooting at them as they shot at us as we went past. She stopped suddenly sideways, and made sure their car was going nowhere.

This girl was cool, badass and so casual, she went back to driving and we took off, soon as we heard sirens she slowed down.

There was moderate traffic and she knew how to blend in. Now most people hear sirens and go faster, but this girl was smart. Police went flying past us and a couple of other cars that happen to be on the street. She drove like a nanna for a while and then floored it again.

"Back to the airport I guess?" she said smiling

"Yeah time to get home" I said "thank you Druantia, if you ever want a job anywhere feel free to give me as a reference"

"Thanks Silver, but I'm good" she smiled "I have my club to rebuild"

"Oh yeah we got the artifacts for you too Sis" Rift said holding on to the dash very tight

I understood why Rift was scared he came from an era of horses, and yes she was going a bit fast but I knew after the first 500 meters she was good at this.

"That's wonderful, but I don't think we'll need them" I said

"Well Lord Ivanovich said," Let her hold them, she may find a use for them," she said very happy with herself as we pulled into the airport and straight into the hanger. She stopped sideways, much to my team's horror right in front of them. literally . It was hilarious to see the looks on their faces.

We got out and Rift kissed the ground a few times.

He looked up at me getting out of the SUV

"How the fuck are you so calm?" He said

"Well I wasn't for the first part but I figured she knew what she was doing" I laughed

""I am sorry Druantia, but I am with Rift" Hemi said looking a bit pale "You should not be allowed to drive, except in emergencies"

"You boys are a bit weak aren't you?" Sylvia said coming round the back of the vehicle

"How can you two not be affected?" Rift said standing up

"Maybe it's a girl power thing" Silvia laughed and got on the plane.

"Thank you Druantia for everything" I said shaking her hand

"That's cool" She said "to be honest it has been my honor to meet you, my ...father talks about you all the time"

"What?" I said in shock "He talks about me in a good way?"

"Yeah, he said you have saved the world a few times, lost everything, got it back and more and yet you maintain your humanity even when others don't deserve it, him included" she said "He really admires you, mind you I have heard him curse your existence too"

"Now that's what I expect" I laughed

"Anyway, did you want me to tell him you have the sword and cup or should I wait" she asked

"Let me get them home then tell him" I suggested

"Done" she smiled

"Rift are you coming or do you want to chill here a bit?" I asked my brother

"But don't you need me?" he asked

"Well no I want you there, but I think other things are more important, and I want to see you happy" I said

"Then I will stay, I'm just over the ditch from home" he laughed

I gave him a hug

"I think she is a good one brother, good luck" I whispered in his ear

He blushed

Everyone said their goodbyes and we got on the plane and left for New York.

Arriving home the front yard looked much like a trailer park, our newer guests were decorating the entry and driveway for halloween. They all seemed very happy.

I got inside and Julian came at me with a huge hug

"Hemi has the sword" I said snuggling into him

"I had a thought," Julian said "where are we going to put these artifacts?"

"That is a good point" I said looking back at Hemi, Lucian was coming in with him and he had the bag that held the artifacts from Druantia.

"We should get everyone together when Talon gets back and see if anyone has any good ideas" I said

Once inside Hemi pulled the sword out from his jacket

"I dunno why this is so special, just looks like an old sword" he said

I took it from him and held it like I was wielding it

"Because it is a sword of myth" I smiled

"How do we know it's real?" Hemi asked

"I have no idea" I laughed, "I hope it is or we have a lot more work to do and Etana tricked us"

"I think for now we should put them in the safe" Julian said

"We have a safe?" I asked having not seen one

"Yeah in the entertainment room behind the bar we found a trap door that leads down to a basement and wine cellar, and there is a safe that I already reset the combination" he said

"Cool," I said "well can you go put these in it?" I handed him the sword and indicated for Lucain to give the bag to him

"Of course my love" he kissed my check and took the sword and bag and left for the entertainment room

"I'm going to go and have a shower and get changed" I said to the others "I am glad it was easy to do this, thank you guys for having my back"

"It's what we are here for" Lucian said smiling, "I am going to grab a snack and go to bed"

"I will join you" Hemi said

I went upstairs and poked my head in the kids room, they were still sleeping. Today we would find out if these daylight rings worked and I would be able to spend a lot of time with them. Of course, I also wanted to talk to Etana about the priest with one.

I showered and got dressed in jeans and a shirt, just in time for my baby's to wake up.

Julian and Mary-Anne were already there and doing the nappy change thing.

"So how are they?" I asked

"They are not happy, Althea tried doing her zoom crawl and found it doesn't work anymore, so she is a bit pissy today" Mary-Anne said

"Oh my poor baby doesn't like going normal speed?" I said pulling faces at her as Mary-Anne changed her

She blew a raspberry at me, and it was so cute we had to laugh

"Well it's better for all of us if you just stay a baby for now my sweetest angel" I said picking her up once Mary-Anne was down and giving her cuddles

Julian had finished with Angelus and we went down stairs to feed them.

We were sitting in the kitchen doing just that when the sun came up, now in this house that's no biggy for the vampires, my windows are well protected. I watched as Etana did some kind of morning ritual outside and then came up to the front door and knocked.

I went and opened the door for her.

"Come in Etana we are just feeding the kids" I said

"I see you are wearing the ring" she said as she followed me to the kitchen

"Yeah both Julian and I are, and I gave one to my brother to borrow" I said

"Yes Dominic joined me yesterday for a walk" she smiled "he is desperate to go back to his lady love"

"I should tell him he can go, we have more than enough people here" I said

"Oh one of your neighbours has been hanging around during the day trying to watch everything you are doing here" she said looking at the babies as if they were some weird thing that had never been seen before, to be fair they kind of were but they still were just like other babies.

Angelus seemed to like her, he kept going shy and giving her the cutest looks

Althea seemed to not care as long as we were putting food in her mouth.

I went to the fridge and got us drinks

"I spoke with Alipa yesterday while you were gone" Etana said

"She is concerned about my coming out of hiding, which I understand, but I let her see in my mind so she could be assured, I am not here to make trouble"

"That's good to know" Julian said

"My people found your portrait in the garage, may I ask why you do not have it hanging?" she said

"Because I do not know anything about it except an old man commissioned it before I was even a vampire, and the artist died mysteriously" I said "and that creeps me out"

She laughed

"Now I understand" she nodded "You should know it is not mystical enhanced at all, it is just a beautiful painting of an old mans dream"

The kids finished their breakfast and were now crawling around the floor at regular speed.

"I see Alipa's potion worked for now, she is truly a mysterious and interesting woman" Etana said "Do you know what she is?"

"Not really, I know she is old, and has lived longer than any human" I said "but she has helped us and has been so good to us, I hope her life continues for a while yet"

"I would have picked her for human too, except I know her from a long time ago" Etana said "She helped me when I first came out of the hole I was stuck in"

"One day I hope she trusts me enough to let me know her story, I am positive it would be very interesting," I said

"Who is interesting?" Alipa said coming in the door from the back

"You are" I said "and so kind and helpful" I smiled

"Pff I'm not interesting" she said making herself an herbal tea "Just bloody old"

"How old exactly?" Julian asked

"I have no idea anymore" Alipa said thinking about it "I don't even know why I am still here, I am just grateful I am"

"Is that Mat girl your apprentice?" Etana asked

"No I am merely guiding her a little, when she needs it, but she understands things beyond me" Alipa said "She has learned much from the books Silver had found for her"

"You found her some books?" Etana asked "what sort of books?"

"Basically we give her anything we find that is in an old language that is not around any more, she deciphers it and tells us what was in it, whether it be scrolls, stone tablets or old grimoires" I said

"You have old grimoires?" Etana said "from where?"

"We were able to raid Lord Ivanovich's library" I said "I don't know where he obtained them"

"The oldest I have seen was Babylonian" Alipa said "which was a surprise as most paper trails that old have crumbled and turned to dust"

"I have an ancient sumerian text I would not mind having translated" Etana said "Do you think she would mind?"

"You can ask her?" I said "she will be back when Talon returns"

"Have you heard from him at all?" Julian asked

"No but Ivory has" I said "they were securing an access to the Vatican, in daytime"

"Etana and Alipa would you know anything about a goblet that can show you everything if you use the right liquid?" Julian asked

"There are legends of a few like that, including the grail, the right liquid is said to give eternal life" Alipa said

"The cup of Jamshid is more see everything kind of cup" Etana said "But that was lost a long time ago and I have not heard of it in century's"

"Well you could do your thing and find it is in a bag in my vault" I said "But I do not know what liquid it uses"

"Blood dear" Etana laughed Alipa laughed with her, "blood of the earth or you"

"It will show you the universe and worlds beyond worlds" Etana said

"Oh well we don't need to see all the universes and worlds" I said

"There was a group of people along time ago who destroyed any artifact they found, it was very sad the ruined many works of art with no power at all, just because it was not their belief" Etana said

"Yes the terror attacks before vampires came out" I said "Islamic state wreaked shit or sold shit to support their own unjust disgusting agenda"

"Hel had a good laugh at them, they followed her lead, in the name of their god, but their destruction was all her doing as well, because the way they treated woman" Etana said

"What do you mean Hell?" I asked

"The norse goddess dear, she tried to take advantage and it failed her, made her weak, because they gave their belief to Allah and not to her a mere female" Alipa said

"So Allah was made strong by the terrorists" I asked

"You would think so, but no, he was further weakened because their belief was corrupt" Etana said

"Man gods are confusing" Julian said

"They are Gods, they are like entitled children who seek attention constantly and throw tantrums when things do not go their way" Etana said

"I blame the parents" Alipa said giggling

"Who are the parents?" I asked

"Human's" the both said

"They made gods to give them excuses to do and not do things" Etana said

"So what happens if everyone stops believing the god they created?" I asked

"Normally the god pisses off to another world, sometimes they pop back to create havoc and those who created them but mostly they stay away" Etana said

"What if the world were wiped clean and there were no more humans here?" Julian asked

"Any god still based here would die" Alipa said "The ones who have their own worlds to go to would be diminished but could rebuild on the faith of the beings in their world"

"So it is in the gods best interests to keep this world going" I said nodding my head

"There were times on this planet when it was wiped clean, the gods of the time vanished, somehow humans keep coming back" Etana said

"Like a parasite" I said remembering the matrix movie

"Exactly, however vampires were newer" Etana smiled, "We are only 5000 years on this planet and there is none I know of that old any more"

"Well I know we have managed to put off an apocalypse, gained the planet a couple more years with all our sustainable things we helped the council impose" I said

"Yes but humans are flawed and will find a way to wipe the slate clean again" Alipa said

"Well I think we should take the kids for a walk" Julian said watching them as they started fighting over a block, the fact there was a whole box of blocks made no difference because they both wanted that one.

"I could do that now" I said excited

"You know these rings have made me redundant?" Mary-Anne said laughing

"Oh no girl" I said "it just means we can help you more during the day"

"I'm not worried, in fact while you take them for a walk I am going to do some of my other work" She smiled

We picked up the kids and went upstairs to get them changed

and dressed for a walk, it was rather brisk outside. Then we went to the kitchen on the way to the garage and got the big double pushchair Mary-Anne had got the kids loaded in and we went down the driveway.

This area was really nice, clean footpaths, lots of trees, big sections, no one had a fence out the front of their house, I guess we were going to be the only ones.

We walked for about thirty minutes and came across a park. We decided to stop and let the kids have a crawl on the grass.

"It's very quiet at this park" Julian said looking around he was right there was no one else here

"Maybe because it is still pretty early" I said looking at my watch "I wonder what age kids need to be to sit in those swings?"

"I think they would be ok with the baby ones," Julian said picking up Althea and taking her over to the swings, Angelus crawled after them and I followed behind him.

Julian put Althea in the baby swing and secured her, Angelus caught up and was sitting with his arms up to be picked up, I grabbed him from behind and spun him round to face me he was giggling and laughing. I popped him in the other baby swing and secured him.

We started small, just little pushes, they were both loving it and the more we pushed the more they laughed.

A couple more people showed up, but none had kids with them. Now to me that is a bit creepy.

Then a group of people arrived but stayed over on the clear patch of grass and started doing tai chi, which was cool. We took the kids out of the swings and went to the little slide. Holding on to them we had them slide down the slide a few times then stopped for a bit. To let them crawl around.

Althea went to the edge of the playground part and was watching the people doing Tai chi.

She started moving her arms like they were, then Angelus crawled over to her and pushed her over. She grabbed his hair and pulled him down with her.

Julian and I jumped in to stop them.

"Now now you two, no fighting" I said

"How old are they?" I heard a voice behind me

We spun around to see a woman with a toddler

"About 8 months" I said lying

"I think your little girl wants to do that thing they are doing" she said nodding over to the ty chi people

"Yes I think she may become the martial artist of the family" Julian said

"Your pretty lucky" the woman said to me "Your bosses hired a manny for the boy makes life so much easier when there's one nanny per child"

"Oh no these are our kids" I said

Her whole attitude changed and not for the better

"Oh" she said, getting a bit snotty "Why are you people in this neighbourhood?"

"We live here thanks" Julian said

"I just bought two homes up the road, and I am giving our nanny a break because she does a much better job than you will ever do" I said

"I have awards" She said ignoring the toddler she had with her, Julian and I could see this was going to be bad as the toddler ran over to a little pond

"For ignoring your charge as they drown?" Julian said looking at the toddler who was nearly at the pond

She spun around and ran after the toddler and got there just as he jumped in the water

We decided to leave.

"I think we have to investigate these nanny awards, I'm sure Mary-Anne can do a much better job" I said loudly as we walked past the nanny pulling the toddler out of the water

"At least she shares our values, darling that alone makes her 100% better than this woman" Julian said smiling at the nanny as she scowled at us.

I hated people who looked down on others like that. I was beginning to think this neighbourhood was a bad idea.

"Maybe it will grow on us" Julian whispered reading my mind

"Maybe we can make it better"

"Maybe if we just stay to ourselves and ignore everyone " I smiled

"If we are going to be around during the day we may have to make some adjustments to how other people live" He said smiling at me pushing the pushchair

"I suppose so, but we don't have to take shit from people like her do we" I cringed

"No we don't, but we should try to be more diplomatic" he laughed

"Oh dear" I said looking ahead of us.

 The neighbours who had come over a few days ago were making a beeline for us.

"I will handle it darling" Julian said smiling at me we stopped and he kissed me as they got to us

"We just wanted to let you know we have laid complaints against your trailer park," the man said

"Thats nice" I smiled Julian gave me a look to shut up

"They will not be here long, they are distant family just coming to help us celebrate our new home" Julian said

"I thought vampires couldn't do daylight" the woman said

"They normally can't, I am sure there are exceptions" Julian replied

"Oh so you two are not vampires?" The man asked

"You will never know" Julian said "So what is the deal with the park, are locals not allowed to take their kids there?"

"Oh , that one is for the help" The woman said

"Oh so where is the homeowners park?" I said

"People here do not take their children to the park" The man said "This is why we have nanny's"

"Really is this classsest bullshit still really happening" I said in Julians head

"Maybe we can change that in this neighbourhood" he replied

"So did you notice we have started decorating for halloween?" Julian said to the couple

"Yes we have laid a complaint about that too," the woman said

"Why?" Julian asked

"They are not suitable decorations" the woman said

"It's Halloween, they are the correct decorations for the season"

I said

"They are a little too dark for our fair neighbourhood" The man said

"Well maybe your neighbourhood needs an education on what halloween is then, our visiting family would love to help with that I am sure" I said

"How is it that your family is so dark and yet the two of you are so light?" The woman asked

"Because they are from Africa and places that no longer exist" Julian said

"Look this is a fair neighbourhood, but you should really keep an eye on your family," the man said

"Oh that reminds me we are having a housewarming party for halloween, as some of our closest neighbours we were going to invite you , however I do not think you will like it so maybe we will not bother" Julian said

"Excuse me?" the man said

"Well a lot of family are coming and they are black, yellow, brown, vampires, wolves, tigers, panthers, I feel your outlook on life, you will make our guests very uncomfortable" Julian said

"Oh your liberals?" He said

"Yeah lets go with that" I said "Darling we should get these two home it's nearly nap time"

"Yes I agree" he said smiling at me

"Ok let's not be nice" Julian said in my head
I smiled

"Don't worry we won't invite you, in fact we would appreciate it if you do not set foot on my property again and if you see us walking our children, just cross the road and stay away" I said "I do not want you infecting my babies with your misplaced disgusting hatred"

"We are not misguided" The woman said "fact is most people who break the laws are of a different colour or they are vampires"

"God you are full of shit" I said moving around them

"Let's go dear, no need to hang with the riff raff" the man said and they stalked off

"I thought all this crap had been stopped" I said to Julian as we continued our walk home

"Well sometimes intolerant asshats train more intolerant asshats" he said

"I think we should make sure our home warming is an A list event, we need to find somewhere for Etana and her people to put their vehicles so we can utilize all our property and make a Halloween festival thing" I said

"I'll get Ivory on to it when we get back" Julian said

"Except he is sleeping" I laughed

"Oh yeah" Julian laughed "So I dump this on Mary-Anne?"

"No we will help and maybe get Rain and Alison to help out, but first we will have to talk to Etana" I said

We arrived at our new fenced section, and stopped to look at the decorations along the fence, there were shrunken heads, cobwebs, big fake spiders, bats floating in the air (on wire), ghouls and zombies that seemed to come out of the walls, I thought it was fabulous. I looked over to some of the neighbours front lawns...a rocking chair and a carved pumpkin was all that adorned one house, the rest had not started.

We walked in the gate, there was a fake vampire crouching on one side of the gate and a fake werewolf on the other. As we walked through they both did a half leap at us, I jumped then laughed.

"This looks very halloween to me" Julian said laughing at me

"Yup, I think it's awesome" I replied

The kids had fallen asleep

Chapter 7

We got back to the house, so many people around, builders building stuff, plumbers working on the kitchenette, electricians working on solar panels and installation of extra wires in the boardroom for the computer bank we would need.

We put the kids to bed and I went to have a look at what had been done in the boardroom, then made my way down to the garage
I got to the garage and found the painting had been moved
"Hun did you move that painting?" I asked Julian in my head
"No darling, but someone did because it is in the lounge" he said
I went to the lounge and yup someone had hung it over the fireplace
"I really hate that painting" I said
"Why?" Rain said coming in the door with Declan
"Because it looks like me" I said frowning
"It is beautiful" Declan said Rain nodded her agreement
"So those rings work well?" Rain asked
"Yeah we took the kids to the park this morning, it was nice" I said "till we meet people"
"Oh surely the people around here are not that bad" Declan said
"Actually they are intolerant, lazy, greedy, and that's just the help, then there's the racist, narcissistic cunts who think our Halloween decor is too halloweeny" Julian said
"Anyway I have decided we will be having a halloween house-warming party, and I want A listers we like, to attend, the mayor and anyone famous I don't care as long as they publicly don't hate us" I said "I was hoping maybe you could help Alison with it so Mary-Anne is not overloaded"
"I would love to" Rain said with her face lit up, then it dropped

"But Mary-Anne asked me to be her P.A and I start tomorrow"
"That's all good, I wanted to talk to her about the party too since she is my P.A" I laughed
"I must say it is very strange having you vamps around during the day" Declan said
"Oh Declan do you think you could ask Etana to meet me in the kitchen, I have something to discuss with her," I said
"Sure" he kissed Rain on the check and took off
Julian and I casually walked into the kitchen.
I grabbed us both a drink (of blood)
And we sat down at the table
"When this is over I want to escape, now we have these rings we don't need to take an entire team and it will be easier to disappear" I said quietly
"I think they only way we can do that is if we die, and I don't want to do that to our kids" Julian said
"Good point" I replied
Mary-Anne came in the kitchen with Brutus
"Oh shit you guys gave me a fright" she said "I forgot you have those rings" she laughed at herself
"Takes some getting used to" Etana said coming in the other door
"You wished to speak with me Silver" she said sitting with us at the table
"Yes" I said "We need to find another place to park your group, I want to set up a halloween fun park type of thing just for Halloween, have maybe fortune tellers and I dunno rides"
"We could maybe move them to the back of our property" Mary-Anne suggested
"Yes that would be fine," I said "and I already talked to Rain but I want to have an A list party here, something that will piss some of the neighbours off"
"Oh that would be fun" Mary-Anne said "we could set up a huge marque and have a masquerade horror ball"
"If I may make a suggestion?" Etana said "We have many gypsies amongst my people they could set up a gypsy camp as part of it

and do the fortune telling, and display their crafts and things"
"That is a good idea" I said "But only those who want to, and if we set them up near the front gate we could have it so everyday people off the street can come have a looksee and maybe buy some crafts"
"There is one couple we would very much like to not invite though" Julian said smiling
"Yes the couple that came over the other night, they are disgusting people" I said shaking my head "But I also want to invite the "help" of the neighbourhood to come and enjoy as well"
"Oh we could put flyers down at the park" Mary-Anne said
"Oh there's that one woman we saw there today" I said "With all the nanny awards"
"Yeah the one who wanted to one up us and ignored her charge as he went jumping in a pond" Julian laughed "She seems to think only nanny's raise children"
"Yeah I don't want her coming, she is as bad as that couple" I said
"Oh you met Greta" Mary-Anne said "the other nannies are scared of her, no one will go to the park till she gets there, except the tai chi group who seem to spend half the day there"
"Oh yes it seem Althea likes tai chi too" I said "She was copying them today, it was very cute"
"Maybe we should start doing tai chi here" Mary-Anne said "Or ask if we can join their group"
"We could ask" I said
"I have some people who do Capoeira I am sure they would love to teach you all, if you are interested" Etana said
"That would be cool" Julian said "Its one form I have not learnt yet"
"It would be kind of cool" I said "maybe they could do a display for the ball"
"Tell me what are you exactly trying to achieve here with the party?" Etana asked
"A show of how awesome shit is when you don't hate others for the way they look or the income they make" I said
"Maybe you should be focusing on the mission?" Brutus said

looking all serious

"Well there is not a lot we can do for now, we have 2 parts of the 3 and are just waiting on Talon" I said

"So you have somewhere to safely hide these artifacts?" Brutus said

"Well yes ish" I said "That reminds me I have to ask Alipa to ward the place from malicious intent again"

"She did that yesterday" Etana said "I helped her with it to make it stronger, there will be no strangers just popping in without permission either"

"Hay Brutus could you possibly work out how to move some trucks to the back yard" I asked him

"That's not hard just drive them down there" he said

"Yes but there is a lot and we don't want to have giant tire tracks all over the lawn" I explained

"So you want me to make a driveway for them?" he asked looking at me as if I had lost my marbles

"Well no just find the least destructive way to do it, maybe you could guide them down there" I said

"Fine" he said "when are they moving?"

"Tonight would be suitable" Etana said "when my people are all awake"

"Fine" he said "I'll go check it out now"

He left out the back with Etana following him

"Oh Etana" I said chasing her "I was wondering where you saw the collars and bracelets that remove things when a vampire uses an ability?"

"That was in Slovakia, about 2 years ago," she said, "why?"

"Just thinking about checking it out, do you know why they had these collars?" I asked

"Yes so vampires would not be tempted to use their abilities while fighting" she said "They have a whole fight club thing going on"

"You wouldn't happen to know who was running the fight club?" Julian asked

"Someone named cloud I think" she said "He was a miserable

angry little man"

"Do you know where they get fighters?" I asked

"As far as I know they are all willing volunteers" She said "We tend not to question others life choices, in the hope they will not judge us"

"Where as I am suspect of everything" I said sighing "It is bloody tiring"

"You suspect me of something?" Etana asked

"Your motives were questionable, the fact you were so eager to help and you are a very old vampire, in my experience old vampires are more likely to be untrustworthy, hell I don't even trust Ivanovich and I have known him for a long time now," I said

"And you trust me now?" Etana asked

"Not really" I said being honest "I trust you enough to be honest with you and hope you will be with me too"

"I suppose that is good," she said, "even though I showed you my mind"

"Yes but minds can be altered" I said casually

"You have experience with altering minds?" she asked carefully

"Not really, more having my mind altered or someone else's mind altered, with myself it was possession and amnesia" I explained "But if you are possessed and you do something vile...it's still there in your mind, even if you would never do something like that normally"

"That would be the human you killed" she asked

"Yes, what I did to that poor boy was vile and unacceptable and I have to live with that, even though I do know it was not my fault" I said

"I would like to hear more about these fights" Julian said

"Well they fight in a large hexagonal, they fights are to the death, but they wear the collars so the fight is contained, as far as I know they are all volunteers as I said" she said looking confused

"So there's a heap of vampires out there with a death wish" Julian said "I wonder why"

"I do not know" she said

"It wasn't Jason Mccloud was it?" Julian finally asked

"Yes that him" she said with glee "not a very stable or nice person"

"I guess some things were inevitable" I said shaking my head

"What do you mean?" she asked

"Did you see the other timeline when you read me?" I asked her

"Bits and pieces" she said nodding

"Well it was Jason who had the prison boats and ran the Hell fights, prisoners fighting to the death for their freedom, the collars were how he controlled everyone" I said

"Oh so you think he is actually controlling the vampires who fight for him?" she asked

"I don't know" I replied "But I will make sure someone checks it out"

"If he is doing something illegal what will happen?" she asked

"He will be arrested and dragged before the council" I said

"And if he is found guilty?" she asked

"He will be put down like the dog he is" Julian said smiling

"Oh you know this man?" Etana asked

"Sadly yes we do" Julian said

"But you knew him in the other timeline you experienced?" Etana asked

"Yes" I said "And from what I have seen there is no difference in the person's character for either timeline"

"And you are not investigating yourself because?" She asked

"Two reasons" I said, "First we are retired, and second we have enforcers who can deal with it"

"They are good reasons" she said

Brutus came back in

"I found a sort of path to the back, but that side is not fenced yet" he said

"That is fine we can be the fence till it is done" Etana said "I am going to go take a nap, I shall see you this evening"

She left.

Mary-Anne brought the twins downstairs, they had finished their nap and seemed eager to get food. Julian and I jumped into action and prepared them lunch.

By the time they went for an afternoon nap Julian and I were nackard and headed to bed.
This daytime thing was going to take some getting used to.

That evening we were able to move most of the bigger vehicles to the rear of our two properties and they formed a line around the back of our section some smaller ones were lined up in front of those so there was a street in the middle of the two. They all had their own power set up and they had water reservoirs. They really were a whole mobile community and they had plenty of technology like computers and satellites.
The more gypsy styled ones stayed at the front and formed a circle near the entrance, there were about 9, I let them start making a bonfire in the center, which they would light on halloween. I thought about putting the painting in it, more than once.
Talon came in the door around midnight. He did not look happy, and neither did Mat.
He handed me a case that held the trumpet.
"I take it you have somewhere to keep this?" he said kind of gruffly
"Yes I do thank you" I said handing it to Julian who took it into the entertainment area "Dining room both of you now," I said to the pair of them and went to the dining room
They followed behind me
"What's going on?" I asked sitting down and indicating the same
"It's nothing" Talon said
"Talon found out that we cannot get married in a catholic church because he is a vampire, unless he wears the ring and pretends to be human and we have it during the day" Mat said
"And?" I said not seeing the issue
"I when I was a kid, I always wanted to get married in a big flash church, now I am in love I do not care where we get married" Mat said looking at Talon
"So why not use the ring, it would be yours anyway?" I said
"I will not get married in a lie" he said
"Fair enough then get married somewhere else" I said "I am sure

there's a big flash church that will do it"
"I did some checking and none of the well known ones will do
it" he said grumpy
"But I don't care now, I would be happy to get married here in
the dining room, with just your family" Mat pleaded
"But I want you to fulfill your dreams" Talon said
"What about a big flash castle?" I suggested
"You mean your home?" Talon asked
"Well there's not just mine, there's Rift's and Dom's and Ana's We
have a family of castle owners, surely one would suit, and even if
we ask nicely maybe Ivanovich has a place" I suggested
"To be honest I thought it would be at your place in New Zea-
land" Mat said
"Fine" Talon said "But I don't want you to resent me for not giv-
ing you your dream"
"My dream changed when I met you Anton" She said smiling at
him
"Fine next family vacation will you Matiana be my wife?" he
said dropping to one knee smiling at me and winking he pulled
out a small box and opened it
"Yes" she said her eyes nearly popping out of her sockets and
then she saw the rock
Her jaw dropped
"This is to much Anton" she said as he slipped it on her finger
"Nothing is too much for you" he said smiling at her
"You know we are meant to be having our annual vacay next
week?" I said suddenly remembering
"Yeah" Talon said "But everyone is coming here this year, I
sorted it when we were in Rome"
"What?" I said "And where are we going to fit any of them?"
"I can't do the wedding thing that quick" Mat said panicking "I
can't even get a dress that quick"
"No I meant the next holiday, when we are back at Castle Alex-
androv" Talon said soothing his fiance
"Shit" I said "and Mary-Anne has gone to bed"
"Don't worry about where to fit everyone, I have it sorted"

Talon said smiling

"So next week everyone arrives we will have a party for your guys engagement" I said

"I want to have a handfasting ritual I was going to ask Alipa to do it" Mat said

"That's a cool idea, we could do that as part of the party. But that means you need 1 year and 1 day before the wedding so what day will you guys do it" I said all excited

"I think if we handfast on Friday, so we can have the wedding on the Saturday would be a good idea" Talon said

"I can do that" Mat said smiling

"Ok so an engagement party on the Friday which gives us a week then our hallowed ball on the 31st." I said writing it down "I might see if Lily and Luca can take the artifacts home when they go back"

"Oh yeah Mat and I will be going too" Talon said "she needs to go back to school and I want to be close. But I can also run the enforcers easier from there"

"That's fine, everything should be sorted by then for our security " I said "I was hoping you guys would be here for halloween"

"I would like to go to the hallowed ball" Mat said shyly

"Ok then we will go back after that" Talon said

"Savannah has already sent your costume too " I laughed

""Are they coming for the ball" mat asked

"No they are busy, but they will be here for the engagement party" I said

"Etana has a lot of people here" Talon said

"Yeah they will all be here a while it seems" I said

"She has some interesting talents" Mat said

"Yes I am loving this whole daylight thing, I get to spend time with my babies" I mused

"So how are you going to educate them" Talon asked

"Carefully" I laughed "we may have to get them tutors that can keep up with what they need. They are growing twice as fast as they should which worries me so much I mean when they are 9 they will look 18 and we need to make sure they are at least semi mature by then and I have no idea if my daughter will hit puberty at 6 or actually when she is 12"

"And with this being the first vampire babies there's no one that can advise you" Mat said

"Yup no one has been through it and no one knows if or when they will become full vampires, or if at some point they get a choice, or if they will be fae like or god like " I said "But it does mean Julian and I need to spend as much time possible playing with them teaching them compassion and kindness."

"Your such a good mum" Mat said smiling

"I kind of feel guilty for getting Alipa to restrain their abilities" I admitted

"You did the right thing there, but when they are a bit older maybe more capable of understanding what they can do will you reverse it?" Talon asked

"Once we can train them, we will" Julian said "They will need to be able to defend themselves"

"And now I don't know if Sin will come for them when they appear to be 18 or still just when they are 18" I said

"At least he doesn't know they already have some abilities, and we have them well trained before he gets near them again" Talon smiled

"You guys know kids need kid time too ah?" Mat asked looking concerned

"I have actually already started making plans for that" Julian smiled "their training will be more like play for a few years, so they can still be kids as well"

"I know my training was pretty intense" Mat mumbled

"That is because you were already old enough to understand what was happening" Talon said "and your magic is a bit different"

"I was just talking about the defensive training" Mat said

"Most of us had a hard time in training at the beginning like me I sure was not used to being so fast and strong" I said, "but I was lucky in the fact I had sort of learned to defend myself as a human"

"From what Talon has told me you had a pretty strange life before becoming a vampire" Mat said "and that you guys were together when you were human"

"Yup," Julian said with a huge grin on his face "and she is sexier today than she was the day I met her"

"Oh shut up" I said

"How do you think you know he is the one?" Mat asked

"Well we have been together forever, but to be honest I see him in my future, and well we must have been destined, being brought back together right around when I was turned" I said

"I wanted to talk to you about something Talon, Enforcer business"

"Ok" he said "what?"

"Do you know where Jason Mccloud is and what he is doing?" I asked

"No I can't say I do, he's not been on any of our watch lists for a while" He said

"Oh, why is that?" I asked

"He lived an ordinary life without that access to your blood and the deal with Ivanovich, he was overthrown as boss, and just sort of drifted away" Talon said

"Ok well he may be behind a vampire fight club thing that uses the collars from hell" I said "about 2 years ago Etana saw them in Slovacia, and he was running the show"

"Why would they need collars?" Talon said "fight clubs are allowed, as long as everyone is willing"

"That's what I was thinking, he may be enslaving Vampires to fight" I said

"Ok I will go tell Ivory to look into it now, he can get all our contacts in seconds, if he is being dodgy we will find him" Talon said

"I am going to go to bed I want to talk to Alipa in morning" Mat said getting up

"Do you need me for anything else?" Talon said also getting up
"No go" I said

Dominic walked in the door gave Talon a nod as they left

"Big brother," I said, "What can I do you for?"

"Just returning the ring, I did what I needed to do" he smiled and handed it back

"Ok" I said "you can have it a while longer if you want"

"Nope I'm good" he smiled "I saw the sunrise and I saw the sun set and I partied hard with the rich and elite of the city"

"Really?" I asked

"Yup and man it was great" he smiled "Oh and they are all coming here for halloween, at a $500 entry fee"

"Why are you charging them?" I asked a bit annoyed

"Oh I wasn't going to but they seemed very eager to buy their way in" he smiled

"How?"

"I said to a couple about the party I was going to go to for halloween and the ones I told others and then people were asking how much the entry fee was...one guy offered 3000 just for him but I said no vip because it is all vip" he laughed "I had no idea it was so easy to get people to throw money at you"

"Well then we better make sure it is the best scariest damn party ever" I laughed

"And the kids?" Julian said

"Upstairs will be totally off limits" I said "and I want the biggest scariest guys guarding all the staircases"

"They should be asleep at that time anyway" Julian added

"And you know we have a few people who will be looking in on them" I said

"So I am going to bed daylight sure makes one tired" Dom said getting up

"That is true" I said yawning "I think we should go to bed, we have to get up to the kids in the morning" I smiled and stood up

"Let's grab a drink first" Julian said going to the fridge, he opened two bottles and handed me one "Here's to us, may we make it through the next few weeks and then puberty"

"Christ hun" I said shocked "they are not hitting that next month, so let's just deal with what we have got" I laughed

"We got this hun" He said "*It's destiny,*" *he said in my head*

Chapter 8

The next day was chaos, I had all our were's helping the builders with the fence, and a plan to get all able vampires to do the same come nightfall, to be fair some would just be scary with a hammer and nails, for now the fence was just a timber box with a thick wire every couple of feet it would be about 1 foot thick, they would be pumping in concrete, and then covering it with rocks making it about 2 foot wide in total.

Etana was setting up her Gypsy camp and bonfire, as it was some of the gypsies were not vampires, so they were helping her.

Mary-Anne had found a marque that would fit around the back and could be done and decorated the day before the party.

Rain found a caterer that could handle the short notice, and had wolf and vampire for wait staff along with humans.

The kids were sleeping through the night most nights but both Mary-Anne and I had the baby monitors with us anyway.

One good thing about being rich, is that you do not have to leave your house for anything in America, we had party planners and event organisers coming through with their ideas, so far we didn't really like many of them, they all seemed to think we needed to have a light party, and remove the scary stuff.

We had 3 hours of interviewing people when a chick dressed like some punk school girl walked in the door. She took a look around.

"So you want it to match the entrance?" she asked suddenly turning to face us

"Yes that would be preferable" I said

"That will scare the shit out of this neighbourhood," she said

"You know there was a time it was not so bad out here, but that's gone, what's the budget?"

"We were hoping to hear ideas at this point and see what the price is, but the budget is a good sized one" Mary-Anne said

"How many people?" she said looking bored

"About 300 at this point" I said
She brightened up
"300 of the elites?" she asked
"Well no about 70 are our friends and family" Mary-Anne said
"Oh yeah I love the gypsy thing you have at the front is spectacular" She said "And the ball is masquerade?"
"Yes" I said
"Ok my crew can do it for say one hundred and fifty thousand" she said
"And the plan?" Mary-Anne asked
"I have a whole film studio of props, every real Halloween looking thing I can bring, I will, witches making a brew, fully automated, can even be programed to move to sound, hellhounds that snarl and sort of jump, dragons that puff smoke, sadly the fire breather doesn't breath fire, when it was in a movie it was cgi'd, I have zombies, mummy's, all things dead and not quite dead, gods of death, goddess who love them, and there's this awesome devil coming out of a volcano, but that one is pretty big" she said quite fast "But what I was thinking is, the other side of the drive from the gypsy fair we could have a hell set up I think I saw a spot the volcano might fit, then about halfway to the door we could have it going to zombies and mummies and then inside the door one room of Anubis, one for Hades and Persephone, and around the back here have the marque done old austria style, but with headless people, some moving some not, and the holographic projectors will be in each room so ghosts can be everywhere." she went on and on...by the end Mary-Anne and I were inthralld.
"Done" I said
"Awesome well I need 30k up front," she said, "So I can get to the warehouse and bring the stuff back"
"No problem" I said "I can put the money in your account as soon as we sign a contract"
"Do you want non disclosure so no one tells anything before the event?" she asked reaching into her backpack
"You are well prepared" I said

"I do try to be" she said "I am also extremely organised, I will need 1 week to set up" she said pointing out where the guys were working on everything"
"Oh we will be having guards on all the stairs no one is to go upstairs" I said
"No problem" she said "I can take fifty thousand off then"
"Even better" I said
We looked over the contract there were blank spots for the details and we filled them in and both signed it. Then I transferred the money to the account in the contract.
"So we will see you when you get back" I said as she left
"Yup see you in two weeks" she said

"You know for someone who wanted to disappear you are putting yourself in the spotlight" Julian said coming up behind me as I closed the door
"Yeah I know" I said turning to face him
"But this party is going to be epic" Mary-Anne said
"Oh I am all for having a party" he said smiling, "I just find it funny"
"I find it funny we retire and Ivanovich drags us back in" I said
"Have you spoken to him yet about the artifacts?" Mary-Anne asked
"No but he hasn't rung either" I said "I'm sure he will at some point"
"Well I am going to bed" Mary-Anne said seeing Brutus heading upstairs "See you guys in the morning"
"So my love what do you need to do right now?" Julian asked
"I need a drink and then I think we should go to bed to" I suggested
"Sounds good to me" he said heading to the kitchen
Etana was in there going over some paperwork
"Oh Silver can I speak with you for a minute?" She said looking up from what she was doing
"Sure, how can I help you?" I asked
"I need to go to England for a few days, is it ok if my people stay

here while I am gone?" she asked

"Of course" I said "as long as they know if shit happens I'm in charge"

"Of course I will let them know, I am sure they will not cause any trouble though" she said looking concerned

"I am not worried about them, just shit happens a lot" I said

"Arh I understand" she said "my people will help if shit happens and you need them"

"Thank you Etana" I said

"So why are you off to London?" Julian asked

"I believe you met one of my brothers and I am going to visit him" She said

"The priest?" I asked

"Yes" she said guardedly "and I must decide if he conning an entire religion, or if he really has turned around"

"Fair enough" I said I knew she may have to report him or dispose of him somehow but it was not my problem
She seemed surprised.

"You are ok with this?" she asked

"I am sure it's a family matter" Julian said smiling at me

"Come home safe" I said touching her arm in a reassuring gesture

"Thank you" she smiled

It was this point I felt a shift in the air, it was nothing bad but something had changed in that moment, like a turning point in a war when we had no idea we were fighting

Did you feel that?`` I heard Julian ask in my head

"Yes " I said so pleased it wasn't just me

"What do you think it was?" He asked

"I think she just chose a side" I said

"Well we are headed to bed" I said "If you need anything just ask one of the twins or Talon or whoever is in charge now" I laughed

"I will thank you again Silver and have a good sleep" she bowed her head and left

"Lets go to bed before someone else wants us" Julian whispered in my ear

The next day we spent with the babies, they were growing too fast, we knew it would not be long enough before they were off doing their own thing.
We had started reading to them as they dozed off.
We had got into a good routine with them, and whatever spell Alipa had done was still working.
By the time my whole family arrived the next evening the babies were pulling themselves up on things.
Etana came back the next day and she seemed happy.
"So how did it go?" I asked
"It went well I feel he believes he is helping people however I do not approve of his chosen way as he knows too well that the christian god is not the only one" She said "I also ran into your Lord Ivanovich"
"Really and how is he?' I said sounding like I didn't want to know
"He was concerned that you had not contacted him about the artifacts"
"Phones work two ways" I said
"Apparently yours have not been" she said "He asked me to tell you to ring him as soon as you have them secured"
"Cool well I don't feel they are secured yet, I am hoping they will soon be" I said
"I thought you had what you needed?" Etana said
"We do, but they are not as secure as I am going to make them" I explained
"Oh also he will be here Thursday for the family feast on the weekend he just has some things to do" she said
"Oh fuck" I said "I forgot he's family too now" I laughed "I better call him once it's dark"
"I must ask a favour of you" she said as if she were looking for the right words "I do not wish for Ivanovich to have a ring, there is something I do not trust about him"
"You noticed too" I said
"We learnt the hard way how careful we had to be around that man" Julian said "but he is one of our family, he has been

through a lot with us"

"And put us through a lot" I said "the old saying keep your friends close and your enemies closer sort of applies but he has been behaving for a long time"

"Just be careful who you give them to" She warned

"I will be" I said "last thing we need is someone like Cleo getting hold of one"

"I did not see your brother again today?" she said

"He gave it back last night" I said " he was happy he saw the rise and setting of the sun, and it was enough for him"

"That is a good vampire there" she laughed

""Everyone here is a good person, we may have all slipped once or twice, but those here and now they are good people, vampires and shifters" I said

"I have noticed this and you do listen to them so they are all happy as far as I can tell" She said

"I treat them the way I want to be treated, they are my family" I said

"Our Family" Julian said grabbing me around the waist "We are in this together after all"

"God yes" I said "There's no way I could have done any of this without you"

I leaned into him

"Have you two always been this..." she said waving her finger at us

"Sickening, soppy, puke inducing" Alipa said coming in the door. She smiled at Julian and I.

"As long as I have known them" She said

"Only since they day they found each other again and Silver was a vampire" Dom said walking in the door with a big grin

"I need a drink" I said heading to the fridge as the rest of my vampire family walked into the room

"It would appear you are about to be very busy" Etana said getting up "I shall go rest, it was a long trip"

"Thank you Etana" I said

"So I have done some research and I think the spell will wear off

when they are five human years old, which might make them ten" Alipa said "And I could given the right tools make them each a bracelet or earring that will keep their abilities in check, but I cannot find anything that will slow their rapid growth"
She looked exhausted my family were all chatting and catching up
"That's ok no rush" I said "You have given us some time please don't over do it, get some rest"
"May I have a look at one of the daylight rings" She asked me quietly
"Of course" I said
"And tell me who are you giving them to" she said
"Well Savannah could use one" I said "Talon has one and since he is marrying Mat I think it makes sense, but I honestly don't know"
"You are not giving Ivanovich one?" she asked
"No" I said
I saw the relief wash through her
"Your a good girl" she said smiling, "I'm going to bed"
"Sleep well Alipa" I said getting up
She waved a hand in the air as she went out the back door to her sanctuary next to the greenhouse

The next few days were hectic.
The babies loved having so many uncles and aunties doting over and spoiling them
Ivanovich arrived on the friday. I managed to avoid him for that day
I had already spoken to Lily and Luca about storing artifacts in the vaults at Castle Alexandrov and they agreed.
Talon would take them with him when he went back after halloween.
He and Mat had spoken to Alipa about the handfasting ceremony to mark their engagement, she thought it was a wonderful idea and saturday morning she and Mat prepared themselves, Talon felt left out till Etana explained there is this whole process Alipa was doing to purify and prepare Mat, but he did not need it as he was a vampire and unable to be pure anyway.

That party went off without any issues, and I still managed to avoid Ivanovich.
The ceremony was beautiful and Talon and Mat were so happy.
On Sunday most of us were just relaxing, our staff had taken care of cleaning up and there was nothing to do.

I had barely noticed when it got dark, till I saw Tatiana and Dom headed my way. I was lounging in the family/dinning room with the kids and Julian.
"You have been very hard to pin down Mrs Gustavo" Tatiana said in a stern voice
"I have been busy, it happens when you have kids and life to deal with" I said
"Well I have been sent to get you and take you to Ivanovich" she said sharply
"Well now's not a good time the kids have to have dinner and be bathed and put to bed" I said
"Their father can do that," she said very sharply "Ivanovich said you must come now, before he leaves"
"Oh when is my lord leaving?" I asked
"At midnight" she said
I looked at Julian
"Get it over with hun" he said in my head
"Are you ok with the kids?" I asked
"Of course Mary-Anne is here too" he smiled
I gave him a kiss and got up
"Lead the way" I said to Tatiana

We went over to the other house where they were staying and he was waiting in the dining room. There seemed to be no one else around at all which was weird considering how many people were here.
"My lord" I said sitting down
"Finally I can talk to you" he said "I have heard rumors that you have somehow obtained a way to move in the light"
"Yes I have" I said cautiously
"And you have found all 3 of the artifacts I asked you about?" he

asked

"Of course" I said

"When will you be able to bring them to me" he enquired

"I won't be" I said "We have found a safe place to house them"

"They would be safer with me" he said looking unhappy

"Really?" I asked "Did you not just recently lose one of them?"

"Things are happening that you know nothing of, I need them" he said looking more angry than unhappy

"Then you should make sure you have Talon in your corner" I said "He can judge if they are needed"

"And the artifacts that stupid girl gave you" he said narrowing his eyes

"You mean Dru?" I asked

"Yes" he snapped

"She is not stupid, she gave them to me to keep safe, and I thought we had your approval for those" I said "Anyway they are in a safe place"

"I want you to know I am not happy about this situation" he said seeming to calm down a bit

"Well, you made me go get them I am keeping them" I said sternly

"Yes" he said pausing for a moment "Now how did you obtain the ability to be in the daylight?"

"Sorry I promised you would not get that ability, kind of part of the deal" I said

"You are doing this for your...children" he said cringing at the word children

"Yes Uncle Ivanovich" I smiled "It is so Julian and I can be there for them, we are extremely blessed to have found this...ability"

"Yes" he looked at me as if he were trying to get in my head "It was Etana wasn't it?"

"Yes" I said seeing no reason to hide that information

"You have the rings off her dead family members" he stated

"How did you get in my head?" I asked him

"I did not get into your head, this is something I have known for many centuries, her bloodline is truly ancient, there were often rumors about her family's rings, and how she, once released, went after the more evil of her siblings. I believe it was some way of making up for some of the things she had done" he explained

"I do not judge people on their past my lord or you would not be here" I said

"Yes I know, but still you do not trust me" he said looking sad

"Ivan do not take it personal" I said "But you are never fully honest with me and you are always working on something in the background, always have ulterior motives, it makes it hard to trust you fully"

"What do you mean?" he asked

"You want Julian and myself back working for you, you know we have other very important responsibilities and yet you still try so hard to draw us back in, we do not want to" I said being as firm and plain as I could "But you did and worse, you used my children to do this, So I need to tell you, We will no longer be at your beck and call, you have people for this Ivan you do not need us, and if you use my children like that again I will personally take care of you"

I saw Ivanovich look very hard at me.

I looked hard at him too

It was the first time I had ever called him by his first name.

Why you may ask because I no longer see him as being above me, and if anything we are equals.

"Silver, I understand what you are saying, but in order to keep the children safe in the future things may need to be done now" He said

"I believe that Julian and I with our extended family will manage, and now we have the daylight rings so we can raise them"

"So you no longer wish me to assist your family" he asked seeming a bit sulky

"I did not say that Ivan, you are part of my family, I am just telling you Julian and I will not be going on missions, no matter how you contrive to try and get us to."

"So you plan to be a stay at home parents?"

"Well yes" I said

"Surely you will let Julian work" he said

"We have no need to, but if he decides he wants to that is his decision, also you have the rest of my family at your command"

"But your family do not have the skills you have"

"Are you seriously underestimating the abilities of all the people here?" I asked

"They do not understand what they are up against, what you are up against, For fucks sake Silver we are dealing with a GOD"

"Yes a god who wants my children for god knows what"

"And he found you when you were out in the forest off the grid, he will find you here and anywhere you go"

"I am working on that" I said

"You have just bought these two houses, do you think he will not be able to find you here?"

"That is why we will not be here much longer"

"Where will you be?"

"No one knows yet, not even me, but Julian and I will be taking the kids away from all the crap"

"Silver you and Julian are vampires there is no hiding that"

"Actually I think we can live normal lives with these rings"

"And how will you feed?"

"Same way we do now" I said

"People will always be hunting you" he said

"And if they find us we will disappear after we kill them"

"I'm sorry Silver" Ivanovich said sternly and almost as if he were trying to command me "I must insist that you stay in contact with me and continue to do what it is you do, you are needed for what is coming"

"I must prepare and prepare my children for what they will be facing in the future" I said back

"There is a greater threat happening now, Sin is banding together vampires to move in and take over as soon as he gets your children" Ivanovich said

"Which is not until they are 18, so I have time to prepare them" I said

"If it can be stopped before then don't you think you owe it to them to try?" Ivanovich yelled getting up.

"Do not raise your voice at me my lord" I said sternly but quietly

"If Talon finds good reason for me to come back and help then he will find me, you underestimate the people we have here and that is your mistake"

"They do not have your abilities" he said storming out of the room

"Well that went well." Julian said

"Better than I expected" I said

"So do you think he will back off?" Julian asked

"Nope" I said, "but once this month is done you, me and the kids are out of here"

"I agree" Julian said "But we should still take some human or beast to help during the day"

"Someone who knows about raising kids would be a good idea" I said

"Yes it would be, I mean we can watch all the videos we like but they will need an education and normal school is out" Julian said

Talon came in

"Well you two have managed to piss off Lord Ivanovich" he said

"His problem not ours" Julian said

"So he told me when you two disappear I have to tell him where you are" he said

"Say you don't know, even if you do" I said

"You know I will" he winked "so when are you two leaving us?"

"I am not sure but after this month" I said "we have to find some-where to go"

"How about buying a homestead somewhere?" Julian said

"Sure can you sort that out, so no one else knows" I asked

"Of course my love" Julian smiled at me

"You should get one near Jay and Savannah" Talon suggested "that way if shit happens they will be nearby to help"

"Talon we know people everywhere so no matter where we hide

someone will be nearby" Julian said

"What about Rain and Declan?" I suggested

"They are a bit young to have child experience" Julian said

"Actually Rain was teaching before her life got all screwed up by a vampire" Talon said

"I should really talk to her about what happened and what lead her to being out in the middle of nowhere half dead, but I didn't want to push her too much" I said

"I would love to know why Declan is so protective of her" Talon said

"Aren't they a couple?" Julian asked

"Not according to them" Talon said

I laughed

"So they are both in denial" I said

"Pretty much" Talon laughed

"Well I shall make time to chat with Rain tomorrow" I said "See how we can help her and Declan more, and see if they would be interested, but I will talk to Mary-Anne first"

"Good move" Julian said

Chapter 9

The next month was hectic. We had people coming and going
with the building and the public coming to see our Halloween
decorations and little gypsy village.
All the family that had left came back for the party, except
Ivanovich.
 The fences were finished as was all the security.
The builders had done an epic job on everything.
The early evening of the party while everyone was awake we
gathered in the lounge.
"Ok guys" I said "after tonight we are leaving"
There were looks of confusion and some understanding
"I am not telling any of you where we are going" I said "we are
doing this for the safety of the kids, we will no doubt be back in
18 ish years, but I hope you understand this is about protecting
our future"
"But where will you go?" Brutus asked looking concerned
"I can't tell you that, you know Ivanovich has ways of getting
information and Sin has ways of getting information so we are
going to keep you all safe by not telling you, we will be taking
one of the RV's"
"Are you going with the gypsies?" Ivory asked
"No" Julian said "we will go and find our own way around"
"But you're staying in America ah?" Ebony asked
"Don't know yet" I said shrugging my shoulders "we are going to
just go and see what happens"
"What if you need help?" Ivory said concerned
"I am sure we will be fine" Julian said
"And if Sin finds you?" Talon said
"Then we will take care of it" I said
"So if we see you again you will have more kids?" Ebony asked

"NO" I said "Julian and I have ways to make sure we are ourselves"

"Sorry but your like our mum, we love you and want to keep you safe" Ivory said

"I promise we will be safe" I said

"Tell you guys what" Julian said "if shit happens with us, we will be sure to call you first"

"Raising these kids right and keeping them safe is our first priority" I said "You guys together are more than enough to handle anything that happens"

"Is that why Ivanovich did not come for the party?" Dominic asked

"Probably" I said "he's probably trying to find a way to make me stay, but you would have more info than me on that"

"Tatiana hasn't said anything actually, just that Ivanovich and her are too busy right now to attend some silly party" Dom said

"Well guests will be arriving soon, and we have to get ready" I said

"It's not going to be the same here without you" Talon said to me when nearly everyone had dispersed

"I am sure you guys will cope" I said

"You are not alone Talon, you and Mat have a great life ahead of you" Julian said

"I know everyone is sad about this but I truly feel it is the best thing we can do for the kids" I said "They need to have a normalish life, not one where mum and dad disappear for months at a time and are too busy to be parents"

"I hear ya sis" Talon said "Are Rain and Declan still going with you?"

"Yes" Julian said "They are over at the other house with the kids"

"I thought they were staying for the party?" Talon asked "and isn't Rain Mary-Anne's PA?"

"Rain doesn't like crowds, so we agreed to meet them later" I said "she even found our family holiday a bit overwhelming, and Mary-Anne thinks it is a good idea since the kids will be

homeschooled and she has some teaching experience"
"Well we had more people than normal here with Etana's lot" Talon said
"Yup and tonight there will be sooo many more than that" Julian said
"Most of the street will be here tonight as will about 40 celeb's, good mix of vampire and humans" Ivory said "and a couple of politicians, just local ones, the wolves are on security, all the attraction rides and things were done by lunchtime, and I think the woman who did all that is currently going around lighting them up, guests will start arriving around 10"
"Well then we better get ourselves sorted" I said smiling at Julian
We were going as Isis and Osiris.
We had a change of clothes waiting at the other house for when we made our escape
Everyone that was left went off to get ready.
We had some people come in to do hair and makeup, and we set them up in the war room so everyone could have a chance to have their look for their costumes done to perfection.
Some of the wolves dressed as vampires and a couple of vampire were werewolves. Everyone looked amazing.
The mayor of the city came, and a few of the current a list actors, musicians for all sorts of genres.
At midnight Julian welcomed everyone and thanked them and invited them to enjoy the festivities, and everyone seemed to be having a lot of fun.
At 1 am Julian and I slipped out the back and over to our other house, Rain and Declan were in the R.V. with the kids when we got there.
"We thought it would be better to settle the kids here than wake them" Rain said
"Yup good move" I said smiling at her
"So are you two really ready to disappear?" Julian asked "This is your last chance to go live a normal ish life"
"I never fit in this world" Rain said "I see things, people freak out"
"I have nothing holding me here" Declan said

"Your family?" I asked

"They don't need me now and I doubt they will in the next 20 years" He said

"Jay and Savannah will miss you" Julian said

"Not really I never fit in with the pack, I haven't been with them much" He said " I mean dad is great and all but I need to follow my own path"

"Fair enough" Julian said

"Did you talk to them?" I asked

"Yeah I told dad, he won't let it slip" Declan said

"Yeah and Savannah wouldn't either" I said smiling "Ok let's go" Julian jumped in the driver's seat and I went back to watch my babies sleep

We stopped at some truck stop around breakfast time. We all got out and had a feed.

Then it was back on the R.V. Declan and Julian swapped driving duties and slept, we only stopped to get gas and eat. We stopped at a second hand dealership and got a van and a car.

Then we went straight up to Canada and Montreal, Julian and I used our abilities to make sure the border guards had no record of us at all.

Julian had a house here and we went there for a couple of nights, we had to find someone who would forget us to make us new identities, Julian knew someone but he didn't feel right making innocent friendly vampires forget shit.

"We need I.D.'s to get out of the country hun, we can't make customs and airport security forget everything" I said

"I might know someone" Rain said quietly

We all looked at her.

"If we are going to wipe his memory it shouldn't be too much problem" she shrugged

"You don't look like you want to contact them" Julian said

"He will want a lot then he will want you to buy me off him," She said

"Is he a vampire or a human?" I asked

"Human, but he works for some vampires" She said

"He was taking your blood wasn't he?" I asked
She nodded.

"He was the one who left you in the wilderness wasn't he" Declan said looking like he was trying to bury a fast burning fuse
She nodded.
"And lord Ivanovich telling you to find me?" He asked
"In a vision" she said
He nodded like that explained a lot.
"I will kill him" Declan said barely holding his temper
"That shouldn't be happening" I said looking at Julian "That sort of shit is illegal"
"Lets met him shall we " Julian said with a cruel smile
"He will make our ID's and pay for what he has done," I said "I hate to do this Rain but we need you to ring him"
"I was prepared for that" She nodded picking up one of the burn phones
She took a deep breath and dialed the number, putting it on speaker phone. It went to answer the phone.
"It's me" She said "You might want to call me back on this number" She hung up
We waited a few minutes then the phone rang.
She took a deep breath again before answering it. Straight to speaker phone.
"Rain?" The male voice said
"Yes" she said "I Need your help"
"Are you a fucking vampire or some shit?" He asked "there's no way you survived"
"Someone found me, saved my ass but I am not a vampire" she said
"So what do you think you can just call on me for help?" He said
"Or I could report your activities" She said
"You wouldn't dare" He snarled
"I know more about your operation than you think, I would think some vampires might like to know what you're up to, you know Lord Ivanovich?"
"You don't know him" he laughed
"Actually" Julian said in Ivanovic's voice "I believe she does"
"Lord Ivanovich...I " he stammered

"We need your assistance" Julian said "I am sending some people to you they need new ID's immediately, I am willing to turn a blind eye to your activities at this time if you do this"

"I don't do ID's for vampires" he said boldly

"These people are not vampires" he snapped "in fact it would be better if they could come during the day"

"It will be costly" the voice said

"Money is no object they will bring cash"

"How many?" He asked

"4 adults 2 babies" Rain said "you will get the rest of the info when we get there"

"One hundred and twenty thousand, you know where I am Rain" he hung up

 "Ok we have a few hours before daytime, I suggest we sleep" iIsaid

"Good idea" Julian said and we all went off to bed.

The next morning we got up and had breakfast and went to see Rains tormenter

We pulled up to a factory of some kind, With armed guards outside we knew this was the place

"Great so he's not a small time crook" I said

"He never had guards before, he's scared" Rain said smiling

We carefully got out of the van, gathered the carseats and went to the guards

They nodded towards the door, which opened to reveal a short chubby man in a smoking jacket and boxers and cat slippers.

"Rain darling" he said coming to greet her Declan and Julian both moved to get between them

"Touchy" he snorted coming to a halt about 2 foot from them "Let me see the money"

Julian opened a bag we had with 120 thousand dollars.

"Ok come in leave weapons at the door" he said turning his back on us we didn't stop to put weapons down he stopped and turned around.

"Weapons at the door" he said pointing to the door

"We didn't bring any" Julian said honestly, against humans we did not need weapons

"Do you think I am stupid?" He asked indicating to his men to search us

"No sir" Julian said "I think you are making us ID's to get out of here and I did not think that meant we would need a weapon"

"Why are you so pale?" He asked looking suspiciously at me

"Genetics would be my guess" I said "My mum was this pale"

"Where are you from?" he asked

"Australia" I said "but I spent most of my life in the US"

His men finished patting us down and stepped back indicating we were in fact telling the truth.

"You know I could use a couple of good men like you two" he said beckoning us to follow him

We went into some offices at the side of the factory.

There was camera gear set up and a computer and printer

"Ok I do passport for mother and the children together, I give you birth certificates, drivers license, marriage certificates where do you want to be from?" he sat at his computer

"Nova Scotia" I said off the top of my head

"Good place" he said "will explain all your different races, mother first" he nodded in front of the camera.

I moved over there

"What name do you want?" he asked

"Doesn't matter" I said

"Well you are more likely to remember one you like" he explained taking the photo

"Fine Katrina Marie McDonald" I said off the top of my head

"What if I want to be a Campbell?" Julian laughed

"We are McDonald's now dear" I said smiling at him

"And the babies?" He asked as we tried to get them to sit still for a second

"Julian James, and Alison Marie" Julian said

"And you" he nodded to Julian to get his photo done

"Jackson James" he smiled after thinking for a minute

"You next" he pointed at Declan

"Angus Mackenzie McDonald, his brother" Declan said

He took the photo. And went back to his computer

"You forgot someone" I said looking at him with intense dislike

"No" he said "I didn't forget"

Rain went and stood in front of the camera

"I am not doing hers" he said without looking up

"SIr"Julian said getting closer "You will do hers"

"I don't think so bud" he said looking at Julian

"You will do her ID" Julian demanded

A change came over him.

"Yes I will do hers now" he said getting up again "What name will the young lady be using?"

"Alana Bonnie Mcdonald, I am Angus's wife" she said

"Ok they will be ready in the morning," he said, "you will have to do bank accounts and shit but once you have Id that shouldn't be an issue"

"You will tell no one what you are doing for us" Julian demanded of him

"Of course sir" he smiled

We left and went home.

The next morning Rain stayed back with the twins and the three of us went to the factory.

We pulled up fast and freaked out the guards.

Julian got out laughing holding up his hands as the guards were pointing their guns at us.

"Sorry guys been a long time since I drove such a fast car" he said acting dumb

The door opened and we were searched and shown to the office.

"Good your here" the guy said smiling still in the same clothes from yesterday

He was sitting at a desk with an envelope in front of him.

"The price has gone up," he said

"Why?" I asked

"Because I can" he laughed

"How much ?" Julian said "I will call Ivanovich" he pulled out his phone

The guys face went pale

"Never mind just take the IDs and go" he shoved the envelope over the table

I picked them up and checked them, everything looked right. I nodded to Julian.

He leapt over the table at vampire speed and picked up the guy by the throat so he was looking him in the eye.

"You will forget we were ever here, you will forget Rain was here" Julian said

The guy just looked entranced.

I got up and went to the computer, I erased everything about us, including the security video feed. The bag of money was still sitting here.

I picked it up, couldn't have him wonder where the money came from.

"Now you will wake up and call Lord Ivanovich and tell him everything you have done that is illegal and accept your fate" Julian demanded

"I will ring Ivanovich and tell him everything about my business" The guy said

"Are we sure this will work?" Declan said

"Yes" Julian said "There are tells to people who pretend to be entranced"

"Why did you say that when he wakes up?" Declan asked

Julian smiled at him then punched the guy in the face, knocking him out. He put him back in his chair.

"That will sting when he wakes up" I said smiling

"Not half as much as he will get in prison" Julian winked at Declan

Declan opened the door and we commanded every guard to forget us, got in the car and drove away

The next couple of days we made a bank account so we could get a credit card in Julian's new name.

Then we booked flights to Spain and bought a property 42 miles southwest of Valencia, it was a huge property 12500 odd square meters, it had 2 houses one for Rain and Declan and one for us it was near a place called Ayora, it was already self sufficient. A family were building it the kids had now left and the wife had died so the husband gave up on it, it had been more her dream

Chapter 10

We arrived in Valencia looking like a family who was over traveling, the kids were screaming and being fussy, we had to wait for things to be finalized with the property so we stayed in a hotel for a few days.

We were looking into rentals for the short term in case the old owner had to have time to move, we got lucky our 4th day there the agent rang and told Julian the owner had moved out a few months ago and we could move right in.

We would have to find furniture.

Julian and Declan went and bought us new cars and we got ready to drive to our new place, it was a long 2 hour drive.

We found a furniture shop and bought us beds and the basic's we would need, it was good that the owner of the shop knew exactly where we were moving to and was happy to deliver that afternoon.

Then Rain and I went looking for linen and food, Julian and I discovered getting blood out here was going to be near impossible without using the people of this town, lucky it seemed to be a tourist spot so we could sneak down here and feed when we had to.

Over the next few weeks we got settled into our new home.

Here in Europe people were not so vampire friendly, yes they tolerated them, no they would not willingly help them, and some extreme groups would actively hunt them and get away with it, I was so glad we had daylight rings so no one knew we were vampires.

With what we heard around town this was an anti vampire town.

Even though it was daytime we were watched with caution.

We went to our new house, it was nice. There was a pool and it needed a lot of maintenance work done. But it would do.

Soon as the furniture arrived we quickly set up the beds, put food in the fridge freezer, while the delivery men watched carefully as they helped us to see if there was anything that seemed out of place, we just kept being tired from moving countries.

"So what brings you to Ayora?" One of the delivery people asked with a thick spanish accent

"We wanted a change" Julian said in spanish but translated in my head "we were living in Montreal for too long then my wife came into some money and we decided to move country, we didn't even know where we were going to start with, but we wanted to be self sufficient mostly"

"This place will be good for that," the man said in spanish looking surprised, again Julian translated in my head

"That's what we thought, and they are halfway to what we want already so it makes my job easier" Julian laughed "And here we have a house each already"

"You looked at places here with no house?" the man asked confused

"No we looked all over the world, some were going to need too much work, We still have limited funds" Julian continued speaking in spanish. I was glad I left most of the talking to him when I could. The locals seemed to like him

"I am going to teach my wife Spanish" Julian said in english smiling at me "And the kids of course"

"Cee cee good idea" the man laughed

He seemed much more at ease now.

By the time they left the kids were playing up, they were tired and hungry.

We got them sorted and put to bed, we too felt exhausted, Declan seemed ok so he offered to keep an eye on things tonight.

The rest of us went to bed.

Changing time zones is hard on a body, and when you are using up double your energy, all the time it takes it out of you, even if you're a vampire.

The next few years were pretty slow.

Julian and I had to break the law, we were feeding on the townsfolk and wiping their memories of it, we had become popular as very helpful friendly people. Human people.

I was able to learn Spanish in months living in this area, we were teaching the kids english as well, Julian and Declan spent a lot of time making our property secretly secure and making sure we could live mostly without the town. We had the internet but used it really only for the kids' education, and Rain was teaching the kids a lot, 5 years in Declan and Rain had their first child, 2 years later their second.

By now the twins were 14 in apparent age

Angelus was wild and moody but respectful of us, and he was not a bad kid, Althea was intelligent and beautiful.

When they were 10 we had explained that they were different and had powers that may start to show, they didn't until they turned 15, but they took to training like a duck to water.

Even though we had been able to slow climate change compared to the other timeline, the damage had been done and the world was making sure us humans knew. We were quite lucky in our little place.

Because we did not feel the temperature so much the extreme hot and cold did not really bother us, Rain noticed it, but we had a good air con system set up in the houses.

We also built an underground passage from their house to ours, and when snow storms hit it turned out to be a great idea.

We watched the world fall into chaos, Ivanovich was overthrown, and vanished.

I suspected he was somewhere in the background controlling one side of the fighting, while the other side had an equally powerful leader who believed it was time for humans to be as cattle, then there was the human side of the fight who wanted all vampires elminanted, Humans for humanity had formed, only this time it was really humans behind it. Hunters of vampires mostly.

Adam's chosen came out preaching peace and love for all, but they did not fight, they held peaceful sit-ins which were largely ignored and laughed at.

They believed we were all god's chosen, we are all here to serve god, not sure which god but it seemed harmless.

We were back to the brink of the world having a nuclear winter scenario.

9 years in and the kids were now 18 in their years.

They were very mature for their age, and we had not hidden the truth from them about who we were and where we came from, and who they were.

We were having a quiet celebration dinner in the middle of a freak storm, for their birthday.

"Mum" Althea said "Ang and I have been talking about it and we want to go and work with uncle Talon"

Julian and I froze.

Rain and Declan looked like they were watching a movie and it just did a massive plot twist.

"May I ask why?" Julian asked very calmly

"The world is falling apart, he needs some good people with good skills that he can trust" Angelus said "we can't keep hiding here pretending it's not happening and not affecting us, our family are out there fighting and we should be with them"

"Have you spoken to Talon about this?" I asked quietly

"No we wanted to talk to you first" Althea said

"And we should get some world experience before the donor comes for us" Angelus said

"Can you give us some time to talk alone?" Julian asked them

"Sure" They said getting up together.

"Do you want us here?" Rain asked

"Yes" I said "If thats ok this will affect you as well"

"Althea dear can you take the kids home and get them settled to bed please?" Rian asked her

"Of course aunty" Althea smiled and took the kids out of the room.

Angelus followed her and closed the door behind them.

"Well?" I said

"I thought they might do this" Julian said "And they are not wrong"

"But they are only really 9 years old" I said "I think they are to young"

"They do have a point about the state of the world though and I am sure Talon could use all of us" Declan said

"Have you been talking to him?" Rain asked

"No" Declan laughed "But I can see what's going on out there and

I have spoken to dad"
"What does your Dad say?" I asked
"He wants me home, but understands why we are here" Declan said
"How do you feel about this Rain, I mean you have 2 kids yourself" I asked her
"I have to say I am torn, I can see both paths, and honestly both are not great" She said
"But which would be better?" Declan asked "staying here ignoring the world, or joining the fight"
"I do not know" she said looking sad
"What are you not telling us?" I asked her
"Either path there is a lot of death, but it must be your decision, till you chose, I can't say for sure," she said
"Why must it be me who chooses?" I asked
"Because you and your children could change things" she shrugged "On the other hand , I want our children to be safe"
"The war will hit here sooner or later, it is only a matter of time" Julian said
"So you want to go back?" I asked him
"I feel we should, those kids of ours are ready, and Angelus is right they will need some world experience" Jualin said "And if I am honest I have been feeling on edge lately, like I could do with a good fight"
"I will have to think about it" I said starting to stress
"Lets sleep on it and see what happens" Julian said patting my arm "Whatever you decide I will stand by you"

The next day we headed to town to get food supplies.
Waiting in line at the check out I overheard a starling conversation in spanish.
"Did you hear about that school for vampires?" the checkout girl said to the guy in front of us
"Good job I say fucking vampires should be all forced into the sun" the guy said
"How can you say that?" the girl said "There were kids there,

like human kids"

"It was a school for vampires and other weirdos who shouldn't be here" the guy snarled "besides if they were not doing illegal things why was the school a secret" he finished paying for his shopping, then he grabbed it and stormed out the door
It was our turn.

"Let me guess you hate vampires too?" she asked

"No" I said shaking my head "They have just as much right to live as we do with all the laws they were meant to follow"

"What was this about a school being attacked?" Julian asked her

"Oh somewhere in New Zealand" she said that got my attention I tried to act cool but was panicking like a mad woman on the inside "A school for young vampires and stuff to help them adjust"

"Sounds like a good place" I said wishing our shopping would hurry up

"Yeah I don't have a problem with supernatural beings learning to be good citizens, and those that follow the laws have just as much right to live their lives as we do," she said then she started babbling and I tuned her out.

"We need to get home and find out what's going on" I said to Julian in my head

"Stay calm honey" He said "let's just get our shopping and not panic, just a few more minutes"

We both noticed Declan and Rain waiting at the door of the supermarket, we paid for our shopping and went right to the car.

"Did you guys hear?" Declan said helping load the shopping into the car and I got in and sat in the passenger seat.

"All we heard was a school in New Zealand was attacked, do you know more?" Julian asked

"Yeah" Rain said "It was Castle Alexandrov, a few guards were killed but none of the students were harmed"

I breathed a sigh of relief. At least that was something.

"Silver has made her decision" I heard Rain say.

Julian got in the car and put his hand on my leg

"Hunny?" He said

"We are going back," I said with a stone cold straight face. I didn't speak at all for the trip home, the others hardly spoke as well.

Soon as we got home I went to the phone and rang Talon.

"Hello" a person snapped into the phone

"I need to speak with Talon" I said

"Yeah doesn't everyone" the person snapped back at me

"Tell him it's Silver, his sister" I said staying cold and detached

"One moment" he said still pissy

"Silver is it really you?" I heard a female voice say

"Mat?" I asked

"Yeah Talon is a bit busy" She said "What's up?" I could tell she was trying to act calm

"I heard what happened" I said "we are coming back"

"Oh Silver that would be wonderful, but it's ok we have everything under control" she quickly added

"The school was attacked it is not ok" I said

"We were ready for it" Mat said "but in saying that we really could use your help"

"Are you running?" I asked as she sounded a bit puffed

"Yeah" she said stopping "I am taking the phone to Talon"

"Ok" I said "so how is everyone?"

"We lost 4 of our guards, they were decoys" she said "They didn't get near the school they just think they did"

"Have their families been taken care of?" I asked noticing the four kids come into the room

"Yes Silver" she said "Hold on here's your brother"

"Silver?" Talon asked

"Yeah" I said "we are coming back"

"Thank the fucking gods" Talon said "You do not know how happy you just made me sis"

"The twins want to work with you, and Julian and I of course will come back to work too"

"Right how old are they now?" he asked

"18 and they have done really well to learn their powers, and what we could teach them" I said watching my baby's faces light up

"So how special are they?" he asked

"They make me look human" I said

"How soon do you think you can be here?" Talon asked "I really have a lot going on"

"Maybe a week?" I said

"Ok well come here, I can arrange a plane to get you" he said

"That's ok we can do that" I said

"No I insist, I will have the work plane come get you" he said

"Ok we are in Spain, easiest airport is in Valencia"

"Ok I will need the names you are using and a time" he said
I gave him the information.

"How about 3 days, afternoon flight" I said

"Done" he said "my plane will be there in 3 days at 1 pm waiting for you"

"I will see you soon brother" I said and we hung up

"So it's done?" Julian said

"Yup we are going home in 3 days" I said trying not to cry. "I'm going to go lie down" I said escaping to my room

"It is ok my love, somethings in history cannot be changed, and at least this time the attack was a fail" I heard Julian in my head

"I know" I said sobbing "I just need a few minutes"

"I know, it cuts close, I love you" he said

"I love you too"

I went back to bawling my eyes out

Hearing the school was attacked gave me visions of the other time when my home was attacked, all the lost lives and history.

"Mum?" I heard at my door

"Come in darling" I said loud

Althea walked in

"Are you ok mum?" she asked coming to sit next to me

"Yeah I will be fine hun" I reassured her

"You don't really seem ok" she said putting an arm around me "is this because of something that happened in that other time you told me about?"

"Partly" I said "and guilt for feeling relief at only 4 guards lost, instead of grieving their loss"

"Well it was four guards you didn't know personally, and you were not responsible for some idiot killing them, so you don't need to take that all on you mum" she said snuggling into me "Your family were there and they were safe, so relief is expected, "

"How did you get so wise?" I asked her

"I had great parents" she said smiling

"Really do I know them?" I laughed

"Look mum I am glad you have decided we are going back, and I don't want you to worry about me and Ang, we can take care of ourselves" She said looking at the floor

"I'm your mother it's my job to worry" I said hugging her

"I know but we can handle this" she said more adamantly

"I know hun" I said

"And don't take offense or anything but I think me and Ang need to do this on our own," she said, biting her lip

"Oh you will be mostly hun" I said "we will be around but I am sure Talon will send us on different missions"

"And when the donor comes back?" she asked

"We should still have 9 years before that happens, the agreement was 18 years" I said "and I will not let him cut that short"

"We should look into how to stop a god" she nodded

"I think when the time comes we will be able to handle anything he tries, and I am hoping you two will be stronger than him when that happens" I said

"I think Ang is stronger than him now, I know he is stronger than me" she said

"It takes more than physical, and yes Ang is stronger physically and with physical abilities but you have smarts, and you will need that" I said

"I can't wait to meet our family" she suddenly put in all excited

"They are a pretty amazing bunch of people, I know I have missed them so much being out here" I said

"I think you did the right thing, raising us out here," she said, "and you made sure we were not deprived of anything we needed"

"You know I love you both ah" I said

"Yes mum" she said hugging me "I think you did a wonderful job, I am spectacular and Ang is ok" she laughed

"I think I am spectacular too thanks sis" Ang said walking in

"I'm still better than you" she poked her tongue out at her brother

"Ok this is an argument that could go on forever, you are both pretty wonderfully spectacular kids, it has been my honor and privilege to raise you" I said

"What do you think the people here will say when they find out they have been living with vampires?" Ang said

"They will probably curse us and not allow us to ever come back" I said

"Was there really ever a time when there was no discrimination?" Althea said

"Maybe when there were so few people that there was no room for it," I said, "But as long as I have been alive it has never changed, there's always too much hate out there, it's all power plays"

"I can't wait to meet our family" Althea said again "We are just so diverse"

"Is there any species we don't have a representative for?" Ang asked

"I think we have a few but I am sure there's others out there" I said "Anyway I need to pack, and so do you two, we only have 3 days 2 cars, only take what we need, we can get other shit when we get there"

They left and Julian came in.

"Are you ok?" He asked sitting next to me on the bed

"Yeah" I smiled at him, "Our kids are pretty awesome, aren't they?"

"They certainly are" he smiled "Look I know you don't really want to go back to all the drama, but I am sure we are doing the right thing"

"It's ok" I said "I just hope we can make a difference for the better"
"Again" he added
"Yeah again" I laughed

Chapter 11

Things had changed a lot at my old home.

There were more buildings, they kept in style with the village but were bigger, As we came in to land I noticed the whole area had got a bit bigger, to accommodate the extra people here.

I noticed a lot of single room buildings that seemed to only act as doors, probably to underground storage.

It was early evening when we arrived so there were a lot of people lining the drive to the castle, the time of day everyone is awake.

It was like I had seen on tv with famous people and red carpet events. We got off the plane and a huge cheer went through the whole crowd, sort of like a mexican wave but of sound.

I was so glad there was a car waiting for us to drive us up the hill to the castle.

"You seem pretty popular mum" Althea said smiling at me

"I don't know why?" I said feeling very uncomfortable

"Maybe because your home" Julian said kissing me on the check as we pulled up to the castle doors

Julian got out first thankfully and helped Althea out, Ang got out. And offered his hand to me I took a deep unnecessary breath and took it.

The crowd near the doors erupted in cheering and we love you Silver.

I waved and Julian was quick to get me inside away from the crowds, I was so grateful.

Inside the door my family was waiting for us.

They all started clapping.

"Ok stop" I said "What the fuck is all this ?"

"Well this is to welcome you home" Rift said coming over hugging me

"It's too much" I said "it's not deserved or necessary"

"You should be grateful this is it, many many more wanted to come, we just don't have room"

"Why?" I asked

"Because of everything you did before you disappeared, and the fact your back" Talon said "Sorry I thought at least family should be here to meet our twins, they seem to have gone a bit overboard"

"Everyone meet Althea and Angelus" I said indicating the twins

"Kids meet everyone" Julian laughed

There were lots of hugs from that point on. My family really is too big.

"Ok it's been a really long trip and I need to relax a bit, I don't want any big fuss save that for the kids" I said "And my coming back to work, I don't want to be anywhere near the top of the food chain, I am lazy and out of shape"

They all laughed

"Your old room is ready for you, the kids can use the other rooms in your suite" Lily said smiling and hugging me some more. "I am so glad your home"

"Where are Rain and Declan?" Talon asked

"They decided to stay" I said "they have young kids now and want to bring them up out of the drama"

"They have kids?" Lucian said shocked

"Yes" Julian said pulling out his phone and showing pictures to him

"I have great grandbabies and no one told me" Lucian said letting a tear slip out "Does my son know he has grandkids"

"I think so" I said "I'm sure Declan would have mentioned it to him at some point"

"Wait" Lucian said "all this time you have been gone Jay knew where you were?"

"No" Julian said "He knew we were safe, Declan didn't keep him fully up to date, but he checked in every month or so"

"He told me nothing" Lucian said looking a bit disappointed

"Don't worry Lucian" Talon said "even I knew nothing of their children or where they were, I didn't even get update calls" he looked mad too

"I'm going to my room" I said "if you have an issue with what we did or how we did it, you need to get over it and move on, what's done is done and frankly I think it was the best decision we could have made.'

"Meanwhile the world fell apart" Dominic said

"It's not our fault that Ivanovich couldn't maintain the balance" Julian said

"Yeah the problems turned out way bigger than anyone knew" Talon said

"Well we can talk about that later" Julian said "My wife and I are going to our room, I am sure all this can wait till tomorrow"

Everyone slowly dispersed and Julian and I went upstairs with the kids.

This wing had been my grandfathers, and even though I had not lived here in such a long time it was kept exactly the same.

The records from the fireplace vault had been moved to an underground storage area, I opened it up just to see what it was used for now.

Artifacts, the shelves were full of artifacts. Including excalibur, the grail and the horn.

I was pleased they were still here.

Julian came up behind me and gave me a hug.

"Whats up sweetness?" he asked

"Nothing" I said

"I know that nothing," he remarked, turning me around to face him "Now what's wrong?"

"I don't want to be in charge again, I don't want all the attention, I wish we could have slipped in unnoticed" I said

We walked out of the vault and closed the door.

"Darling you will always be noticed" Julian said smiling "You radiate an amazing light that brings people to you, like moths to a flame"

There was a gentle knock at the door.

"Come in Lily" I said

"Hay Silver" she said "Look I know you have had a long trip, but some of the students want to show you around, some things have changed since you were here last"

"Ok but please tell people not to make a fuss, I'm just another pleb trainee" I said

"Are you really that out of practise?" Talon said walking in

"Yes I am" I said "And I don't want to be a leader, or considered special" I said

"But darling you are special" Julian piped up

"So you haven't trained the kids?' Talon asked

"Oh we trained them as best we could" Julian said "But they have so much untapped potential"

"Do they have wings?" Lily asked

"Not that we have seen" I replied

"Do they know you have wings?" Talon asked

"I had no need to pull them out, honestly I had forgotten about them" I said

"They know" Julian said "They haven't seen her wings but they know she has them"

"Do I still have them?" I asked popping them out

"I guess so" Talon said looking in awe

"Oh wow" Althea said walking in with Ang

"When do we get those?" Ang asked

"You probably don't" I said "I had a talisman to get these, to be honest it's kind of weird they are still here since the talisman was destroyed about 40 years ago"

"Well you guys should take the students tour, all of you, and then I need to update you on everything that's happened" Talon said "Like Ivanovich, who was nearly overthrown, but vanished instead, no one knows where he is or what he is doing"

"So who is our world leader now?" I asked

"Some human called Jonas, he still believes vamps and humans can cohabitate but he has no clue how to stop all the hate and shit" Talon said "And he is very susceptible to others ideas, especially if commanded"

"So who has control of him?" Julian asked

"At the moment Tatiana" Talon replied "Oh and she is not with Dom anymore"

"She is probably being a go between for Ivanovich" Lily said "But we can't prove it"

"Isn't it illegal to control human's?" Althea asked

"Yes it is, but sometimes we have to bend the rules" Talon explained "and it was Tatiana or a guy called called Boris who wants vampires to take all control away from all human's"

"Ok let's go do this tour" I said "Then we can talk politics"

Lily took me downstairs to meet a group of very excited children, most were teenagers, but one stood out, she was only about 5 and cute as a button.

The teenagers being teens mostly ignored her, I did not. They showed me around the class rooms, there were only 18 classrooms, and most of the kids lived in the village. The 5 year old lived in the castle, I noticed how Lily smiled at this kid, like it was hers.

"So what's the story with the little one?" I asked Lily quietly while trying to listen to the lead teen talking about what they do in the classrooms

"Luca and I adopted her when she was a baby" Lily said "Her father was killed while her mother was pregnant, her mother only just got out alive thanks to Talon, and he brought her here, then her mother suffered some serious complications, we only just saved Alana, we named her after her mother"

I hugged her.

"I am glad she has you" I said

"Alana" I said to the girl "What's your favourite part of the castle?"

"The library" she said her face lighting up

"Do you think you could show me the library?" I asked her

The look on her face was like all her Christmases had come at once.

The teens looked a bit put out, but they would get over it.

We went downstairs to the 2nd floor and across the foyer, when I was here last the library was 1/4 the size it was now, every room on this level on this side was a library now, not just the main room.

Alana lead us to her favorite part of the library, strange to me a 5 year old was so interested in ancient tomes, but that was the room we were in, I could tell by the smell of the books and the age of some of them, hell there were even scrolls in here from before times they had books. Mind you this was Lily's favourite part of the library too.

"Alana has a natural affinity for languages, and can read about half what we have here" Lily said beaming with pride

"I thought new vampires came here as well to learn?" I queried

"Yes some do, Luca normally has charge of them, right now I believe they will be training in the gym" Lily said

"Well kids" I said "it has been lovely but I need to go and unpack. Thank you for showing me all the changes that have happened since I was here last, I'm so glad you have a safe place to grow and become the best you can be"

"Why didn't your kids go to school here?" one of the teens asked

"Originally it was to keep you all safe, then it was just to keep them safe" I said "But now they are considered adults, so they decided to come here and work with their uncle"

"So they are joining Talon?" Lily asked

"Yeah" I said not to happy "I am hoping Julian and Declan trained them well enough"

"I suppose they will start at the top" one of the boys sneered quietly

"Actually they will be starting, with me at the bottom" I said

"So you are coming back full time?" Lily asked excited

"Yeah" I said "now why don't you all go enjoy the rest of your evening, I really want to get unpacked before daylight"
I went back to my rooms.
I found Julian sitting on the bed looking through some photos. I sat with him.

"Do you remember when they were born?" he asked

"Kind of hard to forget" I smiled at him

"They grew up so fast" said closing the book of family photos

"Funny human parents say that and they take twice as long" I said

He looked at me smiling

"I can't believe I am feeling like we need to have more" Julian said

"Oh hell no" I said

"Are you ok darling?" I said to his head

"Yeah it's me I am just feeling …clucky I guess" he smirked

"Don't do that to me, you know what happened to get the two we have" I said

"Yeah and I never want that to happen again" Julian said

"Maybe when we are old and wise we can adopt some" I suggested laughing

"Hay youngin, I am old" he objected

"Yes, yes you are" I laughed emphasizing the you and tried to run

"Now listen here whippersnapper" he said grabbing me and throwing me on the bed

"It will be daylight soon, and I am taking off my ring" I said

"You want to go back to living just at night?" Julian said seeming shocked

"Yeah" I said "the kids are grown up now, and I was never a fan of daytime anyway"

He got up off me

"Are you sure?" he asked looking really serious

"It's not like i'm throwing it away, I will still have it if I need it" I said

"I don't want to take mine off" He said looking worried

"That's fine" I said honestly

"Are you sure that's not a fuck you kind of "i'm fine?" he asked

"No darling if you want to keep yours on that's your choice and I am ok with it" I climbed on his lap and gave him a kiss.

"What if I need you?" he said ripping my top off and going for my neck

"Then you can wait till I wake up" I laughed pulling the ring off

"Can't we have sex first" he said

"We have an hour before sunrise lover boy" I grinned

The next day I slept all day and when I woke in the evening Julian was waiting for me.

"Evening sleepy head" he smiled

"Hello sexy" I smiled back at him

He handed me a goblet of blood prewarmed.

 I skulled it back and got out of bed.

"So what's on the agenda for tonight my love" I asked him while looking for some jeans and shirt

"Well Mary-Anne and Brutus now have 4 kids" he said sort of smiling

"And the bad news written all over your face?" I asked

"It was discovered the attack on what they thought was here was to get them, so they are being hunted, but they are not here" Julian said

"Are they safe?" I asked

"Yes for now, but Talon suspects we have a leak, the last 3 places they moved to were compromised within weeks" He said "he is the only one who knows where they are now, so they should be safe"

"So why are they being hunted?" I asked

"Jason Mcfucking cloud" he said looking mad as hell

"I thought the elites were taking care of that when we left" I said

"Turns out, Jason had moved on, and the elites have been one step behind all the way, he has gotten a lot stronger, like he ate a few vampires far above him" Julian said

"Fuck" I said "So what is it he is doing exactly why hunt Mary-Anne and Brutus?"

"No one is 100% sure, there was rumor of him building a huge fight club with beasts, all leads went nowhere, another is he is building an army, and while it has not been proven, that is still on the table, however if the council election goes badly he will be in the perfect position to become a very rich man" he said "there's semi confirmed rumors that he is trading in humans as well"

"Fuck" I said "why did we come back again? Ok so Jason is behind the attack?"

"It looks that way" he said

"Fuck" I said again

"I believe you said that already my love" he said

"So what's the plan?" I asked

"Talon wants to talk to both of us about that" he said "he has someone on the inside, but they can't make contact often, but he has reported back Jason is apparently obsessed with you for some reason"

"My blood?" I suggested

"Possibly, but how would he know?" Julian said

"So many people do know about me, that it doesn't surprise me he found out" I said

"Well let's see what plan Talon has" Julian said hugging me

We went downstairs together, Talon was in the gym watching some of the young vampires train, our kids were with them.

"Hay Talon" I said standing next to him

"You guys did a good job training your kids" he said not taking his eyes of them

"The boys did all the hard work, i'm so out of practise" I confessed

"Told you to train with us" Julian smirked

"Get in there sis" Talon said nodding at me

"Yes boss" I said heading towards Luca and Rift.

"Alright kids the lady Silver has decided to finally join us" Rift said

"I wasn't expecting to be training today" I poked my tongue at him

"Ok kids Silver has a bit more experience than you lot, but she got lazy, so Sil lets see what you got" Rift said getting ready to fight me

"Boots on or off?" I asked him

"On is fine" he grinned and then he vanished

I knew exactly where he was behind me and I ducked his first throw, and spun to face him but he was behind me again, I kicked my leg back as I ducked his second blow.

"Fuck" Rift said as I connected with his leg. Then I was behind him and had him in a choke hold.

"Maybe I don't need as much training as I first thought" I said smiling as I sensed someone behind me. I let go of Rift and rolled out of the way and onto my feet. In time to see Talon almost punch Rift in the head. He saw me move at the last second and pulled his blow.

"Really full hit?" I said "oh brothers it is on"

"Sit down and watch everyone, this will be fun" Luca said moving to where the students were

That was it 2 brothers on me.

There was a flurry of kicks and punches at speed, Talon flew backwards across the room and Rift had me in choke hold.

I was about to do a full headbut back into his face when he let go

I turned to see my darling Julian pick Rift up off me by the neck.

"Two on one is not fair" He said smiling and putting Rift down on the ground

"That's why your here ah old man" Rift said going to punch Julian in the gut

Julian was next to me by the time Rift's fist made it to where Julians stomach had been.

"You guys need to up your game" Julian laughed

"Wait, " Talon said "You two" he pointed to my kids "Do you fight to that standard?"

"I don't think we are that fast" Althea said

"Says the girl who beat me last week" Julian laughed

"To be fair Dad, Ang had you distracted" She said

"To be fair nothing should distract you that much" I said

"But Ang beat Uncle Declan" she said

"It's not hard to beat a werewolf, he's a dog just scratch his belly" Ang said laughing

"Ang" I said shocked

"What it's what he told me" Ang said defending his racist comment "Along with best time to take them down is when they are mid turn"

"Did he also tell you they are a lot more powerful when in wolf form?" Talon asked

"Yeah we spared when he was wolf" Ang said

"Did you win?" Rift asked

"Sometimes" Ang said

"Ok, later tonight we need to test you two see how much you really know" Talon said

"Wow day 1 and already taking the test" one of the other students said sounding bitter

"They have an advantage over you Simon, they are not new vampires and they have been training from a very young age" Luca said

"We don't want special treatment" Althea said "we will keep training"

I could tell brother and sister were talking to each other in their heads.

"That's fine but training beneath your abilities would be going backwards" Talon said "so we will test you both see what you need and go from there"

"Talon can we can talk about the thing" I asked

"Sure" he said "you guys keep up the good work and I will see you two at midnight"

We walked out of here and into the receiving lounge.

It was now a large office for Talon

"So are you still running the elites?" I asked

"It's now just the enforcers and not really" he said "they do still send me reports and shit of what they are doing, but it's more a supervisory role"

"So what's going on with this Jason situation?" I asked

"They lost 10 enforcers going after him and they stopped" her said seeming very annoyed "They decided he was no threat"

"How do they lose 10 people and decide he's not a threat, I would think they need to send better people" Julian said

"Yeah and if I had been in charge we would have, they just don't have the skills needed to get the job done and they keep losing track of him" Talon said

"So do we know who he ate to get the power he has now?" I asked

"Yeah" Talon said "Cleo, and Etena"

"How the hell did he get Etena?" Juliana sked

"Someone in her camp drugged her, about 3 years ago now, the report I got from her childe was that the matter had been dealt with internally and the traitor was no longer an issue, a guy called Timon is now leading them, he is her childe" Talon said

"Does he follow the same path as his sire?" Julian asked

"Yeah, he's been really good helping us out a few times" Talon said "he sent one of his childe here to help teach gypsy law in the cultural part of the kids education, her name is Athena"

"Would he have gained her skills eating her heart?" I asked

"To a lesser extent yes, if he could find someone to hone those skills he could be almost as dangerous as her" Talon said "his plan was to use the traitor in their camp to do that after but it didn't work out for him"

"Do you know why he has become obsessed with me?" I asked

"That started not long after you vanished, I kept getting reports he was looking for you, but no one is sure why, but I think we can guess" talon said

"My blood" I said

Both he and Julian nodded

"Ok so I hear you have mole, any clues as to who?" I asked

"I have some ideas, and I have only just set in motion some traps for them, I set up a team in a couple of empty houses, letting only one other person here know about each house, we will know who it is if the houses get attacked" he said "if not I will let it slip to another couple who could be involved until we find them"

"Good plan" Julian said "but the teams you sent what if the leak is on one of them?"

"I borrowed some wolves off Jay, ones he trusts" Talon said "only me and the suspects know anything outside of his pack, so there's no one connected through here"

"Ok well what is your plan for Jason?" I asked

"You" he said "now you are back I need to use you as bait"

"Figures" I laughed

"If he was able to get Etena he can take you too" Talon said very seriously

"I am aware of how strong he must be now, Does he know I

have...you know" I asked nodding to my back

"Not that I know of" he said

The phone on the desk started ringing. Talon picked it up.

"I see" Talon said "Yeah not good but now we know where he is" He hung up

"It seems Jason is in England, he just killed Etena's priest brother" he said "We can assume he now has a daylight ring"

"Wonderful" I said "well who are you sending?"

"You, Julian..." Talon said as he was interrupted by the phone again

"Yeah" he answered annoyed

"Lord Ivanovich" he said looking shocked

"Yes my lord that is true she is back" he said

"No the children are not" he said looking at me

"My lord respectfully you no longer run things, and you have no place to command anything from me, my staff, or my family anymore" he said

"Very well I put her on" Talon said then handed me the phone

"How did I know if we came back you would come out of the woodwork?" I said

"Intuition" he said "the same reason I knew somehow you were back"

"What do you want, Lord Ivanovich?" I asked bluntly

"You need to stop Jason, he now has 5 daylight rings and 4 other vampires who have been slowly turning people and training them for war" Ivanovich said

"I believe Talon is working on that my lord" I said

"He will be no match for Jason now, he has consumed the hearts of all these vampires who had the rings and they are all over 3000 years old" he said as if I did not get the seriousness of it

"When did he take the rest of Etena's family?" I asked

"Over the past 6 years, they have each disappeared one by one" Ivanovich said

"And the enforcers what have they been doing?" I asked

"Nothing" he scowled

"Look we will be doing what we can, but you can't lead this as far as the world knows you no longer exist" I said

"Neither do you" he snarled

"I would say Jason knows I am alive" I said

"Yes I wonder why it is he has become obsessed with finding you" he said

"Too many people know what I am, that's how" I said

"Do you still have…the wings?" he asked

"Nope" I lied "I tried to pop them out the other day and they no longer work"

"That is a shame" he said

"Look I have things to do, I have to check in with the babysitter before it gets to late" I said

"How are the gods children?" he asked

"Fine last time I saw them" I said

"They are not with you?" he asked

"My lord what kind of parent would bring a child let alone 2 into this mess" I asked

"I guess not you" he said

"Well Alipa's spell she did is still working so they are better off out of this" I said

"That is surprising" he said

"Anyway as I said I have to go, Talon will do what he needs to as will I, just don't get in the way" I hung up

"He has 5 daylight rings and 4 generals by the sounds of things, How about we don't go to England but make him come to us somewhere" I said

"Etena had 13 siblings" Julian said "so there's 3 more rings out there somewhere"

"Who has the rings now?" I asked

"You two, myself, Savannah, and we have one in the vault in your room" He said

"Ok who do you think would be best to come with us?" I said

"Ebony has turned into an exceptional warrior and his brother of course" Talon said "Also I trust them with my wife's life so I know they are not the mole"

"How is Mat?" I asked

"She is doing great, she teaches here still, she's pretty busy, right now she is probably getting ready for bed, so if you will excuse me I am going to go say goodnight" Talon said getting up. "When I come back down I will tell Ebony and Ivory we have a mission, and then I will test your kids"

"I will tell the twins then I will watch as you test my kids" I said smiling

"Ok then" he said leaving the room

Julian and I went to find Ebony and Ivory.

Down in the basement we had a new really flash looking security room and that was where the twins were.

"Hay Silver, Julian" Ebony said as we came in coming over to give us each a hug

"Hay Eb's, guess what you two?" I said

"What?" Ivory said not even looking up from his computer

"We have a mission, Jason Mccloud has gained way to much advantage and is about to throw an army of vampires at the world" I said

"And who is all going?" Ebony asked

"Us 4 and Talon I think" I said "We may need a couple of wolves as well, I will call Savannah and see if we can borrow her daylight ring so all 5 of us can do the job, but Jason now has 5 day rings and 4 generals who have been preparing an army, so we will need all 5 rings"

"Days like this I wish Alipa was still with us" Ebony said as Ivory tapped furiously on his keyboard

"What happened to Alipa?" I asked

"She passed away, peacefully in her sleep about 2 years ago" he said "None of us were expecting it, we had thought she was somehow immortel, but turns out she just had a magically extended life"

"Etena's people will help us if we need it" Ivory said "Timon specifically said if we go after them he wants in"

"I need to talk to him about exactly what happened" I said

"We have his full report here" Ivory said grabbing a tablet and handing it to me

I read through, I could not believe she did not see this coming, but it was in the report she knew something was going happen, and to prevent it she had her caravan moved around when everyone was sleeping, she had extra guards, but it was one of those guards who betrayed her, and after reading his mind Timon found out what had happened.

He had gone into her caravan to "check on her" and staked her in her sleep that he had induced by giving her a poison in her blood. Then he killed the guards nearest to the caravan and took the caravan about a mile away, where Jason was waiting, he watched Jason rip her heart out and eat it, then Jason bolted leaving the guard behind.

They had found the guard shortly after, he was muttering all kinds of nonsense and no longer was able to function as a person like Jason had done something to his mind so things no longer connected properly.

It took Timon and 3 others to get things in the guards mind sorted enough to find out what happened, by then Jason was long gone.

They killed the guard for his betrayal.

"Ok so what is our next step?" I asked

"Make our own army?" Julian suggested

"We have that already" Talon said "we need to find who are his generals and take them all out"

"Any idea where to start?" I asked

"Yup" Ivory said "Sedona Arizona, for some reason he booked a flight on a public plane"

"Ok well let's get sorted and get there" I said looking at the others

"Are you sure you want to jump right in at the deep end?" Talon asked

"Have I ever done anything else?" I said heading out the door Julian and I went upstairs where we ran into the kids.

"Oh good we need to talk to you" I said

"We are about to go get ready for the test whatever that is?" Angelus said

"Yup and we will be there to watch you" Julian said "but we are

going on a mission, back to the states”
“There's a lot of unrest in the states at the moment” Althea said
“Especially in our circles”
“Oh what have you heard?” I asked
“Powerful vampires have been disappearing, there's calling to take control of the humans, and kill all the half beasts” she explained
“Isn't that going on everywhere?” Julian asked
“Not as bad as in the US, some guy called Jason has been putting viral videos online for the past week, saying humans ruined the world and vampires brought it back from the brink so humans no longer have rights and shit” Angelus said “He has started one of those fight clubs for vampires and werebeasts and is advertising that as well”
“I guess some things are truly fated” I said looking at Julian
Talon came up behind us.
“I was just coming to tell you” he said “Ivory found it just now, seems he is having a meeting in 3 weeks in Houston Arizona, for all vampires at Hermann park on the full moon”
“Why Arizona though?” I asked
“Close to Sedona I guess but bigger population” Julian suggested
“His test would we be able to come with you?” Angelus asked
“I have no problem with that” Talon said “But it's up to your parents”
“It may be better for you guys to stay here and learn some more” I said
“They've already got a head start on all the other recruits, they had you guys training them” Talon said
“Talon is right” Julian said “And they will learn plenty from us, besides if there's anything really dangerous to do we can leave them with Ivory”
“Ok then” I said “But you have to pass this test thing first”
They agreed rather enthusiastically and raced off downstairs. Talon went with them.
Julian and I went down to, may as well watch the test first.
Everyone was headed outside, Talon was at the door with the

twins.

"You guys should go watch from up stairs, much better view from the roof" Talon suggested. We laughed and went to the elevator.

We hardly ever used this, but it was the closest exit to the roof.

We went the the rear end of the castle , Talon was right, the view from up here was amazing, it was set up like a massive survival training course, with all kinds of obstacles, some would require them to work together others would require them to do their own thing, some obstacles were puzzles, there was even a computer simulated part.

The one at the very end was a gauntlet of all the higher level students, the last one Althea would face was Simon.

A lot of the younger students were also up here to watch.

The kids made it through each obstacle quickly working out what was needed and if they had to help each other, it was set up for two people to complete. Both stumbled a couple of times but persevered and got through to the gauntlet.

My kids training had been much more effective than we could have imagined, as we watched them kick the ass of each student, some they did together some separately, they moved like a well rehearsed dance.

I was so proud.

Julian's face was beaming as well

"That's our babies" he said inside my head

"Yes they are" I said smiling

A huge cheer went up in the crowd when they completed and Althea made Simon submit and give in so she was ecstatic.

"That was record time too" Ivory said leaning over a fence that had been put up

"What did you feed them on?" Ebony asked

"Normal food actually, they have never had the need to drink blood, or eat hearts" I laughed

"Can you train the rest of our recruits please Julian?" Lily asked

"Not at the moment" he smiled "Maybe at a later date"

"We need to get Dom and Rift in here more" Luca said "We just need more of us here helping out, Talon and I can only do so much"

"You should also remember the twins have been training forever" I said

"True" Luca said "I guess 9 years training you get a lot of advantage over 4 years training"

"In truth we had nothing better to do" Julian said "Delcan and I were keeping sharp, training and then the kids started joining in"

"I should test their abilities more" Talon said joining us on the roof

"I can give you run down" Julian said "They are basically day walkers, with the addition of being a bit strong and faster, they have a lot of mind abilities, they can make you see and feel things that are not there, they can command humans way to easy and they were able to command Declan, Rain can't read them at all, but she has been a great help with the kids keeping humanity"

"I bet that was fun when they hit the teen years" Luca said

"Yeah we had to do a lot of damage control a couple of times" I said "But mostly they were good kids"

"And they don't need blood" Julian added "But if they do we suspect their abilities will be further enhanced"

"So they haven't yet?" Talon asked

"No they have both decided to abstain from that for now" Julian said "We want them to get a bit older before taking that step"

"But if they need to and you don't know what happens, that could be dangerous" Lily said

"We hope we will have warning enough if it comes to that" I said Lily looked at me as if to say yeah right.

"Technically they are only 9 years old" I reminded her

"Right and they should be 18" Lily said

"And I am pretty sure Sin would find them if they tried before then" Julian said

"Well what did you guys think?" Althea said bounding over

"You guys were amazing," I said, smiling at them and going to hug them, so did Julian everyone else was cheering for them.

"So when do we leave?" Angelus said "We did pass"

"Tomorrow night" Talon said handing them a folder each "Read it, gather the supply's it says and we will see you at the front door 1 hour after dusk"

"Welcome to the big leagues kids," Ivory said, walking past and shaking their hands.

Everyone made their way downstairs where a huge feast had been set out, not just in the ballroom but outside as well.

It seemed everyone was celebrating our return and now the kids' success as well.

So much for no fuss.

We partied till an hour before dawn and then Julian and I went and packed our gear.

The next evening we flew to Auckland and then on to Arizona, I gave my daylight ring to Ivory and Ebony got the one from the vault, I was going to continue without it.

The kids were really excited, so Talon and Julian explained that they needed to calm down, and going on missions is not always fun, and it was dangerous.

We arrived in Arizona and it was daytime, I slept while the boys did some reconnaissance.

When I got up they were rearing to go.

As it turned out there was some kind of mystic festival on, right where we needed to go, so the boys hired us an R.V.

"Jason will know who I am, and you too Julian, and probably you as well Talon so we will need to make sure we stay well out of his way" I said as we drove to the site

"We can mingle with the crowds and get info" Talon said

"Um guys I just tracked down the host of the event" Ivory said looking concerned "after going through shell companies which are now illegal, I found Jason is the host"

"Shit" I said

"The whole schedule is here too and at midnight in 2 days, he is having an enlightenment celebration of some sort"

"What do you mean enlightenment?" Julian asked

"It doesn't say but he guarantees everyone will be enlightened by the end of it" Ivory said

"If I had something of his I could get into his head" Althea said eager to contribute

"You know you two could get close to him, he has no idea who you are" Talon suggested Jualin and I gave him a filthy look. "It's the best option we have to get close to him and find out his plan" he defended his suggestion

"So you want us to act like dippy teen hippy's and pretend he is some kind of god?" Angelus asked

"Unfortunately he is right, you two and the twins could easily do it" I said

"I'm staying in here and keeping an eye on things" Ivory said

"I will go with the kids" Ebony said "been a long time since I had any fun at a festival of any kind"

"We're here," Colin announced from the driver's seat.

"Ok Kerry and Colin can you just spread out and keep your ear on things in the crowd" I asked

"Of course" they both said

"Ok Julian and I will stay here for now" I said "any issues let us know"

"We all have coms patched into Ivory's computer so you will know" Ebony said

"Cool" I said

Everyone went about their job while Ivory, Julian and I all sat in the camper van watching video feeds from them.

It seemed like any other massive music festival, there were stages everywhere for all types of music. The main stage had the most famous acts though.

We hung out and enjoyed the festivities, Julian and I were very careful when we were out and about moving through the crowds.

The good thing was there were vampires, humans, wolves all partying together and hardly any trouble.

The second night, was more amped people were going hard and most were on some drug or other.

Ebony and Talon had been scouting the surrounding area, there were hills and valleys through here. We saw what they saw on the video.

A small army of vampires were hiding behind a hill ready to pounce on all the unsuspecting people here.

Ebony had gone to try and infiltrate them while Talon made a beeline for us.

Soon as he got in the RV he grabbed the phone.

"We have a code red, 1 hour all hell will break loose" he said into the phone and to us

He hung up

"Fuck" he said to us "Did you see them?"

"Yeah" I said "Do you think he is going to turn everyone here who is not already a vamp?"

"Or slaughter everyone" he said "either way reinforcements will be here in 40 minutes, I just hope we can stop this in time"

We were watching the video feed from Ebony.

We saw the generals and Jason standing at the head of this army. Giving orders to spread out but stay on this side of the hills.

We noticed one of the generals seemed to be giving Jason orders, but his face was never clear on the video.

Ebony used the spread to get back to us.

Althea and Angelus were back too.

"You are not going to believe this" Althea said looking worried

"This enlightenment shit is the enlightenment of Syn" Angelus said

"Wait, that General who was giving Jason commands?" Ebony said "The one we couldn't get a clear shot of"

"Probably him, does this RV have one of those anti magic radar things?" I asked

"Yes it does" Ivory said

"He will know I was here if he was here last night, or even today" I said worried

"So what do we do?" Julian asked

"I had the twins put out some small easy to hide cameras around so we can watch them while we wait for reinforcements" Ivory suggested

It was 10 to midnight and our reinforcements had not shown, there had been some small issue at an airfield they refueled at.

"We cannot sit here and wait" I said jumping up

"What are you going to do against a small army?" Julian said

"We have taken on worse odds and won" I said

"But what about Syn?" Althea asked

"I will take care of him" I said determined

"Oh no you will not" Julian and Talon both said

"I think it would be better if Althea and I took care of him" Angelus said

"No" resounded around the RV

"Look he is a god, we are part god we have a better chance than you" She argued

I walked over to one of the storage beds and lifted the lid. I moved some blankets around and pulled out something wrapped in a cloth

"I have excalibur" I said carefully unwrapping it and holding it up

"If you gave it one of us we could get closer to him" Angelus said

"Apparently only certain people can hold it without burning into flames" I said admiring the workmanship

"Mum we are part you I'm sure we can wield it" Althea said

"I don't think this is the right time to confront him, and it's starting" I said looking at the monitor.

The man whose face stayed blurred even when looking directly at a camera was enthralling the people, vampires were being moved to one side and wolves top the other.

My phone rang

"What?" I snapped

"We are here" a russian voice said in the phone

"We have to move now, Syn has them enthralled. Does anyone know how to not get caught in it?" I said

"Yes we have protection from that in all the suits" he said "I am almost at your RV open the door"

I opened the door and he stepped in hanging up the phone

"So you have the sword?" he said looking at my hand

"Now I do yeah" I said

"I thought you said no good mother would bring their children to something like this" he said looking at my twins

"They made their choice and past Talons test" I said

"Well done" he said to the kids "Now give one of them the sword

and let them go kill daddy"
"No" I said "I will kill him"
"Very well you two will go with your mother and kill your father" he said "We are forming a perimeter around the vampires who think they are about to feast, you need to get to the stage before we attack"
"How are we going to get there that fast?" Angelus said
"Well you two should be able to make yourselves light enough your mother can fly you in" Ivanovich said
"Like the painting" Talon said
"Can you two make yourselves that light?" I asked
"Yes but how would you carry the sword as well?" Althea sasked
"On my back" I said "let's do this now"
I took one of each of my children under each arm,extended my wings and flew straight up.
I went over the crowd, we saw the line of Ivanovich's men, the line of Jason's men, the way the people had been sorted and the stage where Syn and Jason were getting the crowd all worked up and excited.
I came down behind them so the crowd saw and thought it was some display they cheered louder and Syn and Jason thought it was for them till we landed.

Syn spun around first and saw the 3 of us and grinned a mighty evil grin.
Jason turned a second later.
A huge explosion went off on each side of the stage, I could see in the edges of the crowds people were fighting.
Syn and Jason came a little closer.
"I am so pleased to see you my children" Syn said looking at the twins
"Julian is our father" Althea hissed
"Oh dear has your mother been lying to you?" he asked
"No but you were only a sperm donor" Angelus said
"That is more than enough" he smiled all his teeth were fangs
"This ends tonight Syn" I said
"Oh no dear this is just the beginning, come to me my children" he tried to command them

They both laughed a bit

"Fine if you will not come I will take your mother" he tried to pull me closer, I could feel it but I wasn't budging.

Then I decided to pretend to be pulled forward.

The kids grabbed me to pull me back.

"Trust me, let go" I whispered

They did and I edged forward pretending I was fighting the urge

I got close enough to draw my sword.

I pulled it out and attacked with everything I had.

He pulled a sword out of god knows where and blocked the attack. Jason tried to attack the twins but was blocked by Julian who had run forward when everything started.

Angelus went to help Julian and Althea came over to help me.

Then 2 of the other generals came on the stage so the twins went to deal to them.

The wolves that were here tried to split when things got heated only to have ¼ of them slaughtered, if it hadn't been for Ivanovich many many more would have fallen

The vampires had been herded near a fence, and they were fighting back against anyone who attacked them, Jason's people were in camo so it was not hard to tell them apart from the all black of Ivanovich's people or the clothing styles of the festival goers so casualties were at a very minimum and the only innocents killed were by Jasons men.

Jason had very high casualties and a lot of surrenders.

The battles on stage raged on, Althea and the general she had were now in front of the stage, with Julian and Jason.

Chapter 12

From the stage we could see when the tide turned in our favour, Most of the people who had fought were now standing around the 4 of us left fighting.

Syn saw this and yelled "enough"

Everyone froze except me and him

"If you do not stop I will wipe out everyone left here" he said sounding exhausted

"Why are you tired?" I asked him

"You fight hard" he said in his defence

"Not really" I said having not tired at all

"You know I will win in the end" he said

"Not the way you are now" I said "And what kind of father threatens the lives of his children"

"Oh no they will be with me" he said "I was hoping to have taken over the world before they turned 18, but I see earth age has changed?"

"No they grew fast" I said "Too fast"

"They are demi gods and vampires to boot, let them do what they desire, what they need at their very core" he said

"I do not own my children, they are free to do as they please" I said looking at both of them standing behind Syn.

He turned around and I drove my blade across his neck taking off his head.

Everyone unfroze.

The body fell down.

The head rolled towards me.

I could see the shock in his eye.

The twins rushed at me and hugged me, Jason gave up and so did his remaining generals, turned out Talon had one in the carpark.

I didn't notice the pause Althea had before she hugged me.

"I think we need to burn it" I said quietly to Julian sitting next to me

"That's a good idea" he said getting up "Can we get some fuel here please we have a god to burn?" he said into his com link

"I'm going back to the Rv" I said smiling at him "don't leave till he is all gone, gone"

"I won't" he smiled back to me "I'll see you back there"

I was about half way back, by now most other people who had attended the festival were all crying at their tents and vans or comforting someone crying. There was a cue already of people leaving too. Suddenly back at the stage I heard a huge boom.

I froze as the shock wave hit.

People were falling all around me.

Then I felt a hole inside me, like someone was missing...or two someones were missing

I slowly turned to the stage, then I ran at my full vampire speed back down there.

No one here was standing but there seemed to be no damage.

Syn's body had gone, as had his head and my children.

I searched for Julian and Talon.

They were unconscious but alive.

Jason and his generals had vanished too.

"FUCK" I yelled at the top of my voice then I melted to my knees and cried.

It was obvious now this had been a ruse to get my kids, but we still had wiped out or arrested most of their army.

Ivanovich had his men interrogating some of them.

He came rushing to the stage at his full speed.

"Where are the children?" he asked me

"Gone" I said crying hysterically

Julian came too and rushed to my side.

"What the hell happened Julian?" Ivanovich said

"We were about to burn him and he got up, I don't remember anything after that" he said "Did the kids go back to RV?"

"HE FUCKING TOOK THEM" I screamed

"It's ok hun we will get them back" he said trying to comfort me

"Really how the fuck do we do that, he has made sure he got what he wanted this whole time we have been 10 steps behind how the fuck do we save our kids from a fucking god who can do anything he wants?" I cried

"You will find a way" Ivanovich said standing in front of me "Now get up, get angry and let us find the children" he said with a venom in his tone and stature I had never seen or heard from him

"How the fuck do we find someone who could be literally in any dimension of time or space?" I snapped

"I believe you have a cup that can help you" Ivanovich said calmer but still angry

"And how do we get to wherever he is without him already knowing we are coming?" Julian said

"We will find a way" Talon said coming to join us

"Ok so how do we kill him?" I asked

"We will find a way" Talon said

"Let's go home and start figuring it out then" Julian said "putting his arm around me

I just went in silence back to the RV

I felt like a complete failure, I let the kids come here and they are gone. I knew it was a bad idea for them to do this work.

I was quiet all the way home and when we got back to Castle Alexandrov I went to my room and crawled into bed. I couldn't do this again, I started thinking maybe Syn had this planned all along, giving me my family back so he could take advantage and then do this, the pain I felt was so much worse than when I lost my chosen family.

Ivanovich had gone home to see what artifacts he could find that may help.

The first 24 hours back everyone left me alone, but after that no one would leave me alone.

"You have to snap out of this if we are going to find them darling" Julian said

"I am so glad you think we have a hope in hell, but seriously we don't he is a fucking god" I said

"Hunny look at everything we have accomplished, all the times we thought we were done and we pulled through kicking ass and not looking back, we can do this but only if we all work together" He said looking very serious "But we need you on that team"

"What fucking use am i… I couldn't even protect my baby's" I cried

"Darling our babies are capable of handling themselves, I'm sure Sin is right now wishing he had never taken them" he said

"Oh god what if they annoy him and he obliterates them, we won't even know, I can't feel them" I said

"Look how about we go down to the kitchen grab a drink, then hit the war room lets work this together to bring our babies home" He said offering a hand

"Fine" I said giving in and getting out of bed "But I have to get dressed first"

I got dressed and we grabbed a bottle of blood from the kitchen and headed to the war room.

Mat came running over and hugged me and then went and sat down.

"Ok so what do we have so far?" Julian asked as we sat down

"Ok we have the cup that can show us anything anywhere anytime, but I think Silver needs to try it because she has the closest connection to the kids" Mat explained "and we do have weapons that might hurt him, but I'm not sure I mean excalibur only half worked, but I do know of ways we can trap him and render him useless, but it is only any good till someone finds him and sets him free"

"I think we should see if an old friend can help, he has a record of hating on gods he may know how to kill one" Talon said

"Who?" I asked

"Luci" Talon smiled

"No we are not making any more deals with the devil" Julian said

"Actually I think it is a brilliant idea" I said quietly

"Silver you know he will want something you don't want to give" Julian said

"I really don't care" I said "I want my kids back and that mother fucker who stole them dead, I do not care if it costs my life or my soul"

"I think that's a bit extreme" Talon said "but we won't know what he wants till we ask"

"How about we see what the cup says and go from there" Julian suggested

I lost my kids too and I am not losing you" he said in my head
I blocked him

Mat got up and went over to a special vault and got the cup and brought it to me.

"Ok just put liquid in it and ask to see what it is you seek" She said

I slit my wrist with my nail and let it run into the cup. Half the table were shocked, the other half nodded in approval.

I closed my eyes and focused on my kids. I looked into the blood. They were in Syn's palace. I could see he had both of them tied up and gagged.

Althea was on the wall and seemed unconscious.

Angelus was strapped to a bed. He was awake and looked terrified; he kept looking at his sister with worry.

This made me see red. The vision blurred out and I smacked the goblet right across the room nearly hitting a few people, but leaving a massive blood trail down the wall.

"What did you see?" Julian asked

"He has them tied up and Althera is unconscious, they are in his palace" I said getting up "Someone call Luci and come get me when he's here, I'll be in my personal vault"

I went upstairs to my fireplace vault and went in.

I looked for the oldest texts I could find and started reading what I could,

Then I found an ancient sumerian book and I took it to find Lily. I found her in the library, she too was reading ancient texts to find something useful

"Hey Lily I found this in my vault" I said putting it on the table next to her "Do you think you can have a crack at it?"

"Of course" she said smiling she picked up the book and within the first few pages started getting a wide eyed surprised look on her face.

Then she started writing bits down. I looked over her shoulder to see what she was writing.

The words I kept seeing were enlil, ninlil, Inanna, and Nanna.

"Ok Nanna is actually Sin, and Inanna is his daughter but she is also goddess of love, beauty, sex, desire, fertility, war, justice, and political power, Enlil and Ninlil may be his parents I'm not sure." she said

"Wait" I said "When I was captured by sin for some reason I called for Inanna and he got a bit paranoid, but how do we get Inanna to help us?"

"I may have some ideas about that, I will need to do a bit more research though" she said

"Ok well you keep working, and if you can find anything about traveling to other dimensions that would be great" I said

"I will get some of the more experienced students to help, there are a few who have shown a real aptitude for this kind of thing" she smiled "don't worry hun we will get the kids back"

"Any idea where else I could look?" I asked

"Anything on sumeria and mesopotamia, it seems he was a god in both times" She said

"Ok I'll be back in my vault" I said

It was strange to me how I could read some languages without thinking and others I knew what they were just not how to read it.

I gathered a small pile of books when some strange well dressed guy walked into my vault

"Wow this place really is quite interesting with all its hidden places" he said I spun around to see who it was.

"Good day miss Alexandrov, I hear you have a godly problem you want help with" He said leaning on one of the shelves

"Do you know how to kill a god or get to other dimensions?" I asked him straight out

"Well maybe, there is a question of price" he smiled

"Oh come on Luci, it's me, surly you could just tell me?" I said

"What god and what has it done?" he asked

"Sin and he has stolen my children" I said angry

"What else is he doing?" he asked "because gods stealing kids is not really uncommon"

"How the fuck would I know, he's joined with a vampire who wants the world at his feet so I guess he plans on taking over and using my baby's to do it?" I yelled

"Hey hey girl calm your farm" he said almost laughing
I walked up to him and slapped him

"Don't tell me to calm my fucking farm my babies are being held against their will by an asshole" I yelled

"If you don't calm your farm I will not help you at all" he said nonchalantly "Now how old are the children?"

"9" I snapped trying to focus on breathing through my anger

"Good age that" he smiled "however if I am to help you with this, I will have to go and talk to my family and that will be costly as fuck"

"Like what?" I said

"Mmm well I would really like to walk the earth in my own body, or your soul" he smiled

"Well if you come here in your body you know what happens so no, you can have my soul but only when I no longer have a use for it" I said walking out of the vault

"But you are immortel, so that's not fair" he frowned following me out

"I'm not immortel" I laughed "i can still die, it will just take a while if I have my way"

"You know you could talk to my family and get them to let me wander the earth in my body" He suggested

"Fuck off" I laughed "They will not listen to me iIm a vampire they think I am evil"

"This is true" he said "so what exactly do you want to do?"

"Kill Sin if possible, if not somehow stop him interfering on earth, and getting my kids back" I said

"And you a vampire have kids because?" he asked

"Because he did voodoo on Julian and I and got us pregnant" I said

"Well in his time he was a creation god, I am puzzled how he got a foothold back here, but I shall talk to my family for you and I shall have your soul when you eventually die" he smiled

"Maybe you could find out why he did come back here, what does it take to bring a dead god back anyway?" I asked

"Some grand gesture of faith, so some human would have had to do something pretty amazing" Lucifer said

"Could a vampire do it, or a shifter?" I asked

"Possibly but they would have to have unwavering faith in him and still the grand gesture would be required"

"Wait in the other timeline, he wasn't so much here, until after time went back, would that have been due to the deal the stupid lords did?" I asked

"Yes but didn't you kill all of them?" he asked

"Yes I thought we did" I said

"Do you know if he has any other followers?" Lucifer asked

"Yeah a guy who wants my blood"

"He may have used the time here to gain the new followers, while he was getting you pregnant and you were killing every-one" he said

"We only took out the lords who turned back time" I said "you should know you got them back at your place"

"Yes" he smiled sadistically "and they are not enjoying their afterlife very much"

"Ok enough banter can you please go get me some answers" I asked

"Fine" he said raising his hands "i will be back when I have some-thing"

"Thank you lucifer" I said politely

"You are most welcome" he smiled then the body he was using fell to the ground

Julian came rushing in

"Why was your door locked?" he asked frantically

"Oh must have been Luci" I said "can you help this guy"

"Luci's leftovers?" he asked

"Yeah poor guy will be so lost if he wakes up in this strange place" I said

"I'll get Ragnor to take him to town" he said

"Yeah just hope he doesn't wake up halfway there" I laughed

The next few days everyone was on edge, we were all going about our thing trying to find ways to trap or kill a god, to slip through to other dimensions and how to help the kids.
It made the way Jason was able to take down Etena and her siblings without any problems all the more clearer.
If only we had a god working on our side.
It was late at night and I was standing on my balcony looking down at the airfield and the village. I looked up and it was a full moon. I closed my eyes and begged the god or goddess or anyone to help me.
Nothing happened so I went inside and sat on the couch and watched some tv.
It was some late night early morning news.
It was awful, anti vampire rally's were being held all of a sudden, everyone was going crazy over what happened at the festival, never mind it was vampires who saved everyone.
The bigger threat was coming though, I could feel it.
I changed the channel.
Some 80"s sitcom was on so I watched that, or more had it in the background while I thought about everything.
I wondered where I would have been if I had not come home, would I still have been living one hand to the next, helping others where I could, moving on when I was bored.
Sure now I would probably be dead, but I sure as hell would not have all these complications, all the beautiful people I know, the love of my life, or my children.

I must have dozed off because when I woke up Julian was sitting beside me gently shaking me to wake up and some strange woman was sitting opposite us.
"And you are?" I said when I saw her
"You asked for my help?" she smiled she was radiating pure white but not burning vampire white more moon white
"I am sorry" I said "Which goddess are you?"
"I have many names, in some cultures I have more than one, but you may call me Ishtar" she smiled
"Do you know why I need your help?" I asked
"Of course" she said "you need help to destroy my father"

"Oh" I said "not necessarily destroy, disabling forever would be ok as well"

"It is ok, I understand why you feel the way you do" she said "that is why I am here to help"

"Well then Ishtar I must say thank you" I said

"My father is not a good man" she said "he has become more and more twisted over the centuries, like with the game he played with you, and the forbidden time travel thing. He has gone past the edge, and your friend Lucifer, will not be of any use, his family do not want us to have existed so they do not acknowledge anything about us, he will probably be severely punished if he utters the name of Sin to his family, there is a reason they named evil doings as sins"

"What price do you ask for your help?" Julian asked

"Nothing" she smiled "I have had to watch his abuse for millennia on many different planets, he is a disgrace to my family and an abomination to the world's he seeks to destroy so he may gain more power"

"So he knew what would happen if the vampire lords got that spell that took us back in time?" I asked

"Oh yes, he planned it that way, then you were defrosted and started trying to fix things, he had seen a very different future till you resurfaced and things changed" she smiled

"If you knew all this why didn't you help earlier?" Julian asked

"Normally we let him go and do his thing" she said "he has destroyed many worlds before this, we normally do not interfere with each other, we all have our own favourite world we protect, however this time he has broken our rules and it was requested I help"

"By who?" Julian asked

"By her" she said looking at me

"This is not the first time I have called for help" I said quietly

"And it is not the first time I have helped you" she said

"When did you help me before?" I asked

"I helped you escape the last time he had you in his place, I helped you hide from him once the babies were born, and if not for me you would have no memory of that time when you were frozen" she said

Before our eyes she transformed into Alipa and back to herself.

"I have been helping you for some time" she smiled

"How...?" I said confused

"Your friend Talon knew a wise woman called Alipa, but when he came to find her she had passed, by my father's will, and I took her place without his knowledge" she said "Alipa was the last true follower of mine"

"She died because he saw the future with her helping us?" Julian asked

"I believe so" she said

"Does he know you are helping us now?" Julian asked

"Oh no this is not something he has seen, just as he did not foresee Silver" she smiled

"So how do we save my children?" I asked

"Well first we must find some artifacts, ones that will enable you to go into his realm as a whole, so that he cannot manipulate you" she said

"She's not going alone" Julian said

"Yes I know and I can tell you this team must be the two of you, the young girl Rain and Declan" she said

"No Rain and Declan will not be coming" I said

"My dear you will need Rain and her wolf, I know my father and both will be needed to get to his palace" she said "Unfortunately if I go he will notice me straight away, because it is his realm and he is my father"

"Ok so what artifacts do we need?" Julian asked

"The Codex Gigas for a start, it holds a ritual that can entrap my father" she said

"Ok so where do we find it?" I asked

"Currently it is on loan to a library in prague, but you will not be able to remove it without making a scene" she said "If I can get near enough to see the words I should be able to memorize it in a few minutes"

"And realm jumping?" I asked

"Sadly I need another rare book for that and it has not been dis-
covered yet" she frowned
"I may have a way to discover it" I said
"Really?" she said with interest
"We have a cup that can find lost things" I said
"You have the cup of Jamshid?" she exclaimed
"Yeah I think thats what its called" I said
"Next you will tell me you have the book of Thoth" she laughed
"Actually we don't but we can get it" Julian said
"Really?" She asked looking very interested
"Will it help us?" I asked
"Very much" she said
"Can I ask why excalibur didn't work?" I asked her
"Because he was not his his own body" she smiled "that is one
reason he needs your children, he cannot yet be here in his own
form"
"Ok well how about we go have a look at the cup and see if you
can't find the book you need?" Julian said getting up
"Ok then" she said getting up
I noticed she didn't walk but floated.
We went down to the library
"So where is the cup?" she asked
"I will get Lily to get it, she studies all the fun things we have
here now, and is currently reading through some old books we
have here to help us" I said "so I would like for her to be in-
cluded"
"Very well"
We walked over to where Lily was reading, she looked up
"Lily can you get the cup from the vault please" I asked her "we
need to locate a book"
"Ok," she said getting up, "may I ask what book?"
"It is the original, Libre creaturae, I think would be the closest
you would know it as if you knew of it" she explained
"You mean a book of creation?" Lily asked
"Yes you know of this book?" she asked
"Maybe" she said "what is the original language of the book, be-

cause there are a few and it really depends what era"

"It is written in ancient sumerian" Ishtar said "but not the same as the cuneiform everyone thinks is ancient" she smiled

"We have a number of books here I still have not deciphered, it could be one of them" Lily offered

Ishtar tilted her head interested

"Please show me?" She asked

Lily got up and took us to a back room in the library.

Ishtar's eyes lit up as she went through our rather vast section of rare books.

"This set of shelves holds the books I have yet to translate either because I do not know the language or it is to faded or delicate" she said

"Do you have any idea the amount of power you have just on those shelves?" Ishtar asked

"Well no" Lily said "hard to know that when I cannot read them"

"Oh of course" Ishtar said "I will give you that, actually I will give you both that, there will be things in these books that can help you in the future"

She touched Lily's forehead and then mine, I don't know what Lily experienced but for me there was a flash of light and a moment of seeing visions of people speaking, the visions were different, because at the start I could not understand what they were saying but then it all became clear, and then the script work started, it seemed like it took forever but when I came back to the room, it had only been 1 minute.

Lily looked a bit dazed, I was guessing I did too.

"Well?" Ishtar asked

Lily picked up one of the books she had never read and started reading it aloud and fluently.

I picked up another book and started reading it.

"This is amazing," Lily said "how can you do that?"

"Magic I guess" Ishtar said "Now I know the book I need is not here, shall we get that cup?"

"Of course" Lily said excitedly running off to get it

She came back with the cup and handed it to Ishtar, who took it and right away cut herself to bleed into it.

"You know it works with any liquid?" Lily said

"Yes but blood is always the most powerful" Ishtar smiled
We all looked into the cup.
"It is in a place called London, this vampire I see has it in his possession" Ishtar said
I looked and saw the vampire, it was Lord Ivanovich.
"It is in his vault in his study" she continued "we must go and relieve him of it"
She put the cup down and turned to face me.
"I take it you have some expert thieves in your band of merry vampires?" she asked me
"There should be no need for that" I said "I will ask Ivanovich for it"
"I will get a team to go and retrieve it" Julian said "just in case"
I pulled out my phone forgetting time zones and rang Ivanovich
"Lord Ivanovich's residence how may I assist you" the voice on the other end said
"It is Silver here, please tell Ivanovich, we are on our way to see him when he wakes" I said
"Yes my lady" the voice said "And how many of you should we expect?"
"Let's say 10 to 15 I am not sure yet" I replied
"Very good and when will we be expecting you?" the voice asked
"Probably tomorrow night" I said
"Very good my lady Silver we shall see you then" he hung up
Ishtar smiled.
"What is so humorous?" Lily asked her
"My father will not be expecting this, and I am happy I can finally be of more help" she said
"So are you coming with us?" I asked
"Ofcourse" she smiled at me

Chapter 13

We went and got ready to leave, organising the flights was the most annoying part but not my job.
It was an uneventful flight to London and we landed at Ivanovich's private airport just before dusk, and waited on the plane till it got dark.

A small bus had arrived by the time we left the plane and we got on board and went straight to Ivanovich's.
He greeted us at the door of his stately home
"My lady Silver, Julian, and friends, may I ask what this unexpected meeting is about?" he asked in his thick accent
"We need to speak with you in private" I said
"Very well come to my office" he said turning around and heading inside
Julian, Ishtar and myself settled in the office and he asked Tatiana to wait outside, which I thought was weird.

"So what is this about?" he asked me
"We need a book that you have" I said "It's in the vault behind your portrait"
He looked shocked I knew about this vault but only showed that for a nano second
"I have many books you will have to be more precise" he said
"You do not know the language of the book so how could you know what it is truly called?" Ishtar said
"Oh one of my very rare collection then" he said looking at her with speculative eyes
"Look we need this book to defeat Sin, he has the kids as you well know and they are not in a good way" I said

"Calm down Silver" he said to me "My problem is that I know there is no one alive who can read the books I have in my private vault"
"That is where you are wrong" Ishtar said "I can read it and so can Silver here"
"Oh really you two can suddenly read texts that are so old they outdate everything man knows about history?" Ivanovich said
"I am history" Ishtar said
"Really and as history who would that make you?" he asked carefully
"I am Ishtar or Inanna, or so many other names I have been called, I am the child of Sin, and the one who is helping Silver and her husband get their children back" she said
"So you claim to be a goddess, how do we know you are not just helping your father?" he asked
"You would feel the decet in me if I were not speaking truth" she said getting annoyed "I must say I am not accustomed to being accused of dishonesty"
"I do not trust anyone I do not know" Ivanovich said looking at her intensely
"Look either you can retrieve the book we need or I can" she said
"I would like to see you try" he said with a glint in his eye "But I do not wish the contents of the vault destroyed so I will get it for you"
He stood up and turned around moving a picture to reveal the vault.
He opened it and brought out 6 large old looking books
"I know these books are older than the historic invention of paper, which is why when I found them I took them in and saved them as best I could" he explained carefully putting them on his desk "Now which one is it you think you need?"
"The one written on animal hides that you have not brought out of your vault" Ishtar said without even looking
Ivanovich smiled and turned back to his vault he went in and when he came back out he had a massive book with him.
"This is probably the best preserved book I have," he said, put-

ting it on his desk.

The pages were really thick, but thinner than I expected animal hides to be.

"It does not look like it will last too much longer" Ishtar said frowning at it

"Maybe while you borrow it you could translate it for us and put it on the computer or at least on better paper" Ivanovich suggested

"Or Lily and Silver could do it " She smiled "Now we are taking this to her castle, thank you for your cooperation Lord Ivanovich"

"No" he said firmly holding his book "It stays here"

"This book belongs to my family, and as the only sane one left I claim it as my right" Ishtar said standing up

"Why do you need it so bad?" he asked her

"So I can finally rid myself of my father, it is the only thing on this planet at least that can tell me how" she snarled, I would swear she grew a few inches as well

"How?" he asked

"I have to find it in the book to find that out" she snarled

"Find it here" he smiled "right now, then tell me how"

She backed down.

"Why" she asked

"In case you fail, then I can get someone else to do it" he said

"You think there is someone more suited to this task?" she scoffed

"I think you plan to use her like he plans to use Althea" He snarled "But I also think she is unknowingly much more powerful than you even suspect"

"Who?" I asked trying to think of the most powerful people I knew, most were dead now.

Ivanovich looked at me, Ishtar burst out laughing

"You think I am wrong?" Ivanovich asked her

"Very much" she said "I do not need a battery, I was adaptable and worshiped in many beliefs in one form or another, my father was not, he is weak because his believers are few, and you killed

a few of the more powerful ones"
"Now he has thousands of adoring fans waiting to wipe out humanity" I said
"The belief has to be pure" Ivanovich said "It cannot be cohoursed"
"He has drones, nothing more" Ishtar said "Mindless untrained vampire cannon fodder"
"We should have killed Jason when had the chance" Julian said
"Yeah that would have been fair" I said "sentence someone for crimes they didn't yet commit"
"You should know your wife by now Julian" Ivanovich said "If it is not fair she doesn't like it"
"Being a ruthless murderer didn't really get you far now did it?" I said to Ivanovich
"Actually I do quite well" he smiled
"You mean you are still doing underhanded shit?" Julian said
"Sometimes it is necessary as you both know" he said
"He is not wrong" I said "anyway we have a god to stop and kids to rescue"
Ishtar agreed to read the book here and Ivanovich put us all up in his massive manor while she did it, I gave her a break as often as she would let me, there was so much about before history as we know it, there was detailed spells to help the earth heal and grow, some required the blood of Sin himself.
It passed through my mind we could steal his blood, but then wouldn't that make me just like the people I despise.
Turned out I was not the only one thinking about this.
We had been there 3 days, I went into the study to give Ishtar a break.
"I think we should get some of his blood, I think it will help with so many things that are broken here" Ishtar said looking up as I came in
"If we can get his consent for it sure" I said
"That is never going to happen" She laughed
"Then we are not collecting his blood, unless it spills on the ground then we could get it?" I said
"You are so naive" she said shaking her head

"No, I just think more big picture, people go stupid when theres big changes, and I think if we fix the planet like that people would just over consume again because they would think we will just fix it again" I explained

"You have that little faith in your former kind?" she asked

"Hell I have every faith they will fuck it over, if we hadn't stepped in when we did the whole planet was going straight to hell" I said "You know that, you were with us the whole trip back"

"Do you think mankind should be wiped out?" she asked

"No not at all, I still have compassion, besides if there were no humans what the hell would we eat?" I said

"You know you do not need blood at all?" Ishtar said

"Yes I do" I said with 100% certainty

"I have always wondered why you did, but you really don't know?" she asked getting up

"I am a vampire" I said

"Yes and you are not a vampire as well" she said "You will find now you no longer need blood"

"I still feel the thirst" I said

"Or is it a habit?" she asked leaving the room. I sat down and started thinking about it, I could feel the thirst now, even though I had fed.

I shook off the idea and got to translating, we were so close to the end, I had not read anything about stopping any gods, but this page it was on was about summoning one of the seven, or all of them.

I had a sudden horrifying thought, she was going to summon all of them, here. I went back over what she had translated and checked it with the book, it was all correct, and it was how to kill a god the extreme complexity of what needed to be done, and some of the ingredients meant Ishtar had a very particular shopping list and we could find her, if she had gone.

I got up and bolted from the room headed for Ishtar's rooms. Empty.

"Julian Ishtar has bolted she has the spell to kill him, and summon others" I said to Julian's head

"Fuck, why do you think she left though, isn't that what we wanted to do?" he replied
"I think she plans to bring back the other gods, and I don't know why" I said "but it could be to take over the planet"
"You have become very cynical my love" he replied "But you could be right"
"Meet me in the study hun bring Ivanovich and the guys" I said as I headed back there
I told them everything I read and Ivanovich had his house and grounds searched after we found no sign of her on the surveillance.
She was nowhere.
While the search was going on I sat down and went over the translations, it all seemed right, but I had a feeling something was missing.
I came across some pages with rituals to transfer power to objects, and noticed a small bit of leather on the binding, like something had been carefully pulled out, but still left a bit behind.
I knew something important was missing from this page.
The page after was how to make a godly creation weak, followed by weakening animals, including humans.
At least that one was still here, but would she remember everything she read anyway, and if she could do that why take this one page.
All I could think was it was something she didn't want us knowing.

The next evening my crew got together in Talon's room.
"We have her shopping list Ivory, has found out she already got these 3 things, you know she will hit the castle, she needs two items from there" Talon said "but they are ready for her"
"Let her have them" Ivanovich said coming in "I am disappointed you did not invite me to your meeting"
"It wasn't really planned it just happened we were all here" I said
"It may interest you to know Durantia has one of these items in her special vault" he said "I have ordered her to bring it here"
"Cool so what else does she need" I said

"These herbs I have never heard of" Talon said

"New york" Julian said "she was Alipa when we were in New York, she was always tending herbs in the glasshouse"

"And she stayed there the most as well, she also had someone helping her when she was not there, they took over the garden when she passed" Talon said "or left"

"Someone ring them and give them a heads up, but not whoever is doing the garden they may not be trustworthy" I said

"Druantia will be here in 5 minutes, we should probably go to the boardroom" Ivanovich said "It would be more suited to this meeting"

"Thank you lord Ivanovich" I said "I will see you all down there" Everyone left my room.

I was currently confused by this shopping list, there were things on it that would not have even been when this book was written, like a magically imbued sword (all the swords we had were much newer), the voynich manuscript, I am not even sure pandora's box was around when the book was written.

The herbs needed had some common ones like sage, frankincense, angelica and dragon's blood, unless they meant real dragon's blood, which I would have no idea where to find.

I went downstairs to the boardroom.

I got there as Druantia arrived.

She looked awful, like she had been in a fight and not fed for days.

"Druantia what is wrong with you?" Ivanovich asked seeing her

"I was attacked, but I made it and I have the things you wanted," she said handing him her bag before she collapsed on the floor.

A bunch of Ivanovich's men rush to pick her up.

"Put her in her old room and make sure she gets plenty of blood" Ivanovich shouted as they carried her off. "Let us get this moving I wish to tend the child"

He stormed into the boardroom with the bag.

"So you read the translations, what do we do once we have everything?" Ivanovich said gruffly

"Take them with me to my place grab what we need there and hopefully meet up with the people gathering herbs" I said "then

hope Ishy turns up and lets us help or helps us"
"Very well" Ivanovich said "i think you should take the book with you as well as a copy"
"But you wanted to keep the book with you" I said
"I trust you with it, I do not trust Ishtar" he said "make your arrangements to leave I am going to check on Dru"
He left. Talon started gathering all the things back together and put them in the bag. I went and got the book, I put a copy of what we had with the artifacts and kept the original with me. Julian arranged for our plane to leave before dawn so we could be on board when the sun came up and hopefully land when it was night again.

It was not til we got home I let the others know about the missing page.
"Why didn't you tell us this before?" Talon asked
"Because I felt it was not the right atmosphere" I said raising my eyebrow
"You mean you didn't want Ivanovich to know?" Ebony laughed
"Exactly, he would have gone nuts" I said
"So what now?" Ebony asked
"We wait" I said "I let Lily have a look over the book, see if we got it right, and we wait for whoever is bringing the herbs and for Ishtar to come looking for some of the things she needs"
"Why would she be so helpful and then run off?" Ivory asked
"Good question" I said "I think if we figure out what was on the page she took we could figure it out"
"There's been no word that she has been in new york yet" Ivory said "Mary-Anne has the herbs you wanted and is on her way here"
"Good hopefully she gets here soon," Julian said "we do have the spell to stop Sin ah?"
"Yes" I said "If I translated it correctly"
"You should ring Ivanovich and see if he has a copy of the full original book" Ivory suggested "That missing page could be the most important part"
"Can you do it?" I said asking Julian

"Sure" he laughed

He left the room and rang Ivanovich then he came back in .

"Yes he has a digital copy of the full original, he is sending it through email" Julian said not looking happy

"But?" I asked

"He is really pissed. I told him you didn't notice it till just now" he gave a crooked smile

"AND?" I asked

"She got the artifacts Ivanovich was holding"

"Fuck" I said

"I'll say" Ivory said "getting past his anti everything safeguards is not easy and probably better secured than us now"

"So if she went there without an issue how easy will it be for her to get in here?" I asked

"Way to easy" Ivory said tapping on his pc "Really there's only so much we can do against a god"

"I wish they would just be reasonable and not so .." I said lost for the right word

"Moronic and assholey" Julian said

"Yeah I mean what's wrong with being straight up and honest and considerate" I complained

"Not many people like that get to take over the world" Ishtar said appearing behind us

We spun round to face her

"What the hell Ish?" I yelled at her

"I am sorry but sometimes we are in such a rush we forget to wait for mere mortals" she said putting a large backpack on the floor in front of her. "I have what we need aside from a few bits you already have, we will need to plan the attack directly on his plane"

"Won't he be more powerful there?" I asked

"Yes but it is the only place he will be complete" she said

"So what was on the page you took out of the priceless old book" Julian asked

"A spell I needed to acquire something to assist us" she said

"So we can have it back now?" I said

"No I still need it, but it will not be an issue for all of you, do you have the spell for interdimensional travel? She replied

"I have not read it, but yes it is in the book" I said

"When you are ready to go and have chosen your team we shall need a clear space and a dark night" Ishtar said "while we wait on Mary-Anne I shall prepare all the magic weapons you have so you will be able to fight whatever he throws at us, however I must request I do the final act"

"You're going to kill your father?" Ivory asked

"Yes or at least contain him once again on his plane and get the children out" she said "I am not sure how well it will work, but getting the children back should be easy enough once we find them"

"Can you tell me why he had my daughter chained to the wall and my son to a bed?"i asked

"Yes your daughter is the more powerful" she said as if it were obvious

"Is she?" I asked

"She should be, like all woman she is more powerful because of the god blood she spills every month" she explained

"One thing I do love about being a vampire, I do not bleed monthly" I said

"Which is why you are weak" Ishtar said

"She is not weak" Julian said quietly

"Mayhap I shall test her when this is done and I shall show you how weak she is" Ishtar offered

"Look I do not care if I have power or not right now the only important thing is getting my kids and stopping Sin and Jason" I said

"Why this Jason?" Ishtar asked

"Because he is working with Sin and he is vampire who wants to take over the world" Ivory said

"So will he really use her as a battery to boost himself?" I asked

"Yes he may try to, but transference of power from one to another is a very taxing complicated ritual" Ishtar said

"Thats what was on the page you took wasn't it?" I said more than asked

She looked at me stunned for a second

"Yes, how did you know?" she asked

"I can be clever when I try" I said

"So who's power are you trying to get?" Julian asked

"Sin's of course, if he has his power we will not be able to stop him, so I will drain him and then we can deal with him" she said "once he is drained he will not be able to drain from the children"

"But then won't you become all powerful, what's to say you won't take over where he gets stopped?" Ivory asked

"I am not like him" she said looking angry

"I am sorry Ish, but if you had not just taken off the way you did and if you had told us what you were doing maybe we would have some trust in you, but for now we do not know you, all we know is what you claim and frankly to many all powerful beings are too happy to screw us over for more power" I said

"I promise you Silver Alexandrov Gustavo, I will not as you say screw you over, I am not accustomed to working with others, let alone vampires who don't want power, I am sorry if it appears I am untrustworthy" she said looking like those words were the most confusing she had ever said "I shall endeavour in future to ensure you are notified of what I am doing in regards to my father"

"Thank you" I said "so what is the plan and how do we do this?"

 She went over the spells that would bind her father and the one that would take his power, so we could kill him using excalibur was the right weapon but it needed to be prepared properly for this particular deity.

Lily and I watched her carefully as did half a dozen others but they didn't understand what Ishtar was doing as well as we did.

It took 3 days to prepare the sword, the next full moon would be the time we had to do this so we had a week to find him.

Ishtar laid the sword in my arms like it was a child.

"Now I shall find him and take you and whoever you will have go with you to him and we shall end this" She said

It took Ishtar two days of tracking Sin with the cup before she could pinpoint him and track him personally.

Julian and I thought it was taking too long, after all the longer my kids were with Sin the longer he had to twist them or break them.

The day finally arrived, I had gathered the people I would take with me.

Khan, because he is a tiger, a couple of wolves, Rain and Declan came out of hiding to join me, Talon because he would not let me go without him, his wife Mat because she would not let Talon go without her, Julian of course, Dominic and Rift joined me as well.

We all had magically enhanced weapons, provided in part by Ishtar.

We were ready to go.

We gathered in the war room and Ishtar sat in the middle of the table.

She invited us to gather around her and we did.

She told us to join hands so we did.

Then she started chanting in an ancient language I could understand, thanks to her. And then we were no longer at my place.

We looked around at the desolate place we had been brought to.

We could see the palace quite a way off in the distance.

"Ok we have to get to there" Ishtar pointed to a hill near the palace "there's a secret entrance there"

"Let's get moving then" Talon said taking the lead

"Wait" Rain said "I know this place, if we go around this way we can avoid the traps"

"How do you know this place?" Ishtar asked in shock

"I have been here a long time ago, before Declan found me, and I have been having visions of it" Rain said

"Very well Rain let's go" I said, letting her take the lead

We walked for what seemed like hours working around the main path to the hill where the entrance was meant to be.

There were two guards on the door that lead to under the hill and to the palace.

Julian and Khan took them out before they even noticed someone was there.

"Follow this way to the palace, I am going ahead to create a distraction" Ishtar said "get those kids and get out if you can"

"But I have the sword to kill him," I said, "and I am not leaving here unless he is gone for good"

"Then save your kids and come find me" she said seeming slightly angry. "But if he can still drain the kids of their power you will not be able to kill him"

"How do we get them home?" Julian asked

"Rain can do it" Ishtar said looking hard at Rain "Mat may have to let her use some of her power but Rain can get you all out"

"I can?" she asked stunned

"Yes you can" Ishtar said touching her forehead "see it now?"

"Yes thank you" Rain said looking slightly confused

Ishtar vanished

"Are you sure you got this Rain?" Declan said looking concerned

"Oh yes getting us out will be easy" she said trying to brush off her confusion

"Then what's wrong?" he asked her

"Ishtar was my mother" she said quietly, "she thought I was dead"

"Oh shit" I said "why didn't she say anything when you guys meet"

"What I just saw she didn't realize until she pressed into my mind, as I said she thought I was dead, that's why she wants her father gone, she thought he killed me" Rain said

"Oh dear, if her motivation to kill him is gone, she may not help us when we need it" Julian said

"Oh no she still has good reason, just because I am not dead does not mean he did not try" She said I could see a teardrop in eye

"Let's get moving guys" I said

We made it into the palace itself without too much hassle, we noticed there was a lack of guards we carefully snuck around keeping our eyes out for anything weird, or guards.

I happened past a window and saw why the palace was empty.

The massive empty space outside the front of the palace was full of people lined up facing away from the palace. Like they were waiting for us.

Then we heard Ishtar.

"FATHER YOU HAVE FUCKED ME OVER FOR THE LAST TIME"

I looked past all the soldiers and saw Ishtar standing approximately 20 feet tall, and with her seemed to be an army of her own.

"You will never beat me now child" Sin sneered at her. Then ordered his men to attack, he was in the palace, in the center tower, on a balcony.

Ishtar's army stood their ground, I noticed the generals in Sins army included Jason, they were about to get a face full of Goddess.

While the two armies fought, Ish flew upwards and then suddenly a fireball was headed to the generals.

"Come on hun we have to go" Julian said pulling me away from the window.

"They will be in the center tower where he is" I said

"Ok follow me" Rain said leading the way

We passed another window and I could see Sin had left the tower.

"Ok guys we need to go vamp speed" I said Talon picked up Mat, Julian picked up Rain and we took off into the tower zooming around it looking for the kids.

I stopped at another window and looked out…I could see a thin line of light coming from the top of the tower going to Sin and he was winding up to nail Ishtar with something big.

"Top" I yelled as I raced to the top of the tower.

There was Angelus, chained to the wall. With a thin line of light going out the tower to Sin and another going down the wall.

"Where's Althea?" Jualin said

"Dungeon, I know where I will get her" I said

"Not Without Us" Talon said

"Rain can you get him down and break that line?" I asked her

"Not until we break the line from Althea, I can get him down though, but if that line breaks before we break her line to him, he will be overpowered and possibly explode or give Sin a boost he doesn't need" Rain said

"How do I break that line?" I asked her, she touched my forehead.

I suddenly saw pictures in my head. There would be objects in the room with her to keep her weak and then I saw a thing like a canopic Jar.

"Move all the objects I showed you first, then smash that jar" She said "I will do the same up here once the line is broken, Declan can you stay with me because I will not be able to carry him out"

"Julian you stay too, and carry Rain out at speed if necessary" I said "Khan, Talon and Mat with me"

We took off downstairs, every window we passed showed us the battle was raging hard. Sins generals seemed to be gone, lost in the chaos and rubble outside.

We got to the door of the room I was held in.

"Did you really think it would be that easy and he didn't know you were coming?" A male standing in front of the door said

"Jason?" I asked him

"Yes you know me well apparently, from some other timeline or some shit" He said

"Yeah, you were a cock then too" I said

"Sounds just like what you need, I hear you let anyone in your bed" He said

I laughed

"Look Jason just get out the way" I said

"I don't think so" he sniggered

"I do" Mat said as a fireball hurled towards him

He half dodged it, it caught his clothes.

"Ha fire doesn't incinerate us here like back home" he said thinking he was immune to the fire.

You could tell when the heat got to him though he was jumping around like an idiot.

I took my sword and ran it through him quickly and moved away from him

He looked shocked as he fell to the ground and turned to ash.

I went to go through the door.

"Wait" Mat said "That door is not right"

"We don't have time for this," I said, "Can you make it right?"

"I can try, I just don't know how my spells will work here, after all the fireball did not ash him like I thought" she said

"Give it a shot" I said

She started mumbling and muttering, she stopped and shook her head and started again.

She did this a few times before the door finally opened.

I went in carefully.

Althea was chained to the wall we could see the thin line of light going up the wall, it was getting thicker.

I quickly kicked all the objects Rain had shown me so they were out of place, then I zeroed in on the canopic jar.

I didn't use abilities or magic I walked over to it and kicked it as hard as I could.

It fell over but did not break, so I picked it up and threw it against the wall as hard as I could, it shattered and lots of dust fell out.

The line of light vanished.

There was an almighty roar that shook the building.

Mat unlocked the chains.

I could feel Sin coming towards me at speed

"Get her out of here" I yelled to the others

I headed to the front of the palace.

I reached out to Julian.

"Are you guys out yet?" I asked him in his head

"Nearly at the tunnel" He said back

"Cool" I said "See you soon"

I confronted Sin in a courtyard near the front of his palace

"I knew you would come" he smiled at me "You sent my daughter to end me while you kidnapped my children"

"It is not kidnapping when you remove kids from an abusive home" I said "You broke your deal with me, you promised you wouldn't take them till they were 18 years old, they are only 9 years old"

"They are 18 where it counts" he said

"No they are not, we made the deal in human years and you broke that deal" I said

"What does it matter, you would have done the same thing anyway" he said as we stalked around each other

"A deal is a deal" I said "I'm sure I said I would kill you too"

"You can't kill me, I'm GOD" he yelled, launching at me with a

flaming sword.
I dodged it without a problem and nicked his back with my sword
He howled in pain.
Ishtar came in looking a bit broken
She smiled at me and threw something at him.
"YOU BITCH" Sin yelled at her then he threw his sword at her and it went through her heart
She fell down and disintegrated
"You just murdered your own daughter" I yelled at him
"She does not matter" He snarled "I have my children"
He roared opening his arms wide and increasing in size so he was 15 foot high
I took a chance and threw my sword towards his chest.
He blocked it and flung it somewhere I didn't see where it went.
Then he grabbed me and held me up high
"What can you do to me I'm a fucking god?" he laughed throwing me back to the ground
I landed hard. I felt something give inside me.
Then I felt liquid coming out of my mouth.
Sin was suddenly normal size again.
"While you die I am going to fuck you one last time" he said grinning from ear to ear
I coughed up some blood as he moved on to me.
I knew this was the end for me I was just praying everyone else got out safe
He had an awful grin on his face when I looked at him.
Then I saw Rain behind him with my sword
I smiled at Sin.
I saw his confusion.
Then everything went black.

"Well that didn't go as planned" I heard a voice say
I opened my eyes, I seemed to be floating in the air
"What..." I said feeling dizzy
"Oh" a young looking boy said "How are you here?"
"I don't know where, here is exactly?"
"This is the place of souls that are lost to the world below" an older man said

"I'm not a lost soul" I said adamantly
"Yet here you are" the old one said
"I don't even belong to this world" I said
"Neither did we" the boy said
"Is Sin dead?" I asked
"Nearly" the old man said " it's what we are waiting for"
I looked around we were sitting on a cloud watching the scene below
Ishtar was dead, She hadn't had the chance to take her fathers power before he killed her, Sin was dying, I watched Rain cut his head off with one strike. I saw lines of blue light flowing out of Sin racing everywhere.
The trees planted in pots around the room turned into people
Much to the shock of my family who were all in the room, not escaping this hellhole like I'd told them.
Julian and the twins rushed to my body, I saw blue light flow into everyone.
"What's happening?" I asked
There was no one there. I looked back down at the ground.
A young boy and an old man walked into the room and over to my body.
How did they get there? They were here a minute ago, maybe Sin dying set them free or something
I wished I could hear what was happening.
I tried to get off the cloud, but I was still floating, I tried to get closer but it was like the air had an invisible floor.
I watched as Julian moved away from me and the young boy and old man moved next to me
The twins touched my legs and the old man had one hand while the young boy took the other.
They started chanting or at least it looked like they did.
Then Rain grabbed Julian and rushed to my body slamming their hands into the wounded area.
I suddenly felt really light like I might float away. Then my body or spirit started to melt away.

I woke with a huge pain in my chest and a need to breathe like I was out of breath and my lungs were blocked.
I opened my eyes and Rain and Julian let me go.
The pain went from my chest.
"What the fuck?" I said

The twins and other two stopped chanting and let go
"Welcome back" the old man said "Now you lot must leave, this is not your place or time"
"Yeah we know" Julian said
"What happened?" I asked
"You died" Julian said looking most unhappy
"Ok guys lets get a move on" Rain said
"Thank you for freeing us" The boy said "Life as a tree is not fun"
"Your welcome" Rain said "But we must go before the link between our worlds is gone"
"What?" I said, still dazed and confused.
The twins lifted me up and helped me walk to the portal someone had opened.
"Take care father" Rain said as she stepped through
I looked at the old man and he just smiled.
I felt I was missing something as the twins carried me through the portal.

We were back home.
It was two weeks later
The house was blissful chaos, the school was back in and there were kids everywhere.
I was spending a lot of time in my room, I still was not feeling right but I couldn't work out what was wrong. Medically I was fine, vampirically I was fine, but there was something missing.
"So Darling?" Juian said waking up next to me again
"Yeah" I said sleepily
"How about we have some fun tonight?" he said moving over to my side of the bed
"Oh why Mr Gustavo what are you talking about?" I said smiling at him and pretending I was offended
"I think you know Mrs Gustavo" he said jumping on me so I could not escape
"Oh Bite me" I smiled at him
"As you wish my love" he said before he sunk his teeth into my neck
"Oh Julian" I moaned, loving the way I could feel the blood

draining from my neck
He stopped and offered me his neck. I sunk my teeth into his neck and drank.
 He looked at me funny.
Like he was trying to talk in my head
"Darling?" I asked him
"Can you not hear me?" he asked
"Yeah I can hear you" I said
"No in your head?" He said
"What?" I said he gave me that look again
"I just asked you to take off your nighty" he said aloud
"I didn't hear a thing?" I said starting to panic
I tried to tell him to strip me himself in our head
"Did you hear me?" I asked him aloud
"No" he said looking concerned
"Maybe that's what is missing, maybe when I died, I lost the fae thing" I suggested
"We need to work out why?" He said getting off me
"Right now?" I said feeling disapointed we were not going to be having sex now.
"Yeah" he said grabbing clothes and getting dressed
"Can't it wait just a few minutes?" I said "I mean it's been two weeks it should be able to wait a few more minutes"
"Sorry hun but we need to work out what you have lost exactly" he said "We can have fun later"
"Well I'm gunna sleep in, you go find out what's wrong with me" I said turning over so I was facing away from him
"Hun I can't find out what's wrong with you without you" he said dragging the blankets off the bed
"And I don't care what's wrong with me" I said still not looking at him
"But what if it means you are weaker, what if people find out?' he said
"What that I now might just be a normal vampire, who cares hun" I said
"This is important Silver" he insisted

"No its not, I am quite happy not being an uber powerful bitch with a bad reputation for frying people" I said

"But if some of the others find out they may try to take you out while you are weak" he said snuggling into my back

"And I have you and lord Ivanovich and everyone to help me if that happens" I said still not looking at him

"Look darling I am worried about you, it's an important part of who you are" he said

"And aside from now not having uber powerful blood that vampires are often craving after I see nothing else that could be wrong" I said

"I cant talk to you privately" he said looking sulky

"We can, it's called go to another room" I said

"Yeah but going to another room to drop dirty thoughts in your head isn't the same" he said

"Well you can always use texting, like everyone else in the house" I said

"Who texts you dirty things they want to do to you?" he said suddenly shocked

"No one you dick, other people in the house text each other, you can tell when Khan gets that stupid smile after checking his phone and then has to rush off, Talon does it, hell I have even seen Savannah do it to Jay across the war room." I said

"How can you not see how this is a vital part of who you are" he said "But if you want nookie first then ok"

I moved away.

"Not interested now" I said getting out his side of the bed

"What?" he said shocked

"Go do whatever, I'm going to have a shower and get dressed, I might pop up to auckland tonight see how things are going up there" I said headed to the bathroom

"Ok fine I need a sample of your blood" He said jumping off the bed and coming over to me

"And you can have one when I feel like giving you one" I said slamming the bathroom door and locking it.

Was it really that important, I mean I still fed like normal, still had all my vampy skills, I was still me.

I had a shower and when I got out Julian was standing there waiting for me

"Darling can you please come with me and get you checked out?" he asked so nicely

"Fine just let me get dressed" I said

We went downstairs and to the village where medical rooms had been set up.

The doctor was confused by Julians request to test my blood.

"But if the fae in you is gone, will you not have lost some of your abilities?" the doctor asked

"Yeah I guess" I said trying not to care ...what were my fae specific abilities

"When did you last test your abilities?" the doctor asked

"Not since I became a vampire really, I'd just try shit and if it worked ya, if not oh well try something else" I said

"Ok well I suggest you find someone who knows your whole range and tests you" she said smiling at Julian who looked really worried

"I guess that's you hun" I said looking at him

"You should have Talon do it" he said turning and walking out with a blank look on his face

"Thank you doc" I said "I don't know what his problem is but I will get someone to test me"

"I will call you when I have the result from this" she said holding the test tube of my blood.

I rushed out the door Julian was nowhere to be seen.

And I couldn't feel him nearby, like he had run off for some reason.

I tried reaching him with our connection but there was nothing.

I headed to security, at vampire speed.

"Hay Silver" Ebony said as I walked in

"Did you guys see where Julian went?" I asked

"He took off into the forest just a few minutes ago" Ivory said "he seemed in an awful rush to go nowhere"

"Can you send a wolf to follow him?" I said wondering what the fuck was going on

"Sure" Ivory said carefully "Are you ok?"

"I have no idea" I said, "Can you find Talon and ask him to meet me in the gym asap"

"Sure" Ebony said jumping on a computer

Ivory was on the phone.

I headed to my room to get changed and then hit the gym.

Talon was waiting in the gym when I got there.

"So whats up sis?" he said

"I need to test my abilities and Julian is acting weird" I replied

"Ok why?" he asked

"Because after what happened I think I have lost some" I said

"Why is Julian acting weird?" he said

"I don't know, I asked him to test me and he said you should do it and walked out" I said

"Ok well I have no idea why he'd do that, so let's get to work. Have you still got wings?" he asked

I tried to pop out my wings, they were still there.

"To be fair, that wasn't an ability I should have had anyway" I said "it wasn't fae or vamp.

"Ok so what have you noticed is missing?" he asked

"Julian feed on me this evening and we can't talk to each other in our heads" I said

"Oh can you do the fireball thing?" he asked

"Let's go outside and find out" I said headed to the door

We walked outside to where the pool was and I tried to form a fireball.

Nothing happened

"I think you have lost most of your extra abilities" Talon said "let's go for a run"

He took off so I followed. We ran at vamp speed around the whole property.

"Still got that" I said when we stopped.

"You're a bit slower though" he said "there were some things you could do with the wave of your hand or a spoken word can you still do those?"

"Lets try" I said looking at the pool and waving a hand to send

water over the edge
Nothing happened
I went inside and locked the door.
"Unlock" I said to the door
Nothing happened
"It would appear you have lost your fae abilities I'm afraid" he said
"It would appear that way" I said frowning
"Well you are still a kick ass vampire" he laughed
"But is that enough?" I asked
"You should be fine, you've been trained by the best" he laughed
"So why is Julian so upset about it?" I asked
"I don't know, maybe just worried about your safety?" he suggested
"Then why did he take off?" I asked
"You would have to ask him," Talon said "and where did he go?"
"He went into the forest I have a wolf tracking him" I said
"Why?" Talon asked
"Because something is off, and I wanna know why he left when I needed his help" I said
"Well you should just asked him when he gets back" Talon said "sending someone to spy on him is a bit overkill"
"They are not spying just...ok I guess they are spying for me, I will call them back," I said and headed back to the office where Ebony was.
Talon came with me.
"Hay Eb's can you call the wolf you sent after Julian back please" I asked sheepishly
"No" he said
"Why not?" Talon asked
"There's something you should see Silver" he said turning the monitor he was at around to face me
I saw Julian walking to a shack in the forest, none of us knew was even there.
I saw a woman come rushing out, and hug and kiss him as if they were lovers and then they went inside.
"Who is she?" I asked

"We don't know" Ebony said "Just keep watching"
Then we saw why the wolf would not be called back.
The woman rushed out of the shack and the camera dropped to the ground facing up then we saw a mist slit the throat of the wolf and she stomped on the phone breaking it and killing the camera.
Not one picture showed her face clearly.
I stood staring at the screen in shock.
"What the hell is going on?" I asked
"We don't know, we sent a team out" Ebony said "no report back yet"
"I will ask him when he gets back," I said, turning around and headed back to my room.
"Ok well now I am sort glad you chose to follow him, but we have lost one of ours in the process" Talon said catching up to me
"I can't do this Talon" I said sitting in the middle of a hallway on the way to my room
"What do you mean?" he asked
"You saw the way they kissed" I said trying not to cry "he hasn't kissed me like that for years"
"I thought you two were still strong as ever" he said sitting next to me
"He has been more distant, he no longer drinks my blood during sex, if we have sex, I gave up asking, then today he finally wanted it and he fed on me and i thought we were back to normal, till we couldnt talk to each other." I said
"I figured it's just because he's old but we don't age like humans, I didn't think he was seeing someone else" I said " I mean we've been in hiding"
"I wish I could help you sis, but I had no idea" Talon said as shocked as I was.

I sat there a bit longer, a few people walked past and looked confused but kept going.
Talon stood up.
"Do you want me to stay or do you want to talk to him alone?"

he asked
I looked up to see Julian coming down the hallway towards us as if nothing had happened.
"Stay close but I need to do this alone" I said getting up
I turned and walked towards our rooms.
"Talon?" I heard Julian say as he walked past
"Go talk to her" I heard Talon say as I got to our door.
I went in my room and walked to the balcony
"Whats up hun? He asked coming behind me to hug me I moved away
"Where have you been?" I asked him
"I went for a walk, why?" He said turning away from me
"Dont play dumb Julian" I said looking out at the view
"I'm not playing hun what's wrong?" he asked making me look at him
"Your girlfriend killed one of the wolves today, I guess she didn't realize he was live streaming" I said waiting for his reaction
I saw it, he knew he'd been caught.
"I can explain" he said backing away from me
"Really?" I asked
"You are always so busy and you never have time for me" he started
"We sleep together every day, we have sex when you want it most of the timed, I look to you for advice on everything I do" I said "christ your my everything, you and the kids"
"You havent sucked my dick in months" he yelled "and the sex is boring"
"You haven't eaten me out or drunk my blood in years when it comes to sex" I said calmly back, "and yeah the sex got boring because everytime I suggest some fun you keep saying no I dont feel like doing that tonight"
"You don't listen to me" he said still not looking me
"If I've been making you that miserable for years then why not just fucking leave" I said walking back inside
I stormed over to his drawers and started pulling his shit out
He walked in

"What the fuck are you doing?" he asked rushing over to put his shit back

"I want you gone" I said looking at him "I want you and all your shit gone"

"Babe can't we talk about this" he begged as we wrestled with his clothes

"Fuck you..if you wanted to talk you should have tried that before fucking some slut" I yelled

"Babe it was just one time" he said "I swear"

"Bullshit Julian" I yelled "she has a house in a deserted forest near our home..did you have a house for her when we were in spain too? Is that where you kept going when we were raising our kids"

"Our kids funny we both know they not mine they never were and never will be" he yelled

I fell to the ground. The pain was so unbelievable

"Mum" I heard from near the door I peered over the bed to see my daughter standing there looking in horror "are you ok?"

"No I'm not" I said honestly bawling my eyes out

"Mr Gustavo" she said to her dad "I suggest you get the fuck out and as far from here as you can

I saw the look on Julians face..he was hurt when she didn't called him dad

"Now see what you've done" he spat at me "Turned my daughter against me"

I just bawled my eyes out

"No Mr Gustavo, according to you, I am not your daughter" she said racing to him

She punched him in face and he went down like a ton of bricks

"Now get up and get the fuck out, I will make sure your shit gets packed and sent to you" she said

"Fuck both of you" he said getting up and using vampire speed to leave the room

I burst into tears again

Althea came and held me and I cried for hours. At some point my son came in too and the 3 of us just sat there as I bawled my eyes out

The next few days were a blur, Althea and Ang packed up all of Julians stuff, I don't know what they did with it.

4 days later I was woken by someone yelling.

"Get the curtains open" a familiar voice yelled "Let the big guy in"

I sat up and was thrust a bottle of blood I looked up to see Dominic

The voice I had heard was Tatiana.

"What the.." I said still a bit dazed

"Just drink" Dominic said looking at me so sweetly and caring

"Is she awake yet ?" I heard the voice of Ragnor

I sat up and felt Dominic push the bottle to my mouth.

I drank it looking around the room my whole family were here Rift was standing at the end of the bed looking really mad

"It's time for you to haul your ass out of bed and come join us downstairs, we have a problem" Rift said

"What?" I asked

He threw some clothes at me

"You have 5 minutes to get dressed and down stairs" He snapped and walked out

"What the fuck Dominic, whats going on?" I asked

"Just get dressed and come down" Dominic said smiling at me nicely

"Ok I will" I said

They all left the room except Ragnor

"I will stay to make sure you get up" he said turning around

I got up and went to the bathroom, I decided to shower first.

I got dressed in the jeans and t shirt Rift had thrown at me I walked out and garbed socks and boots

"So what's the big emergency that needs me?"i asked ragnor

"Your family are worried about you" He said

"They don't need to be, I'm not about to wander out in daytime" I said

"No but when you hear the news they have to tell you you might," he said "I will see you downstairs?"

"I don't think I want to go downstairs" I said standing up

"Then I will fly you down" he said reaching to grab me

"Ok I'll go" I said

I walked out my door before he started to head to the balcony so he could go downstairs

Talon and Rift were at my door to make sure I went downstairs

"So sis, you are to have a guard 24/7 now" Talon said as we walked down stairs

"Why?" I asked

"Because your ex knows to much about this place and he seems to think he has been..wronged" Rift said "I swear sis if he does anything I will rip his stinking lying heart out for you"

"What do you mean? wronged?" I asked shocked

"In the receiving room" Talon said

I walked in and my family were all there except my kids.

"Where's the kids?" I asked

"Sit" Dominic said then he pushed a button on his phone

The tv started showing a video

Juilian was standing in front of the camera

"Right now since we have been together longer than 2 years I am entitled to half everything you own and I am taking it, starting with your abominations" He said moving to one side

Althea was lying on the floor chained and bleeding, she seemed unconscious.

Angel was chained to the wall not looking much better.

"How the fuck?" I started to say

"You have till midnight to decide which is mine, I'll return the other" the video stopped

"How the actualy fuck did he get the kids?" I yelled

"He asked them to met with him alone and they did, they wanted to find out what the hell he was on and how long he'd been cheating" Talon said

"He will be well prepared for anything we do" Dominic said "he knows everything about how we do things"

"And he knows the kids weaknesses" I said getting angry "How fucking dare he pull this shit"

"Silver calm down please" Talon said " we need to work out what to do to get both the kids back"

"Do we know where he is?" I asked

"We are narrowing it down now" Ebony said "I think hes just in Taupo, but we are having an issue narrowing it down"

"When you know, tell me" I demanded and started to head back to my room, I needed to change my clothes.

I grabbed a shirt that had no back. So I could use my wings if necessary.

Ragnor was on my balcony. I went out to see him.

"You cannot go alone" he said quietly

"I have to" I said "He has the kids"

"I know which is why I am coming with you" he smiled down at me

I gave him a hug

"Thank you old friend" I said "Shall we see if these still work."

I popped out my wings and gave them a flap.

I felt some pain, I hadn't done this for a long time thankfully it was not far to Taupo.

"You need some practise Silver" Ragnor said laughing

"Yeah on the way" I said giving them a bit more flapping practise before I tried to take off

"Your not leaving without com's sis" Talon said walking in handing me an ear piece I took it and put it in my ear

"And we will be following you in the chopper" Dominic said

"Wait for us when you get there" Tatiana said "You go off like you are now you will get your kids killed"

"If he kills my kids I will slowly mutilate him" I sneered

"No" Talon said grabbing my arm "You wait for us and we will bring him to justice"

"I love you Talon, but get your hand off me" I said

"Don't make us stop you Silver" Tatiana said "You know I will"

"Tat" I started to say fuck off but stopped myself "I will see you all in Taupo"

I gave a final big flap and lifted off, I swooped down the side of the castle and went up over the trees

Ragnor was right with me as we flew to Taupo.

He motioned a spot near the lake where we usually landed the chopper.

I went down and and stood near the building here to wait for the

others
I suddenly felt a strange pull, I knew it was Angel calling to me.
"No" Ragnor said putting a hand on my shoulder to stop me taking off "We wait" the chopper was finally coming in so I nodded
The others got out and came over.

"Ok Here's what we are going to do" I said "I am going alone, maybe I can reason with him, maybe we kill each other, either way I want you guys going for the kids, let me know when they safe"

"This is not a good plan" Tatianna said "You cannot expect him to be reasonable"

"I don't, but I do have an ace up my sleeve, something he doesn't know, and I don't want to do but if I must I will" I said

"What?" Talon said looking at me confused
I touched his face in a caring manner

"Its ok, I will be fine" I said trying to reassure him "Remember we know his weaknesses too"

"Yeah but we know nothing of the woman he is with" Tatiana said

"Ragnor" I said turning to my gargoyle friend

"You want me to take her away?" he said

"Can you?" I asked

"I will dump her somewhere safe" he smiled

"So where do you think they are?" Talon asked

"They are in that warehouse we bought a while ago and never use" I said "well Angel is"

"What if he separated them?" Dom said

"Well lets hope I keep calm enough to find out" I laughed
I walked with vampire speed to the warehouse.
I planned to walk in the front door, however when I got there I felt Althea in pain.
I used everything I had to blow the main door in.
Julian was standing there between me and my kids.

"You really want to do this Julian?" I said so angry I was calm

"Stay back or she dies" he said way calmer than me
I noticed the people he had here with him, one had a sword over my daughters neck.

"Where's Angel?" I asked
"He's safe for now" Julian said
I could feel he was in this building, I just couldn't pinpoint where, which was weird.
"What the fuck are you doing Julian?" I asked him
"Where is your back up?" he asked
"Making plans, trying to find my kids" I said "I came here alone"
"I don't believe you" he said walking towards me
I saw Althea lift her head a little and wink at me.
"I haven't lied to you in how many years Julian?" I said "why the fuck would I start now when something as important as my kids are on the line"
"So are you giving me what is rightfully mine?" he asked "and my name is Jugs"
"Everything was put into trust years ago, you know that and what I had left went into trust last week, just before you fucked me over" I said in that angry calm I do sometimes
"Fucking bullshit" he sneered getting in my face
"What the hell Jugs, why are you doing this, they are your kids too" I said quietly
"NO they are not, they are Sins fucking kids" He sneered
"Your dna, my dna, it was your damn dick that put them there, all the crap we went through to keep them safe and dealing with Sin, you did that as their father" I started crying
"They are not mine, vampires can't have children, they are your abominations" he sneered
"I will give you everything I have, just give me the kids please" I cried
"You get one" he laughed "you get to pick which one you want"
"I can't choose between my kids Jugs" I said feeling depressed suddenly..I felt as if a black cloud came over the whole building
My eyes were so full of tears I couldn't see the expression on Jugs face
"What are you doing Silver?" he asked sounding a bit paranoid
"I think it's called crying you fuckwit" I sobbed
He suddenly grabbed me and pulled me back to him

"If anyone comes after you you all gunna die" he sneered in my ears

"Jugs this isn't us, you know my people" I said not at all worried about the knife at my throat.

"Really Silver?" he snapped "You always find people with new skills and shit, how do I know you haven't found a weather mage"

"I've spent the last few days locked in my fucking room you fucking coward" I seethed at him

"Whatever" he sneered in my ear "Maybe I should take a bite?" he moved his head closer to my neck.

I threw out my wings. Sending him flying backwards ..the knife lightly cut my throat as he went back, he dropped it when he hit the ground.

He would have fallen on Althea but she had taken advantage of his back being to her and taken out the guards

"Fuck" He yelled relizing she was ok and I was spinning around to come down on him

"Mum" Althea yelled "Stop"

I drove my knee into Julians chest to hold him down. My fist was in the air ready to pound him.

"Listen to your daughter" Jugs sneered

"You are in no position to tell me shit Jugs" I seethed

""Mum, let me take care of it" I felt her hand on my shoulder

"You go deal with the other guards and get your brother" I said calmish not taking my eyes off Jugs

"Ok mum" she said "Just don't kill him yet"

"I see no need to keep him alive" I sneered

"There is, I can't explain yet but just wait" she took off

"She'll never get to him in time" Jugs seethed

"I'd be real careful if I was you Julian" I sneered back

I heard footsteps come into the warehouse, I didn't need to look to know it was Ragnor.

"You right here sis?" I heard Talon say coming up behind me

"Althea said I have to keep him alive to find out something, she's gone to get her brother" I said

"Ok well Ragnor can take over" I felt a hand on my shoulder "Its

ok sis you can let him up now"
"Alania is better fuck than you slut" Jugs said as I was about to get up
My fist went into his face, breaking his nose.
Next thing I knew I was being held back by Ragnor.
"That was cunt move Jugs" Dominic said as he restrained him "your lucky we didn't let her keep going"
"Wouldn't matter if she had" Jugs smiled "I'm fucking immortel"
"I'll show you, you aren't you son of a" I screamed trying to get lose so I could fireball him "let me go damn it"
"No Silver, if your daughter said he has information we need to get that first, then we need him alive" Talon said
"Let me drink his blood" I screamed "I'll get it out of him"
"And let him into your head?" Dominic said
"That doesn't work anymore" I seethed, unable to control myself struggling against Ragnor even though I knew he was too strong for me and he was holding me so tight I couldn't pop my wings out like I had done with Jugs.
"Just be patience Sis, we will see what Althea says when she gets back with Angel" Tatiana said
"I knew you brought back up" Jugs yelled "You fucking lying bitch"
"Actually they brought me" I snarled "And you are in no position to call me a liar, How fucking long have you been cheating me?"
"Since Spain, you were too attached to the godspawns to even notice me" he smiled
"They were children, hell yes I put them first, but I still had your back, I still did everything I could for you, How could you do this?" I started crying
"You haven't loved me since we were in hell" He yelled
"I haven't ever stopped loving you" I cried "all the times I planned things for us to do together alone that was for us for you"
"You never listened to me, you never gave me your all once

those kids came along" he yelled

"You need to shut him up" Ragnor said behind me "I don't know how much more I can hold her"

"Maybe take her away Ragnor" Tatiana said gently

"But I wish to see her rip him apart" he said gruffly "He is an unreasonable selfish man"

"Yes he is" Talon said making sure Jugs was well and truly restrained "We all know how much effort you always put into him and the kids and to think a mother should put any man before her kids is just stupid and rather narcissistic"

"She was meant to be MINE, not a couple of snot nosed brats" Jugs yelled trying to escape

"You said you would love me forever" I cried "I loved you enough to trust you all these years, everything we've been through you were my strength, everything I did for you out of love"

"You had your tattoo friend curse her tattoo didn't you Jugs?" Tatiana said wondering over to him

"What's taking Althea so long?" I asked sobbing

"Maybe my backup has killed her" Jugs laughed "Only one to go and I'm sure he'll be dead shortly if not already"

With that Talon bit on his neck from behind, taking his blood. He spat it out

"He's been tainted" Talon said looking calm "I need to go find some fresh blood"

Dominic took over the hold of Jugs

Jugs was laughing demonically.

"I would still like to know Julian, did you have your friend do something in her tattoo?" Tatiana asked going over to him

"Yeah I told him to bind us together, I wanted her to come back to me, so I could turn her" he laughed

"And when Alpia fixed it, she broke that bond didn't she" Tatinan asked

"How would I know" Jugs said

"It would seem that his love was never true I am sorry Silver" Tatiana said

"Please go check on the kids Tatiana" I asked her suddenly becoming calm

"Do not fry this scum Silver, he is not worth it" she said before running off

"She's is right Silver" Ragnor said

"Yes she is, but I would feel so much better, now that I know he has been controlling me from the start" I said "You are no better than your brother, and how many times have we killed him?"

"I am nothing like my brother" Jugs yelled

"Actually the way you used Silver is a lot like your brother, the Tattoo, the deception is very Gustavo of you" Dominic said "and using family to hurt her, is classic of my sire"

"I am nothing like my brother" Julian said, getting pissed off.

"Dom hun can you take his ring off him please" I asked, noticing he had one of the daylight rings.

"Oh and you're a thief?" Dominic said, ripping the whole finger off not just the ring.

Julian screamed in pain, and blood gushed out

 "Thank you brother" I said

"That was kind of therapeutic, would you like to rip something off" Dominic asked me

"Yes I would, but I don't want to touch it ever again" I smiled

"That ring is mine" Julian screamed

"No, this was a gift to those who needed it, you no longer do, as you are no longer working for the greater good of anyone but yourself" I said finding my inner calm

"Fine take it I'll just get another one" he spat

"Good luck with that" Dominic laughed

Lightning and thunder started picking up outside.

"This looks bad" Ragnor said looking outside

"It's not natural either" Althea said walking back in

Angelus and Tatiana were with her

"One of you should be dead" Julian said in shock

"Oh your new girlfriend tried" Althea said "But I stopped her and now she is having a tantrum" she nodded to the outside

"I propose we throw him out the door and see if she is good with

her accuracy" Talon said also coming back in
We all looked out the door

Chapter 14

Lightning was striking the ground outside the door over and over

"It would seem she is just hoping to hit anyone coming out" Ragnor said

"Did we get the info we need from him?" I asked talon

"Yes we have what we need" Dominic said

"Yeah" Talon agreed

"So we have no use for him?" I asked

Everyone shook their heads

"I'll do it mum" Althera offered

"No" I said "this is mine"

Ragnor let me go

I prepared myself to go all out

I walked over and Dominic held him tight

I took over and pushed him to the door.

"So you reckon she'll save you?" I asked him

"She won't hit me" he smirked

"You know I would have saved you" I said "I never stopped loving you Jugs, you were everything to me"

"God your so full of shit" he snarked

We got to the doorway and I stopped for a second

I could feel him start to panic as we watched the lightning strikes hitting everywhere outside the door.

"Good bye Julian" I said as I pushed him outside using all my vampiric strength

He tried to stop but couldn't, tripping as he went through he landed on the ground outside and was hit by 5 lightning strikes

It fried him faster than a deep fryer can cook a chip.

I fell to the ground turning so my back was against the wall

I felt like a giant knife was rammed through my heart again

The lightning stopped so did the thunder
We all heard an almighty scream from outside …so loud it shook the building
"Back door?" Talon suggested
"Yup let's get out of here" I said getting up again. No time to grieve right now we had to move.
We all went to the rear of the building and made our way to the back door using our vampire speed
"I will go out the front" Ragnor said "I can take lightning"
"Ok Ragnor" I said "Just be careful we don't know the extent of her abilities"
"I will be ok" he smiled like a pit bull
He went back to the front
We snuck out the back door.

We made it back to the helicopter without any issues and the weather had cleared completely.
We were waiting on Ragnor.
30 minutes later we were still waiting.
"Maybe we should go look for him?" Tatiana said
"I'll go, I can fly" I said
"Ok but be careful" Talon said
I got out of the chopper and took off back towards the warehouse.
When I got there there was no sign of Ragnor or The witch.
"Guys there's no one here" I said over the coms in my ear "I'm gunna take a look around"
I landed and went to the front door, there were no signs of a struggle, but it's not easy to be a 9 foot tall gargoyle with wings hiding anywhere in an urban environment.
I went to the door, it was still open, I went inside carefully.
I used my senses to see if anyone was around and no one was
"The warehouse is deserted guys" I said over coms
I went back outside and flew up.
"Isn't it a lovely view from here" I heard a female voice say
I spun around to see an old friend.
"Silver?" I said "I thought you had closed our worlds off"
"She did" the woman said almost snarling "I am not Silver, I am

her sister, she locked me on this side of the gate, I guess she decided I was not good enough for her new world"

"Oh" I said "I'm sorry"

"Its ok child I wouldn't want to be there, this world is so much more fun" she grinned

"Your the witch that Julian is in love with" I said with sudden realization

"Well done" she smiled

"Where's Ragnor?" I demanded going on the defensive

"He is safe enough" She smiled "You however are not so much"

"What do you mean?" I said

"Look for yourself, all your friends are fine, they can't see or hear you" she said

"What do you want?" I asked not n the mood for this bullshit

"Well for a start I want your wings" she said smiling at me "Then I am going to take all your blood and sell it"

"Oh really?" I laughed

"Yes dear" she smiled "Your already in my trap, and you don't even know it"

"What do you mean?" I said confused

"Well dear you can see your friends but you flew through my barrier into my world so they can't see you, or feel you or help you" she said calmly "And in my world I control everything, for example"

I felt a sudden cold breeze that turned into a hell gust of wind that blew me to the ground I landed painfully on my back in the middle of my friends who seemed confused, even Ragnor was there but flying

"Fuck that hurt" I said loudly

No one heard me.

They were talking about the fact I had vanished.

I heard laughing above me. I looked up and saw Silvers sister come flying through Ragnor, I saw Ragnor shiver when she did, so the worlds were not fully separate.

I rolled and jumped up as her foot landed where I had been.

I flew through Ragnor he shivered again and looked around.

"Where do you think you're going?" she snarled at me

"No where" I said turning to face her
I gathered myself focused on not bending to her will and waited,
I was going to try a surprise fire attack.
"Get down here" she said snarling at me
This time I didn't move
She looked shocked.
Then she got mad
"How dare you" she screamed lunging for me
I dropped my mental protection and threw a ball of fire at her.
It caught her clothes and hair, but more importantly I saw Rag-
nor react to it
"Huh... fire can't hurt me you stupid bitch" she screamed still
coming
I dove to the left.
She spun in the air and kicked me in the back
I was back on the ground. I rolled and got up in one move
I needed to stay calm and focus.
Ragnor went off to the side as if he were trying to work some-
thing out.
I saw him out the corner of my eye move over to my daughter.
The woman fighting me tried to launch at me with some kind of
spear. I dodged and spun to face her again
"Why do you want my wings?" I asked calmly
"Because they were never meant for you" she snarled
"I know they were meant for a demon, but the demon fucked up
and I got them" I said
"And I am going to take them back" she smiled as she launched
at me again, I dodged her even easier
I noticed she was weakening, as if fighting me and holding this
illusion was taking a toll on her
"Well you better hurry" I said
"Why?" she asked puzzled
"Because any minute now your illusion is going to collapse and
you will be considerably weaker and I might just kill you" I said
"You can't kill me" she laughed
"I wouldn't be so sure about that" I smiled at her
She launched at me again. I threw up a wall of ice.
She hit it hard, my daughter and Ragnor were right there.

Althea waved her hands and the illusion fell.

"So what will you try now" the woman said as she blew the ice wall apart

"Nothing" I said "I have no need or desire to do anything with you, you have too many issues"

She tried to launch at me again and I moved over to Ragnor and Althea

"You know iIm sick of this" she yelled and threw her hands in my direction

Ragnor stepped in front of me while Althea did a similar action towards her.

Ragnor rocked back a step as an invisible wave hit him.

I looked up in time to see the woman fly backwards.

The look on her face was that of great shock.

Althea was on top of her before she could do anything.

"Stay down if you want to live" My daughter said

"You can't hurt me bitch" the woman screamed

"Actually I can," Althea said as she grabbed the woman's head and held it.

The woman started screaming even though it only looked like my daughter was just holding the head and not doing anything.

I knew what she was doing, info first destroy later

I watched as Althea let go and got off her

"Mum" she said turning to me "I fried her brain"

"What why?" I asked

"She is evil as fuck mum, now she won't remember how evil she is and if she recovers she won't know who she is and what her plans were, I suggest we get her commited to an asylim before she heals"

"Oh what asylum would you recommend to hold a fae?" I asked

"We could try take her to the fae land" Ragnor said

"You know we can't" I said

"There may be a way" Althea said

"But?" I asked

"But someone would have to go with her and not come back" Ragnor said

"They would have to volunteer for it to be fair" Althea said

"How do we contain her till then?' I asked

"Mum I fried her brain she will be a mindless fool for a while yet" Althea said smiling

"I hope so" I said

"Let's get back to the castle" Talon said

"No we cant take her there" Althea and I said at the same time

"For safety we need somewhere ...remote and preferably underground" I said

"And she doesn't know exactly where the castle is" Tatiana said

"But she was so close to it" I said

"Yeah but Julian never told her exactly where" She said

"Why would he do that?" I asked

"Maybe the thought of wiping everyone out made him soft, maybe he just wanted to hurt you" Tatiana said

"Ok Tat" I said "What do you mean?"

"He doesn't want her to destroy the entire estate, just you because he feels hurt you kicked him out, and he thinks he deserves half" she said

"He fucking cheated on me" I said shocked

"He blames you for that too" She said

"Is it my fault that instead of manning up and talking to me he went and fucked someone else then plotted my demise, hell no" I said "Everything that has happened to him is on him"

"Including when you pushed him outside?" Tatiana asked with an eyebrow raised

"Actually yes" I said "If he hadn't taken my kids, hadn't tried to kill me, and his girlfriend hadn't been throwing lightning at us he would still be ..." I couldn't say it..."You know"

"Alive?" Tat offered

"Yeah that" I said

"You had no choice" Althea said

"There's always a choice, I could have let him kill you or me" I said

"That's not a choice" Althea said

"Sis you are not to blame for anything that happened here, the love of your life betrayed you you merely did what any of us would in the same situation" Dominic said

"So where do we take her?" I asked

"I know of a place, it's a bit south of here, it used to be a asylum but now it's mostly farmland, there is an underground part where they held the worst patients and it is still there" Talon said

"Ok" I said "It sounds good"

"I'll take her, Talon can fly the chopper" Althea said

"I am going home" I said "I'll fly myself"

"I shall see if I can get a way through to fae lands but I shall fly with Silver" Ragnor said

I got back to Castle Alexandrov and Ragnor went to find out if there was a way back to the fae, I went to my rooms.
I decided to have a shower...and a cry.
All we had been through together and he turned into a self centered narcissistic asshole, finding out he trapped me to be bound to him, hurt even more, he never really loved me at all.
I was just another conquest, something to piss off his brother.
I felt worthless.

I came out of my bathroom and Ragnor was waiting on my deck.
"He is not worth your tears you know?" he said as I walked out to see him
"I know, but it's part of the grieving process" I said calmly "Don't worry old friend I will get through this"
"Yes you will" he said slapping me on the back
"So any luck?" I asked
"Yes I can take her" he said looking down
"Why you?" I asked
"Because it is time" he said "we have been through much together, but I have been here for centuries and I feel it is time to go home, it just so happens I can take Silver's sister and she will stand trial for the crimes she tried to commit here, over there she is weaker, so she will not be able to escape and I'm sure Silver will want an extensive update on her namesake"

"I was thinking I might go" I said looking out over my estate

"You are needed here" Ragnor said coming over and putting a wing around me

"For what?" I said "The kids are grown, this empire runs itself, I'm sick of fighting, if it's not one asshole it's another, my family here don't need me anymore, you on the other hand are a priceless asset, you have helped and saved us more times than I can count"

"I have to say working for you and being your friend has been adventurous, to say the least, but my time is over here" Ragnor said "You now have freedom, if this bores you find something else to be passionate about, you have the resources and skills to do anything you want"

I laughed

"I remember when I wanted to open my own club and just party and have fun" I said

"Then do it" he said "You still have clubs around the world, pick one and do what you want"

"Na I want to start fresh if I do that, Ex abyss is its own brand now" I said

"Back to basic's?" he asked

"Yeah I might think about it" I said

"What else did you love when you were still human?" he asked

"Helping those less fortunate" I laughed

"You do enough of that" he laughed "Maybe you will find someone to really love you"

"Or maybe I will use guys for sex and dump them like I used to" I laughed

"I am sure there are many men who will be happy to be used by you" he chuckled

"Well to be fair guys are easy" I laughed, then I sighed "I'm going to miss you Ragnor"

"And I will miss you too my queen" he said looking at me

"I am no queen" I said shaking my head

"I think your people would disagree" he said smiling at me

"Mum" I heard behind us in my room

It was Althea

"Yes dear I'm out on the balcony" I yelled

"That bitch is secure, and Talon and Dominic decided to stay with her" she said

"Ragnor can take her home" I said "and I'm going to go on a bit of a holiday"

"Mum you can't go to fae land" she said

"No darling I'm not going there, just a regular holiday" I laughed "Maybe it's time I retired for good"

"And who will do all the things you do?" Althea said

"You darling, you, your brother and my wonderful team we have here" I said

"It would seem your daughter doesn't want you leaving the nest" Ragnor laughed

"Don't worry darling I will still visit you and stuff and when I find a place to settle you can come stay for holidays" I said hugging her

"When the fuck do we get a holiday?" she said looking unimpressed

"Ok then you can come stay when your on a mission in my area" I laughed

"Why can't you retire here?" she said looking at me

"Because as long as I'm here I will always be dragged into missions and teaching, it's time for me to have some me time" I said "and I want to workout what I'm doing next"

"Can't you do that here?" Althea asked

"Sorry hun but no" I replied

"Your mum has worked hard trying to keep everyone here safe for such a long time" Ragnor said "A break to find herself again, may be the best thing for her"

"I'm not letting you fall off the face of the planet mum" Althea said hugging me tightly

"Don't worry darling, you and your brother will always be able to contact me" I laughed "no way I can just disappear when you two are around"

"You know we'd hunt you down if you tried ah?" Althea laughed

"Yeah I'm sure you would" I laughed

"So Ragnor you can take the crazy bitch to the fae world, will you be back ever?" Althea asked

"No I will be staying there" he smiled "I am not really needed here anymore, and I will not be able to come back"

"When are you leaving?" she asked him

"As soon as possible" he said "I don't want a big fuss made out of me leaving, so I am thinking tonight"

"You know someone will make a fuss ah?"i said "I'm going to miss you old friend"

"I can slip away before they know" he said giving me a hug

"Well Talon and Dom are waiting for you, I just texted them" Althea said

"Good I shall go then, now Althea don't give your mum a hard time, and make sure your brother doesn't either" he said to her

"I will Ragnor" She said hugging him "if you can ever come back please do, you'll always be welcome here"

"I know child" he smiled hugging her back "Well I am off then, be well Silver, take care of yourself Althea, and watch that brother of yours"

"Always Ragnor" Althea said

"You too old friend" I said giving him another hug

As he left he took one look back and I could swear there was a tear in his eye.

"Mum were you a vampire when you met Ragnor" Althea asked

"No it was just before I became one, I even talked to him about the whole vampire thing when I wasn't sure" I said

"Did he help you make the choice?" she asked

"Yeah, he helped me figure out what I wanted to do without judging me or saying I should go one way or the other" I said

"Why did you say yes?" Althea asked

"It was something I had a fantasy about for a long time, before I found out they were real" I smiled at her

"Was it all you fantasized about?"

"Sometimes yes, sometimes no, I never expected to go through about 90% of what I have been through" I laughed

"Well it's a big jump going from a normal human to being a vampire with demi-god kids" she laughed "Do you think I'll ever have kids?"

"I don't know hun, if you can and you want them I don't see why not?" I said smiling at her "Just wait a while first …live your life and enjoy it"

"How will I know if I'm in love with the right guy though?" she asked

"Julian and I had a long history hunny, I don't regret loving him at all, I regret how things ended but most of our relationship was wonderful, I have so many good memories with him, and a few bad ones, but if your both willing to communicate and be honest about everything you'll work through the bad times" I said

"Do you think you and dad …I mean Julian would have been able to sort this out" she asked

"I think if he'd talked to me before he went and cheated then yes we might have been able to, I had no idea he felt the way he said he did, but also we do have incredibly long lives and people can fall out of love, maybe he'd still be alive and maybe we could have parted better if he'd talked to me" I said "No one is perfect hunny, you have to accept that includes when your in a relationship"

"Will you ever forgive him?" she asked

"Maybe one day" I said "I just wish it hadn't ended the way it did"

"Well it's nearly dawn, I should let you go to bed" she said giving me a hug

"Althea. Thank you for being you" I said hugging her back

"Night mum, and thanks for being you too" she skipped out of my room

The next evening I got up showered and went downstairs to find some sustenance and people.

The kitchen was buzzing with kids who'd finished their school day and were cleaning up after their dinner

"Mrs Gustavo" one said coming up to me "Can I help you with

anything?”

“Please just call me Silver and no I’m good thanks” I said back

“Well I'm in charge of the kitchen, so if you need anything just ask” he said

“OK thanks, what is your name?” I asked him

“I’m James, I’m Shadow’s son” he said holding out his hand

“Nice to meet you James” I said taking his hand

“So what are you doing down here?” he asked

“I just wanted to get some breakfast and some company” I laughed

He snapped his fingers and one of the other students ran off and came back with a goblet of blood for me.

“You have them well trained” I laughed

“The other adults are in the conference room, probably discussing something important you should go too” he said smiling

“Except I retired last night so I am not getting involved” I laughed “but maybe I’ll just go see whats they discussing”

I went to the conference room sipping on my blood

I walked in and everyone was standing around not really doing much

“Ah Silver glad you're here” Talon said “Ragnor took our little problem away, we were just about to start”

“Is it work things or can I hang around?” I asked

“Work things and I expect you to be right next to me” he said looking at me strange

“Oh I am resigning as of last night” I smiled

“I know, but I still want you here” he smiled then turned to the whole room” Ok can we all take our seats please”

Everyone sat down, I went to the head of the table with Talon.

“As you know Silver is leaving us, as of last night, so I want to hold a big party for her, since if it weren't for her we would not be here now” he said once all were seated

“No don't be silly Talon, I’m sure there's more important things to do” I objected

“No he's right Silver, you deserve a decent send off” Dominic said smiling at me

"Have you decided what you are going to do next?" Tatiana asked

"Not yet, except for maybe a deserted island somewhere" I laughed

"You know there are positions available in several places we run around the world that require a caretaker I think would be good for you" Talon said "depending on where you want to go"

"What sort of positions?" I asked

"We have a few small sanctuaries that need someone to just look after the property and make sure the residents are ok and settled" Talon said

"So a place like this?" I asked

"No the ones I am thinking of are much smaller" he laughed

"I think you'd love the ranch in Canada" Dominic said "It's quiet out of the way and there's only like 6 in residence"

"I dunno, I kinda want to not work for a while, that's the idea of resigning"

"You know we will always find you a position any time you want it ah?" Khan said

"Yeah I know" I replied

"And the ranch doesn't need a leader just a caretaker" Talon said smiling "we have a couple of other places you might like too"

"What aren't you telling me?" I asked looking around the room

"Basically we want to make sure your going to be ok, if your at one of our small sanctuaries we will know your ok, and you can enjoy your retirement" Taiana said grinning at me

"Well I suppose I can look at the options" I said giving up "but I don't think we need a full meeting to discuss it"

"Good girl" Tatiana laughed

"Well we are having a party next weekend, to say goodbye so you have time to think about it" Talon said "I can show you the places we think you'd like"

"Where do you guys find the time to sort all this for me when I can't even find the time to think?" I laughed

"We have had the whole crew looking into this for you" Ebony said "at least let Talon show you the options we found"

"Ok then show me" I said giving in again and finishing my blood

They showed me the ranch in Canada , a fully self sufficient quiet beautiful place, somewhere out of the way and secluded, there was also a ranch in Alaska, Arizona, and deep in mexico. A couple of other places around Europe, and a few in more dangerous places like Russia.
In total there were 15 places.
"Can you send them to my laptop, I'll go over them later and see which one I like the most" I said when they were done
"Already done" Ebony said smiling
"Now the party" Dominic said standing up "We have already invited the important people, is there anyone you want to invite that we might not have got to yet"
"Yes but they are all dead now or in the fae world" I said "so not much point, also I don't want a party"
"Tough shit mum" Angel said "You deserve to have a good send off before you leave us behind"
"You know son, no matter where I go you and your sister will always be welcome" I said
"Yeah I know" he replied "But we haven't had a good party in a long time"
"Ok well I'm going for a walk" I said standing up "I'll let all you guys sort this"
"Well if that's the case, Silver you are banished from the ballroom until the party" Talon said "Or I shall be forced to detain you"
"Fair enough" I laughed and left them to it

I wandered through the village which had grown considerably since I first came here, I no longer knew the names of everyone living here, but they all knew who I was. People who passed kept saying hi and evening, some even stopped for a quick chat. Things seemed to be going well down here, with the school keeping everyone busy.
I eventually found myself in the spot where Silver's house used to be, it was now just a lovely garden.
I sat near a small pond and lay back on the grass looking at the

stars.
What am I going to do with my life now?

Night time air traffic around here is pretty high for such a small place with people going out to work or coming home, so I didn't pay attention to any of the aircraft that had landed tonight.
"You know, your going to be very much missed" I heard a thick russian accent say
"Good evening lord Ivanovich" I said without even looking up
"Good evening it is Silver" he said I felt his presence sit next to me "So why are you out here?"
"Just relaxing and trying to decide what to do next" I said "everyone here wants me to go look after another sanctuary, but I don't know what I want yet"
"I want you to come and work with me" he said
"Yeah that's a hard no thanks" I said sitting up
"Why you not want to work for me?" he asked looking serious
"I want to get away from all this, I'm over fighting and drama" I said
"Just because you work for me does not mean you will be fighting or dealing with drama" he said sternly
"But I'll get dragged in again and again, it's actually the reason I am thinking of just vanishing, so I can't get dragged into the next drama or fight and the next one and the next one" I said
"You know I could have you run one of my businesses" he said
"No thanks" I said "I don't need a job, I have enough to support me"
"And what happens if your enemies find you, what will you do then?" he asked
"I'll kick their asses and find somewhere else to live" I said
"Would it not be better to have a whole team behind you?" he asked
"We both know I can handle myself, if all else fails I'll just burn everything and hide till I can fly away" I laughed
"I worry about you Silver" he said "you have so much potential, yet you keep trying to run from it"

"Look Ivanovich this is my life, I have the right to do with it as I see fit" I said

"Yes you do, but you could be so much more" he said

"How, I am already too powerful, in both our world and the human world, I have too much money...and now I want to relax, it may well be at some point in the future I get bored and want to come back, but I don't really see that happening in the next 10 years" I said

"We live very long lives Silver, and you are harder to kill than most" he laughed

"Yeah I know, but right now I need space and freedom, I need to figure out who the hell I am before I decide what my future looks like" I said

"That is fair enough I suppose" he said getting up "May I escort back to the house"

"Sure" I said holding my hand up so I could use him as leverage to get up

He took it and helped me

"I think I might go stay with Mary-anne and Khan for a while or maybe with Savannah and the wolves" I said

"Well they will be here tomorrow so you can ask then" he said "I just would like to know one thing"

"What?" I asked

"Are you pretending to retire and then making moves against us or are you just over it all" he said very seriously

"I am over it all Lord Ivanovich, I would not make moves against my family, and that does include you, but it does not mean I am like you, I will not double cross my family like you have done" I said feeling a little angry

"Good" he said "Then let us go and feast and catch up with old friends"

"Are you going to make a move against me again my lord?" I asked him

"No I have learnt my lessons in regards to you my dear, and yes I did the wrong thing a couple of times but you always came through and did not take revenge like most vampires would,

but at the time I felt it was the only way" he said
"Just remember that ok" I said as we got to the steps leading into the castle
"There are entirely too many children here" he said "I shall be in my rooms" he stalked off

I looked around , there were no kids around right now.
I went inside and made my way to the kitchen, it was empty which at 4am is not unusual
I grabbed a bottle of blood and heated it
"Did you get me one?" I heard a voice say behind me
"Rift you are big enough and old enough to get your bloody own" I laughed turning around
"It's good to see you Silver" he said smiling at me
"Are you sober Rift?" I asked
"Yeah I am" he laughed
I handed him my bottle and went to grab another
"Thanks sis" he said "So how are you doing, and why are you sober?" he asked
"You know me" I said putting the second bottle in the microwave "I just keep moving forward even if I don't know what forward is anymore"
"Yeah miss perfect I don't drink to forget" he laughed
"No I'm not perfect" I laughed
"Maybe you could let loose for your party?" he suggested
"Actually I might just do that" I said "But not to forget, just to let loose and get wild"
"That sounds good, when was the last time you let your hair down?" he asked
"Fuck I don't remember, last time might have been that halloween party in new york, but even then I was busy with other things at the same time" I said thinking about it and sipping from my bottle.
"So what are you going to do with your life now?" Rift asked
"Well everyone here wants me to go run a sanctuary, but I just wanna go find somewhere quiet to live. I've been thinking about

maybe writing my story, I need to really find myself, I lived so much of my life for others. I need to back to me whoever I am" I replied

"So you want to be a stripper again?" Rift joked

I laughed and smacked his arm.

"No, that was a means to an end, I needed money it was a job" I said "Now I have money and I don't need a job"

I would suggest a lot of day drinking" he laughed "But then everyone gangs up on you and forces you back to the real world"

"We did not gang up on you Rift" I said "we simply remind you that you have people who love you and care about you"

He looked at me intently

"Do you ever regret becoming a vampire?" he asked

"I've never really thought about it, I think I accepted it is what it is" I laughed

"I regret it sometimes, the things I've seen and lived through, sometimes it would just be easier to die and not worry about it all" he said

"If only the dead stayed dead ah Rift" I laughed

"I would, I will not come back as a demon or a ghost, I am sure of it" he said

"Do you remember the time I was newly turned and you taught me how to drink booze right here in this kitchen?" I said looking around

"Yeah and how much you threw up" he laughed

"Even with all the crap we went through back then theres still a lot of great memories" I smiled

"Just think now your retiring you might get more good memories and less bad ones" he said

"How long do you think it will take me to get bored and get into trouble?" I laughed

"By yourself..maybe a couple of years" he laughed

"And if I have someone with me?" I asked

"Well I think if its someone you enjoy it could be 10 years, just a friend maybe 5" he laughed

"Our life is so long I would like to think it will be decades" I

laughed
"So have you chosen a sanctuary to take over?" he asked
"Actually I'm thinking of not going to a sanctuary, I'm thinking of moving to some party towns dn partying for the next few years" I laughed
"You know if you want a quiet life a party town might not work" he laughed
"Yeah I dunno what I want yet" I said
"Maybe you should figure that out, before you get muscled into a sanctuary" he suggested
"Yeah like I've been muscled into this damn party" I said
"Yeah there's no getting out without a decent send off" he laughed
"It will be nice to see everyone without the drama of some world ending event going on" I mused
"Yeah it will" he agreed
"Well I'm going up to my room, I have a lot to think about" I said putting my empty bottle in the glass recycling bin
"Yeah I'm gunna go make sure there is no impending drama we need you for" he laughed

In my room again I started looking around at all my stuff, I dunno how I had accumulated so much, my wardrobe was bursting with clothes and boots and a few shoes, I had a dresser of make up, a set of drawers with lingerie, and so much more, I decided to go through and just pick out what I really loved.

Althea and angel came in and stopped
"What the hell mum?" Angel exclaimed
"I'm sorting out my shit" I said
"I had no idea you had so many clothes" Althea said looking around
"Well if you want hun you can go through that pile" I said pointing at the small pile nearest the door "I'm getting rid of them, this pile is my keep pile" I looked down at the pile at my feet which was still considerably large
"You know we could store some of this for you?" Angel said

"I just want to get it down to what I can take with me" I said looking at the huge pile "I think I'm going to need to cut it down a heap more"

"So you taking a container?" Althea laughed

"No just a few suitcases" I said frowning

"Well I can help you go through it all mum" Angel said smiling and evil grin

"No, I'm good thanks son," I said, throwing another one of my favorite dresses on the pile to keep "So what can I do for you two?"

"Nothing" they said

"Then why are you here?" I asked

"We just came to see our mum and see what she was doing" Angel said "you know maybe spend some time with her before she abandons us"

"I am not abandoning you Angel, I am just getting out of the way so you can live your life" I laughed

"He's just being a dick mum" Althea said smacking his arm

"Yeah mum, you are an amazing mum and an amazing woman, and we want you to live for you. you've done a good job raising us" Angel said "You have an exceptional son and an ok daughter"

"Fuck you Ang" Althea said punching his arm

"Ok you two cut it out" I said " I love both of you and think you're both pretty amazing kids"

"You would say that your our mum" Ang said smiling

"I don't want you to go" Althea said

"Yeah neither do I" Ang said

They both came in for a hug.

"Oh my darlings" I said hugging them back "You know wherever I end up you two will be welcome anytime"

"Yeah but it's not like having you here" Ang said

"You guys are old enough now to go out on your own, do your own thing, you know even if it means not working here, in fact if you both took a few years to go explore the world and find who you want to be I think that would be a great idea" I said smiling at them

"But everyone expects us to basically take your place here"

Angel said

"You can always come back to here later, good thing about this family, we can wander off do our thing and as long as we aren't causing problems we can come back and work here" I said "It's not like you two need a babysitter, your kick ass all on your own"

"Yeah so kick ass that dad...I mean Julian was able to kidnap us and keep us prisoner" Althea said

"He merely caught you off guard, trust me darling it happens, and I think you could of escaped at anytime, both of you" I said

"It was that bitch who got us, not Julian, if it had of been just him he would have been dead sooner" Angelus said

"And if you work here with Talon and the rest you will be subject to danger often, we all understand that" I said "but you know what, every person we lost as much as it hurt, helped us all grow and we didn't lose as many as we could have, there were times I thought we were all going to die, but there were more times I felt it was my fault. Everyone worked together to get us out of the situations, and it was not actually my fault, but people who were jealous of what I can do or wanted power over me to use me for their ends"

"How do you deal with that mum" Althea said

"I learnt to understand, it wasn't about me, it was always about them" I said "We are family here, you know that and we are the type of family who will all come together for family, my family keep me safe and when they can't they come save me, no matter how far from you I live, I will always come when you need me"

"So if I decided I wanted to explore the world and find old lost treasures, that would be ok with you?" Althea said

"Don't be daft sis between discovery channel and lord Ivanovich there is no more" Angelus scoffed

"Actually there is always more mysteries to solve, many of the humans don't actually understand what they find, their information is really based on best guesses and attempted deciphering and well since Ivanovich owns Discovery he often removes anything he thinks might be dangerous, like the book that helped us with ..SIN, he has many treasures like that, that he has taken and hidden again, but I know he often has people loyal to him on these human adventures, it would help keep you safe while you explore" I said

"Yeah but with the tech they have now...nothing is actually hidden" Angelus said

"100 years ago they thought they had discovered things which they now know are wrong, 100 years before that they thought they knew those same things and now we know they were wrong too, there are so many places that are still being discovered, like around egypt, all over south america, hell even europe and south africa, the middle east and china are rife with their secrets yet to be found and even things that have been found that are yet to be understood" I said "and there is also other vampires who have hidden treasures from the past"

"I think it would be fun to fund something new" Althea said

"Well if that's what you want to do darling I will support you" I smiled

"Yeah and you know what, I will go where you go sis, Even if I am just your bodyguard" Angel said

I smiled looking at my babies.

"That makes me so happy" I said "Knowing you two have each others back, but angel hun you should also do things you want to do, try things you want to try"

"I will, and I will drag her with me" he laughed

"You two should make bucket lists, I'm going to" I said

"Don't you do that like when you gunna die soon?" Althea asked shocked

"No hunny" I laughed "It's really just a list of things you want to do, for an example, I want to spend a week at a health spa, go on holiday at a resort, go diving with sharks, jump out of a perfectly good plane with a parachute, things like that"

"So are you taking a daylight ring when you go?" Angelus asked

"No I was planning on leaving them here" I laughed

"You should take one mum, especially if you want to go to health spa and resort" Althea said

"You two are so lucky you can live in both worlds" I smiled at them
"Well we have to go" Angel said looking at his phone
He grabbed his sisters arm
"Oh yeah" She said suddenly "we will see you later mum we have something to do"
"OK darlings, just remember I just want you guys to be happy" I said as they rushed out the door

I looked at my piles of clothes...and decided I needed food instead.

I spent the next few days continuing to sort out all my stuff, what I was taking and what I was giving away. Althea claimed a good chunk of it, we had always had similar styles. The rest I gave to the school for the students. I knew some of them were not necessarily from well off families.
We decided the jewelry would go into the vault in my grandfather's rooms, which was now Angel's rooms, except for the costume stuff that also went to the students, and I kept my grandmother's red set. I also found "the boots".
These boots that I loved so much, when I knew Jugs and I was human, and how I had been given these by Talon because he saw my facebook, man we had all come so far from those days. When Gustavo was really in control. When I thought I was so in love with Dominic, and now he had Tatiana, Julian was a fried vampire, Gustavo was dead a few times over.
All the battles we had had, the people we had lost. I finally made up my mind as to what I was going to be doing for a few years at least.
I went to my laptop and googled islands for sale.
I found a nice one that was a decent size, came with a self sufficient, technologically up to date, homestead. It was far away from everything to be just what I wanted, and still close enough if I had to I could come back, or go where I might need to. It also had the internet by satellite. I checked for any weather events that might have occured in all of time, there were not many through that area, so dying from drowning was not going to happen. It did occasionally flood but there was a big hill, probably more a small mountain. The homestead was about half

way up the thing so out of flood range. It also came with electric 4 wheel drive buggies and motorbikes. It really was a rich person eco retreat.

I sent an email to the owners.

Shame you can't just hit buy now.

I was going to have to go through all my stuff again and cut it down more.

For now I went for food it was easier

Someone had decided the farewell party for me was going to be masquerade, my favourite, not that I had decided what I was going to wear. But I had to decide pretty quickly, it was on in 24 hours from now.

The purchase of my island had gone through with the help of Ebony and I was leaving the next night, everyone was here.

There was a knock on my door.

"Yeah" I said before hiding under the covers again

"Silver?" I heard a female voice say

I threw the covers off and lept out of bed

"Savannah" I yelled hugging her

"Hay hun" she said taken aback a bit "I missed you too" she added more excited

"So how are things?" I asked

"Most of the time they are great, but you know wolves" she laughed

"So like vampires" I laughed

"So you bought an island?" she said

"Yup" I said "I'm going off grid"

"You have tried to do that before" she laughed

"Yes but then I had other people and then kids, now it's just me" I smiled at her

"Fair enough" she laughed "Now to more important things" she paused "what are you wearing tonight"

"I have no idea" I laughed

"Well I have just finished a divine bit of costume, mask included" she smiled

"Where is it?" I said

"In my room" she said nodding

"Lets go" I said smiling

"Are you going to get dressed?" she asked

"Na" I said "Everyones here has seen in my pjs" I was wearing a minion onesie

"I thought you hated those?" she laughed

"Oh I do but I'm trying new things" I laughed

"Fair enough" she said

We left my rooms and went down to where she was staying.

She went to the wardrobe and pulled out an old fashioned wardrobe chest designed for carrying womens dresses on long journeys

She opened it and there was only one thing in it.

She carefully pulled out the bodice and handed it to me

It was sleek but had black feathers with sequins, then she pulled out the skirt. It was a slim line pencil type skirt and had a V split in the front and a tail.

"I thought you could use your wings with it" she smiled and then she pulled out the mask.

It was like a plague doctor mask but covered in sequined feathers, it looked amazing. The way it glinted in the light was incredible.

"So what are you wearing?" I asked her

"I'm going as a wolf, to honor my pack and my man" she said sheepishly

"Oh that is so cool" I said "your costumes are always amazing"

"Yeah the business is doing so extremely well now, I've been able to hire other designers, give them their own label within my company, and I've scaled back what I am doing, now I only do one show a year, and I do 3 or 4 outfits for each season in that one show, so I can focus on costumes, I am doing a full fantasey set for a movie at the moment, but i'm not allowed to talk about it" she said

"I am so glad you're doing so well you definitely deserve it" I said smiling at her

She put the costume back in the box and closed it

"I've come a long way since Andre and Damion" she said "sometimes I wonder how I made it through all that, but yes I do deserve my life, I have an amazing man, a great family, and i'm doing what I love"

"Its funny how things change" I smiled at her

"I'm going to miss you" she said

"No need I'll still be reachable, the island I bought has room for guests and I think Jay and the boys would love running all over the island" I laughed "speaking of Jay where is he?"

"He went to see if he could help with anything, really I think the boys are doing a catch up drink or ten" she laughed

"It's been pretty mad the last week, all the family are gathering and they've all come to see me I've been remember old times, both good and bad" I said "But I am looking forward to some me time, who knows maybe I'll write a book on my life" I laughed'

"That's actually a good idea, I mean you've been through a lot of unbelievable amazing things, like your wings" she said

"Yeah,but we all have" I said

"I havent had to fight demons" she laughed

"Yeah and I pray you never do" I laughed we hugged

"This party's gonna be off the hook" Savannah said

"Did you hear I'm going to performing a few songs like I used to when I was human" I said

"Yes I did" I am so excited, I've never actually seen you perform"

 "It has been a long time since I did" I said "I'm kinda nervous about it, what if I can't sing anymore"

"You will be fine" Savannah said "I've heard you at random times sings bits of songs and your voice is good"

"Thanks" I laughed "I suppose I should take this costume to my room so I can get ready tomorrow night when I get up"

"Yup" She said "who's doing hair and make up?"

"I have no idea but i'm booked in for for 10 pm" I laughed

"I think I got 9:30" she said "I should check"

She looked at her phone.

"Ok hun well I will see you later i'm feeling kinda peckish" I said

"I'll come down with you, I want to find Jay" she said

We dragged the large box to my rooms before heading down-

stairs.
Savannah went off in search of her man while I went to the kitchen
There were a lot of people in the kitchen so I just stood off to the side, someone bought me a bottle of blood, I smiled and went back out. I headed to the pool area.
I looked around at my family home while I was out there.here by the pool you couldn;t see the new school rooms additions or the dorms,the center had remained pretty much the same.
I remembered feeling overwhelmed the first time I came here, part of me wished I had known about all this properly when I lost my parents but I had a blessed life really.
Untill I came here actually, and then after the whole Gustavo turning me rape mind controll bullshit, I still had a blessed life.
I had an amazing but huge family.
I didn't have to worry about money anymore which was fantastic.
Sure I was alone but I was not lonely not by a long shot.
I had this awful feeling they would make me do a speech which I was so not prepared for.
I wonder if they will give me a gold rolex I giggled
"Mz Alexandrov" I heard come up behind me
"My lord" I said turning to face Ivanovich
"I have been told you have decided to leave your ring here" He said
"Yeah" I said " they might need it"
"I would ask you to reconsider, running a even self contained off the grid property takes a lot of work, and you will need to be out in the day time" He said
"You could be right, but I don't feel its mine to take" I said
"Then I shall gift it to you as a going away present" he said
"That's not necessary my lord" I said
"You have served the vampire community well, you deserve it" he said then he turned and walked away.

I spent the rest of the night wandering around talking to everyone who wanted to say hi.

The next evening I got up early and showered and started to get dressed. I knew I'd need help with the corset and just like that my daughter came in.

"What are you wearing tonight?" I asked her

"Oh my costume is easy to get into and I have till midnight" she said

"I'm booked in for hair and make up at 10" I laughed

"Yeah I know" she said "I came to see if you needed help with the outfit Savannah made you, I know she has a thing for corsets" she nodded at the corset I had just put on

"Thank you darling" I said turning around so she could do up the back

We chatted idly as she did it up. Then the makeup lady arrived.

"Oh that costume is divine" she said walking in

"Yes it is" I said "Can you do the makeup to match it"

"Oh yes I know exactly what to do" she smiled

My daughter left to get dressed herself and I sat at the dressing table .

I had an hour once my make up and hair were done before I was expected at the party.

I went out to the balcony, Half expecting Ragnor to come down for a chat.

I looked out over the extension and the village, I could see both from here.

I went back inside and had a look for my old stash of weed.

It was still there so I rolled up a joint and took it outside to smoke.

I could watch people as they came to the castle to join the party.

I decided to make my way downstairs to the ballroom, they had banned me from entering that room for a week now.

I was stopped just out of sight of the foyer by a security guard.

It was Khan.

"Sorry miss I've been asked to ask you to wait till everyone is in ballroom" he said smiling

"How is Mary-anne and the cubs" I asked

"Doing well" he said "Brutus has proven a worthy partner for my sister"

"I'm so pleased, are they inside?" I asked
"Yeah" he smiled "I got stuck playing guard till your inside"
I heard a whistle from down stairs
"If you will follow me my lady" Khan said, turning around so he could go down first.

The doors to the ballroom were closed.
Two large guys dressed as maori warriors opened them.
Then someone I didn't know stepped in front of the doorway facing the crowd that had gathered
"Lady Silver Alexandrov" He said then he stepped out of the way and Kahn and I walked in.
A huge cheer went up and I could hear whispers oh oo's and ah's about my outfit. I flicked out my wings, hay if i'm center stage I gotta play it.
That sent another round of louder oo's and ah's.
I laughed and went over to the throne that had been set up for me.
I put my wings away and sat down.
The music started and I watched as everyone in their costumes started mingling and dancing.
Plenty of guys came over and asked me to dance, I didn't turn any of them down.
Around 3 am I was going to be performing.
I was just off stage when Ivanovich stepped up to the mic.
"Ladies and gentlemen" he started "we have gathered this evening to celebrate the life and retirement of one of our greatest assets"
"Silver Alexandrov has been one of the hardest working, loyal, and by far the most interesting person I know"
"Before she performs for us for the first time in a long time I am to present her with our version of a gold rolex, a daylight ring" He said
There was an audible gasp that went through the crowd as I walked onstage.
"Silver" Ivanovich said turning to me "we would like to thank you for your service to the councils, and the world, please accept this gift as a token of our appreciation and respect"

"Thank you my lord" I said back
Then the crowd started chanting for me to do a speech. Ivanovich stepped away from the mic and I stood waiting for quiet.
"Friends, family and workmates" I started "to be fair most of you are all three to me now, we have been through some shit haven't we ." I waited for the agreement noises to stop.
"Well now I'm going away hopefully for a long time, I'm not leaving you all, I'm taking time to explore other options after I spend some quality time on my own finding myself, the place I am going has enough room for friends to come visit but please not all at once"
Everyone laughed
"Anyway I hate speeches I just want you all to know I will be here if you really really need me and I have full faith in all of you to continue the work we have been doing to secure the future of vampires, humans, and shifters alike, now I've chosen a few songs that I like, and some that are directed at ya'll" I said
I started with feel this moment by christina aguliera, then some pink, some ava max, some kesha, primadonna by Marina, cheap thrills by Sia, the good the bad and the dirty and the greatest show by panic at the disco, then I'll be there by Jess Glynn and the finally last harrah by Bebe Rexha and post malone by Sam Feldt and rani. Then we let the band take over and I danced till 30 minutes before dawn, when I begrudgingly went to bed along with everyone else.

The next evening I got up early and it was still daylight. I grabbed my packed bags and headed downstairs. Things were still pretty quiet. It was nearly dusk so everyone was still sleeping, I had arranged for the chopper to take me to Auckland to leave around dusk so I could avoid saying goodbye to everyone and I put my bags in the car waiting to drive me the short distance to the airfield.
Khan was behind the driver's seat.
"You know we gunna miss you sil" he said
"Please don't start, I'm on the verge of tears at it is" I said
"Well you know my next holidays I'm gunna come harass you on your wee island" he smiled

"Yup I'm sure most of you fuckers are, I'll be lucky to get a minutes peace" I laughed
"Probably" he laughed starting the car
We drove the 10 mins to the airfield, the chopper was warming up. Khan grabbed my bags and I got in the chopper.
"Till next time Silver" Khan yelled
I hugged him awkwardly in the door of the chopper
"Tell everyone I love them" I said he nodded
The door closed and the chopper took off
I looked down over my old estate , it was all over to them.
I shed a couple of tears and quietly said goodbye.

Acknowledgement

I would like to thank my friends and family for helping get through this last book in the series, it has not always been easy but you have stuck by me when others failed to and for that I am truely grateful. 2020 was a bad year for many, but it helped me find the focus I needed . Heres to a better 2021 and beyond

Books By This Author

Silver Is Rising

The first book in the series Silver Saga by Silver Moonbeams where Silver Alexandrov finds herself in a way more interesting position in life after the death of her grandfather.

Silver In Hell

Book 2 of Silver's saga
Silver wakes up on a prison boat with no memory of her life before. who put her here and why? and who is this man who cliams to be her husband?

Redemption

Book 3 in Silver's saga
Silver and Julian must find a way to save the world as they knew it, and battle once again for their freedom

www.ingramcontent.com/pod-product-compliance
Lightning Source LLC
Chambersburg PA
CBHW071401150726
48000CB00001B/117